GOBLIN SLAYER

14

©Noboru Kannatuki

"...What's next?"

The music of battle crescendoed, the shouting of warriors mingling with their death cries, and then there was the ocean, boiling up again. Who could be expected to leap straight into this whirlpool of chaos? Who else? Adventurers.

©Noboru Kannatuki

Contents

GOBLIN SLAYER

Volume 14

GOBLIN SLAYER

† CHARACTER PROFILES

"I am to goblins what goblins are to us."

GOBLIN SLAYER

A strange adventurer active on the frontier. He is famous for reaching Silver (3rd) rank hunting only goblins.

"Protect, heal, save."
—The Three Holy Tenets of the Earth Mother

PRIESTESS

Works with Goblin Slayer. A sweet young woman who must put up with her partner's antics.

"Ignorance is bliss, for learning is the highest joy." —Elven proverb

HIGH ELF ARCHER

An elf girl who adventures with Goblin Slayer. A ranger and a skilled archer.

The only things that matter to her are the weather, the animals, the crops...and him.

COW GIRL

A girl who works on the farm where Goblin Slayer lives. The two are old friends.

"How can you go adventuring without pen and paper?"

GUILD GIRL

A girl who works at the Adventurers Guild. Goblin Slayer's preference for goblin slaying always helps her out.

GOBLIN SLAYER

❖ VOLUME 14 ❖

KUMO KAGYU

Illustration by
NOBORU KANNATUKI

YEN
ON
New York

GOBLIN SLAYER

KUMO KAGYU

Translation by Kevin Steinbach ✢ Cover art by Noboru Kannatuki

GOBLIN SLAYER vol. 14
Copyright © 2021 Kumo Kagyu
Illustrations copyright © 2021 Noboru Kannatuki
All rights reserved.
Original Japanese edition published in 2021 by SB Creative Corp.
This English edition is published by arrangement with SB Creative Corp., Tokyo, in care of Tuttle-Mori Agency, Inc., Tokyo.

English translation © 2022 by Yen Press, LLC

Yen On
150 West 30th Street, 19th Floor
New York, NY 10001

Visit us at yenpress.com ✢ facebook.com/yenpress ✢ twitter.com/yenpress
yenpress.tumblr.com ✢ instagram.com/yenpress

First Yen On Edition: August 2022
Edited by Yen On Editorial: Rachel Mimms
Designed by Yen Press Design: Wendy Chan

Yen On is an imprint of Yen Press, LLC.
The Yen On name and logo are trademarks of Yen Press, LLC.

The publisher is not responsible for websites (or their content) that are not owned by the publisher.

Library of Congress Cataloging-in-Publication Data
Names: Kagyū, Kumo, author. | Kannatuki, Noboru, illustrator.
Title: Goblin slayer / Kumo Kagyu ; illustration by Noboru Kannatuki.
Other titles: Goburin sureiyā. English
Description: New York, NY : Yen On, 2016–
Identifiers: LCCN 2016033529 | ISBN 9780316501590 (v. 1 : pbk.) | ISBN 9780316553223 (v. 2 : pbk.) |
    ISBN 9780316553230 (v. 3 : pbk.) | ISBN 9780316411882 (v. 4 : pbk.) | ISBN 9781975326487 (v. 5 : pbk.) |
    ISBN 9781975327842 (v. 6 : pbk.) | ISBN 9781975330781 (v. 7 : pbk.) | ISBN 9781975331788 (v. 8 : pbk.) |
    ISBN 9781975331801 (v. 9 : pbk.) | ISBN 9781975314033 (v. 10 : pbk.) | ISBN 9781975322526 (v. 11 : pbk.) |
    ISBN 9781975325022 (v. 12 : pbk.) | ISBN 9781975333492 (v. 13 : pbk.) | ISBN 9781975345594 (v. 14 : pbk.)
Subjects: LCSH: Goblins—Fiction. | GSAFD: Fantasy fiction.
Classification: LCC PL872.5.A367 G6313 2016 | DDC 895.63/6—dc23
LC record available at https://lccn.loc.gov/2016033529

ISBNs: 978-1-9753-4559-4 (paperback)
        978-1-9753-4560-0 (ebook)

10 9 8 7 6 5 4 3 2 1

LSC-C

Printed in the United States of America

"Before they're polished, jewels and precious metals all look like rocks. No dwarf would judge a thing by its appearance alone."

DWARF SHAMAN

A dwarf spell caster who adventures with Goblin Slayer.

"A naga does not run."

LIZARD PRIEST

A lizardman priest who adventures with Goblin Slayer.

"Train yourself: Kill with the blade. If blood flows, let it be the enemy's."— First of the "Secrets of Steel."

HEAVY WARRIOR

A Silver-ranked adventurer associated with the Guild in the frontier town. Along with Female Knight and his other companions, his party is one of the best on the frontier.

"Only a tangled skein awaits those who carelessly spin tales about love or the universe's mysteries...not to mention a woman's beauty."

WITCH

A Silver-ranked adventurer at the frontier town's Adventurers Guild.

"I won't make friends tomorrow with an enemy I respect. I'll do it today."

SPEARMAN

A Silver-ranked adventurer at the frontier town's Adventurers Guild.

"Love does not consist in gazing at each other, but in looking outward in the same direction." —A poet

SWORD MAIDEN

Archbishop of the Supreme God in the water town. Also a Gold-ranked adventurer who once fought with the Demon Lord.

©Noboru Kannatuki

Loot may be lost, a family may fall,

and my own life will wither in time,

but great deeds

wrought by mine own hand,

precious are they,

for they never fail or fade.

CHAPTER 1

TO WHAT SHALL WE COMPARE THE HEART?

"You think Orcbolg's been acting funny?"

"Orcb—? Er, yes. I do."

Cow Girl was thrown off for a second by the nickname—she never could seem to get used to it, no matter how many times she heard it—but then she nodded.

They were at the tavern just before noon: The adventurers had cleared out, there were no other customers, and the whole place was uncommonly quiet. Under the circumstances, even the high elf—who looked beautiful simply grunting "hmm" and grabbing a handful of leafy vegetables—didn't really stand out. The only people around to see her were Cow Girl and Priestess, along with Padfoot Waitress, who was pretending to take her time cleaning but was really catching a surreptitious break.

The elf's pointed ears gave away that she was less interested in the conversation than she was in soaking up the sunlight, so it was Priestess who, after taking a sip of soup with a thoughtful expression, nodded and said, "Do you think it has to do with the dungeon exploration contest, then?"

"Yeah, seems like," High Elf Archer replied.

So I was right.

Cow Girl let out a sigh. It hadn't just been her overthinking things; the other women in his own party had noticed it, too. Was this a bit of a serious problem?

Or should we be happy that he's turned a little softer?

Maybe the fact that she was even asking the question showed how far gone she was, as well.

"Come on, it's not like acting weird is something Orcbolg just started doing today," High Elf Archer groused, flicking her long ears and nibbling on the vegetables. The mercurial emotions of mortals must have seemed so trivial to an immortal creature like her. Or perhaps she'd learned to see even these little ripples in the heart the way a human would.

That was why (would it be fair to say that?) she circled one finger in the air and smiled. "*Goblins, goblins, goblins.* So he's started to get away from his favorite topic a little. Shouldn't we be happy about that?"

"Do you think we can be?" Cow Girl asked, cocking her head uneasily.

"Sure I do!" the elf replied immediately. It seemed the anxiety she'd felt just a moment before had vanished completely.

The instantaneous shift almost blinded Cow Girl; she squinted and replied, "Ummm, right, then. I'll be happy. Happy, happy…"

"The question is what to do about it, isn't it?" Priestess volunteered. She was sucking on her spoon (most unladylike) and twiddling her fingers in thought. "The issue is, we don't know what caused it. I mean, sometimes you can get depressed for no reason, but…"

"You don't think he was just too busy?" Perhaps bored of nibbling on leaves, High Elf Archer was now chewing on some diced carrots. She seemed very pleased that other long-eared vegetable lovers had recently joined them. The harefolk was one thing, but Priestess sometimes felt the new elf occasionally looked askance at her vegetables…

"*She's just shy!*" High Elf Archer had exclaimed, completely unbothered. Nothing solves a problem like giving it time.

"Think about it. There was the kerfuffle with the wine, then he went to the desert, then the three guys went off somewhere, and then he helped out with the dungeon exploration contest," High Elf Archer said, counting on her fingers; indeed, he had been getting around quite a bit lately. And a fair amount of what he'd been doing was virtually unrelated to goblins. "I'm sure it just got to be too much for Orcbolg."

"I don't know... I kind of like that he's doing so many different things," Cow Girl said.

"So...do we ask him to rest for a while, then?" Priestess suggested.

"If he'd just stay on our farm... I'd like that." Cow Girl's smile took on a touch of self-deprecation to hear herself repeat the same words. It *would* make her happy—but she couldn't ignore the part of her that knew of what he dreamed. Once he settled down, someone as tired as he was might not get up again. She knew he of all people would keep on walking—but she couldn't help thinking, *What if...?*

"I guess maybe I wouldn't want that after all," she murmured.

"You... You wouldn't?" said Priestess. She didn't seem to grasp what Cow Girl was feeling and only cocked her head in confusion.

"Oh, it's nothing." Cow Girl waved it away. "I guess I just wanted to figure out if there was anything I could do for him. That's why I wanted to talk to you two."

"Hmmm...," Priestess murmured.

"Sure," said High Elf Archer as if it were perfectly simple. "It's not that hard."

"It isn't?"

"If his body is tired, he should rest. If his heart is tired, he should do something fun. It's as simple as that."

"Ah!" Even the somewhat perplexed Priestess nodded when she heard this explanation. "You're right. It's one thing if doing something ridiculous or outrageous will be of any benefit, but it's not usually that straightforward."

Cow Girl giggled to hear her invoke those familiar words with such a studious expression. Priestess shot her a questioning look, but— Oh, never mind. Today was...well, it wasn't a bad day by any means, but it wasn't exactly exhilarating, either. She couldn't seem to make herself focus on work around the farm. And yet, she couldn't work up the excitement to come do anything in town, either. Instead, as a sort of escape, she'd invited the girls out on the pretext of asking for advice. (Although, of course, she really did want advice.)

She didn't quite have the courage yet to call them friends, not even just in her own mind.

But being able to see them and talk to them makes this meal worthwhile.

"Let me tell you what that means," High Elf Archer said in a lovely voice, as if she'd read Cow Girl's thoughts. The high elf, whose blood ran back to the Age of the Gods, sat there holding her half-eaten carrot and smiling a smile as bright and warm as the morning sun. "We just have to take him somewhere—on a proper adventure."

§

"So where're y'off to this time?"

"…" Goblin Slayer grunted softly. "Me?"

"See anyone else here?"

The light that drifted in through the window of the cramped workshop glittered with floating dust. He didn't see the apprentice, who would normally have been bustling around doing grunt work. Maybe he'd been sent on an errand, or perhaps he was eating lunch. Goblin Slayer could hardly imagine how other people spent their days.

Thus, after a moment's thought, he took the items he'd purchased—his preparations—and put them in his pouch. Before noon, after noon. It would be time to get going soon; he couldn't dawdle here. He took some gold coins from his money pouch and placed them on the counter, then shook his helmeted head from side to side. "Nowhere special," he said in his typical dispassionate tone, and then recognizing that this was not enough, he added, "Goblin hunting, I expect."

"Hmm." The workshop boss, not sounding very interested, rested his chin on his hands. The coins shone dully in the light, but although he glanced down at them, he didn't touch them. Instead, he fixed his gaze on the helmeted face in front of him. "Never changes, does it?"

"Mm." Goblin Slayer nodded.

No, it never changed, nor did he have the slightest intention of changing it.

Goblins were weak. Say what you would about them, they were the weakest of monsters, hardly threatening. In terms of the danger they posed, even the largest-scale goblin infestation would mean the potential destruction of only perhaps a single village. They were nothing compared to dragons, demons, trolls, or dark elves.

He had been to the Dungeon of the Dead, to the snowy mountain, to the desert; he had faced down a dragon and been a facilitator for the dungeon exploration contest. The world was overflowing with threats, dangers—and adventures—he couldn't even imagine.

But none of this made him any less content with his role, which was to slay goblins.

Goblin Slayer had a thought. "How is the girl doing?"

"Which girl?"

"The one with the black onyx."

"Ah, her…" The boss, chin still resting on his hands, looked disinterestedly out the window at the sleepy midday streets. "She comes by to get oil and whatever else. A real regular by now." He then added brusquely, "Not that I'm going to lower the price for her."

Goblin Slayer's only response to this was: "I see."

The boss's one good eye turned and fixed Goblin Slayer with a stare. "Hope she doesn't pick up all of *somebody's* bad habits."

"I try to buy only what I will need."

"For goblin slaying." The boss spat the words out, sighed pointedly, then shrugged elaborately, provoking a series of cracks from his stiff joints. He swept the coins on the counter toward him, after which the man felt the gaze upon him was somehow softer than it had been before. Or perhaps—softer than it had been the first time *he'd* come into this shop. "What, haven't y'anywhere you'd like to go?"

"Hmm." The truth was, he'd never thought about it. He had no plans to go anywhere. Well, if there was a quest, if goblins appeared, that would be different—but that wasn't something that could be planned.

Somewhere he wanted to go… He wondered if in fact there had ever been such a place for him. Beyond the borders of his country, perhaps? The desert. The elf village. The old ruins. All places he had never even dreamed of.

And were there any hopes or desires within his own self?

"Ah," he said as a place he had never seen manifested itself in his mind. A place that had never been anything but a dream to him. Someplace he had heard of time and again in bedtime stories but which he had never once believed he would really visit. "Beyond the northern mountains."

§

"Beyond the mountains?" Guild Girl asked, her voice bouncing like a ball as she abandoned any attempt to keep the fluttering of her heart from her tone.

"Yes." The helmeted head nodded. It looked rather out of place on the street at noon—the street full of ordinary sights.

He wore grimy leather armor and a cheap-looking metal helmet. On his arm was a small, round shield, and at his hip was a sword of a strange length. One wondered what had happened to the shimmering Silver-ranked adventurer who'd helped out with the dungeon exploration contest.

It was hardly an outfit to wear on a date, even if that date was just going shopping with a young woman. Guild Girl had planned in advance for this day, made sure her request for leave was in early, and gone home specifically to change clothes, and now here beside her was…

I guess we don't exactly look like a pair.

Her in her clean white blouse, him in his armor covered in dark-red stains of unknown provenance—it wasn't a good look. Even her hair, which she'd gone out of her way to comb and braid, looked comical beside the tattered tassel on top of his helmet.

But she liked him just fine this way and felt no displeasure at the situation.

"Beyond the mountains. You mean the dark country of night that extends across a lonely wilderness?"

"Yes."

She couldn't resist a chuckle at this most characteristic of responses. *I might laugh it off as just machismo if I didn't know that famous story.*

It was a tale that had once caused many a pulse to race but which fewer and fewer people now knew. A barbarian of the north, a usurper, pirates, mercenaries, generals…and a king.

This macho man had cut his way through many enemies, conquered a mountain of treasure, and ultimately possessed many thrones. It was the sort of legend one could carve only when the light of civilization did not yet burn brightly, and an iron sword was all one needed to bend the world to one's will. The story of a great man that would make a fine tale to tell to any boy.

And even this man beside me was once a boy who dreamed of being an adventurer, wasn't he?

It was such a sweet thought that Guild Girl couldn't help smiling; it was enough to make her want to give him a hug. Whether or not she would restrain herself—maybe that was the difference between her and his old friend who lived on the farm.

"Hmm…" Enjoying the feeling of his words rolling around in her head, she spotted a shop selling accessories. A profusion of colorful ties. She would pick a few. She wondered which might match her hair. "Which do you like best, Goblin Slayer?"

"…Me?"

"Yes, you." Had it been unfair for her to ask not which one would look good on her but which one he liked? *No, no*, she thought. *That's called strategy.* It wasn't fair for her to fret about his thoughts. Let him fret about what *she* thought a little.

Scarlet. Pink. Black and white. One dark green, another blue. *Even purple might be nice*, she mused.

He studied the ties from behind his visor, taking care that they not be blown away by the gusts, which had begun mingling the breeze of fall and the wind of winter. The shopkeeper shot them a

©Noboru Kannatuki

less-than-welcoming glance, but Guild Girl let it roll right off her back. She couldn't have cared less at that moment.

"I don't know much about colors," Goblin Slayer said but took one of the ties in his gloved hand. She looked closely at it.

"White, you think?"

"Your usual hair tie is yellow, and the Guild uniform is black. I thought something close to that might be good."

Oh, for crying out loud…!

She could almost have laughed at herself for how little it took to get her heart racing. To know that he saw her at "usual" times, knew and remembered her, and was considering that in his decision.

Still, though… Guild Girl tried to keep her feet on the ground as she pointedly pursed her lips. "I asked which color *you* like."

"Hrm…" He grunted, then went silent—and, after some thought, finally concluded: "I don't dislike white."

"I suppose I'll accept that for today." She laughed wholeheartedly and took the white hair tie in her hand. "I'll take this, please."

Goblin Slayer nodded, passing some silver coins to the shopkeeper. The total lack of hesitation was one of his charms.

"Thank you very much," Guild Girl said, hugging the hair tie to her chest and smiling at him. "My goodness, though… The north. You've never been beyond the snowy mountain yet, have you?"

"No," he said, shaking his head. "Not yet." He sounded as if he believed he never would, either.

"Hmm." Pouting again. She didn't think the way he'd said that was very fair. "What would you do if I said you *could* go?" She trotted out ahead of him, then spun to face him. In the corner of her vision, she saw her braid flutter like a tail.

Goblin Slayer came to a halt without even his customary grunt— just stopped cold. Right in the middle of the crowd. Passersby shot the two of them suspicious looks, then swerved around them. He took a step forward, as if forced ahead by the silence itself. "*Can* I go?"

"I'm asking whether you want to."

He grunted softly: "Hrm…" Then he fell silent again and stilled. She could tell at a glance that he was thinking.

I wonder what his face looks like right now—behind that visor. Was he expectant? Did he think this excursion would be fun?

No, no—she'd known him for years. She knew what he was thinking about. His party members (though he still seemed somewhat reluctant to call them that). His farm.

And, she had no doubt, goblins.

None of that had changed in all their years together. But certain things had.

He thinks about something other than just goblins now.

Changes could be either good or bad. But Guild Girl thought this was a change for the better. Someone who had never changed before was making the attempt to become the slightest bit different.

And how can that not be a good thing?

After a long moment, the answer finally came: "…If it's indeed possible."

It was far too passive to call it a promising response. Guild Girl took a breath, let it out, and looked at the ground. No matter what expression she brought to bear on him next, it would take courage. She mustered up her nerve, then almost jumped forward and reached out to take his gloved hand in hers. "In that case, I have just the adventure for you!"

I hope I can get my smile under control by the time we eat lunch!

§

"The north, you say… Hmm, hmm." Lizard Priest shivered and huffed to himself.

It was the next day, in a corner of the waiting area of the Adventurers Guild. The five adventurers sat on a bench, conferring about the quest. It was nothing like the plain sheets of parchment they normally saw—which was to say, the goblin-slaying quests. It was lavishly decorated, the text studded with elaborate, ornamental script; even the ink somehow seemed to be of higher-than-average quality. Notably, it appeared the quest had never even been on the bulletin board; there wasn't so much as a pinhole in the paper.

All of which meant...

"This is a quest fit for Silver-ranked adventurers!" High Elf Archer exclaimed, puffing out her slim chest. Lizard Priest might have been thinking about how cold the journey would be, but the elf seemed in high spirits. "I think it's a great idea. An uncommonly excellent choice coming from you, Orcbolg!"

"I see." The helmeted head nodded.

The high elf grinned like a mischievous child and said, "I'll take it—*we'll* take it. I'm going on this quest, by hook or by crook!"

"You don't even know what the quest is about!" Dwarf Shaman, ignoring the elf's triumphant (but still elegant) gesture with her fingers, grabbed the paper in his own thick hand. It took him a moment to parse the letters that danced across the page, but finally he said: "Survey the northern frontier?"

"Yes." The helmet nodded again. "I don't fully understand it myself, but there was something about a battle, reconciliation, and an alliance... It seems the area recently became part of this country's territory."

"Hoh." Dwarf Shaman stroked his beard, his face darkening. "So there was some fighting."

"Er, um." Priestess placed a slim pointer finger to her lips and looked up at the ceiling. "Major battles with other nations ceased after the reign of the previous king," she said. At least, that was how she seemed to remember it. "There was the situation with the Dungeon of the Dead, and then—you remember, the Demon Lord appeared. I believe it was around that time."

"Don't you think it was basically payback for all those wars?" High Elf Archer said with a touch of sarcasm. Sometimes all you could do with humans was laugh at them.

Plagues and zombies had enveloped the land—a terrible threat, all culminating in a tremendous battle with the forces of Chaos. Well, admittedly, humans couldn't have denied that it was the result of their own insatiable appetites.

Having said that…

Priestess didn't know much about restoring the resources of an exhausted country, but she knew it couldn't be easy. Observations and surveys like this would be an important part of that process. "Are they sure they want to entrust something like that to us?" That was what concerned her.

"Yep," Dwarf Shaman said, shifting in his seat, leaning toward her and handing her the paper. She thanked him and took it; even a quick glance made clear the beauty of the penmanship, an immediate and obvious difference from the average quest. Priestess, however, showed no sign of anxiety or lack of confidence. Perhaps she felt such emotions—just a little—but if so, they didn't make it into her expression.

All one saw in her face were questions—and answers. It was like she was proceeding through a dungeon, testing the floor with a ten-foot pole.

Dwarf Shaman, heartened by the growth he saw in his companion (which he was sure Priestess herself hadn't yet noticed), gave a hearty laugh. "Eh, leave the politicking to the more important people," he said. People could always have a drink and understand each other, so long as no one was bent on starting a fight. To a dwarf like Dwarf Shaman, this conviction was perfectly natural; he accepted it without any discomfort.

Goblin Slayer appeared to agree, for he extended a gloved hand and pointed to something on the paper. "It appears they wish to establish an Adventurers Guild there eventually, as well."

"Huh. And they want us to go have a look first, eh? Well." *Glug.* Dwarf Shaman took a swallow of the fire wine at his hip, licking the stray drops out of his beard. "Sounds like they want to show us off."

"I don't know anything about that," Goblin Slayer said. However, it was clear what this unusual adventurer most likely *did* understand. As someone who held to the basic precepts of a scout—including "know what you need to know"—he must have figured it out.

These five adventurers—the strange-looking warrior, the cleric of a foreign religion, the dwarf, the elf, and the lizardman—would have to look like a most unusual party to the northerners.

Yet, they seem to want to say, we are indeed adventurers.

Silver-ranked adventurers at that—and no doubt they would be expected to act like it. That much, even Beard-cutter here surely grasped. Dwarf Shaman was certain of it. *I s'pose you could call that growth, too, after a fashion*, he thought. They should probably take the quest. Only a truly old person would try to hold back youth when it was finally stepping out into the world.

"Much as it pains me to agree with the anvil, I'd take this job, too."

"I'm no happier than you are, having to go along with a barrel."

"Oh! I-I'm going, too!" Priestess raised a small hand quickly, already ignoring the jabbering argument beginning between the elf and the dwarf. Maybe she didn't feel she needed to intervene, or maybe she was simply used to it by now. "What about you—are you all right?" In any event, her considerate gaze now settled on...

"Mmmm..." His face was blue as if from worry—well, bluish-green—well, it had always been that color, thanks to his scales. Lizard Priest stretched out his long neck. "*Ahem*, they say that the one who gives in to fear is far from a naga, so I suppose I must go. Yes, I suppose I have no choice, but..." A sigh escaped his great jaws, and he rolled his eyes in his head. "Verily, it must be cold indeed beyond the mountains to the north." One could hear in his voice as he forced the words out how profoundly he meant them.

Priestess stifled a laugh at the lizardman's tragic act. All of them understood perfectly well that for him, the chill was a real matter of life and death.

The elf, of course, had an easy answer to this. "What if you bought a new cloak? And maybe some kind of magic equipment?!" She was going to snow-clad mountains but seemed altogether unconcerned about the cold—a very high elf sort of detachment.

Lizard Priest crossed his arms, nonplussed by her sanguine attitude, and grunted. "I cannot rely overmuch on equipment. As one who seeks to be a fearsome naga—"

"C'mon, that's the same thinking that got your ancestors wiped out by the cold."

"Gnrrr..." Lizard Priest was apparently unable to come up with any other rejoinder.

"Ahhh, leave the man alone," Dwarf Shaman said, but even he was wearing a wry smile. It wasn't often, after all, that their lizardman was to be seen hanging his head, at a loss for words. High Elf Archer poked his scales playfully, amused by the unusual sight.

Priestess found Dwarf Shaman looking at her as if to say, *Do something about this.* So she offered, "I've been granted a new miracle; perhaps it might help a little..."

She'd secretly been wondering when to tell them about it. It seemed like it would be childish to sound too proud of it, yet at the same time, to mention it too casually would seem disrespectful. Besides, she did want them to congratulate her for it... Maybe that was what made her such a child.

"That's awesome!" High Elf Archer exclaimed, casting away Priestess's hesitation in a couple of words. Her curiosity focused on the young cleric quicker than a leaf danced in the autumn wind. "So when was this? When did this happen?"

"It was...just after the dungeon exploration contest." Priestess scratched her cheek shyly as her elder friend leaned in. She was a little embarrassed, but she was also joyful—and she'd resolved to stop trying to be humble when it wasn't warranted. The words she ultimately came up with were *thank you*, and she was sure that was the right thing to say. "It felt like...like the Earth Mother spoke to me."

After that experience, she had stayed in the temple and purified herself, observed several days of silence, and finally...

Finally?

This word that welled up within her—could it be attributed to inexperience or to the fact that the austerities were such that any ordinary person would have found them difficult?

I wonder which.

It was hard to feel confident when she didn't know the answer. At length, she decided taking a step forward was better than doing nothing. "Be everything else as it may, I've been granted a miracle... It feels like the Earth Mother acknowledged me."

"Well, that's great. Congratulations!" It was wonderful; the elf couldn't have seemed more pleased if it had been she herself who had been blessed with this divine gift. She gave Priestess a big hug, and the younger girl felt her heart leap at the verdant smell of the forest that wafted from the elf's slim body.

"Thank you," Priestess repeated, graciously accepting the embrace.

Goblin Slayer watched the two happy women intently, then finally said, "...Me, I've only heard of what's beyond the northern mountains in stories." His tone was somber; no doubt he'd been thinking about this utterance very carefully. The helmeted head turned toward Lizard Priest, and he added dispassionately, "I would like to go on this quest, but I won't force you to come along."

Lizard Priest didn't respond immediately. The party shared a glance; then Dwarf Shaman started: "You heard the man. Beardcutter says he wants to go beyond the mountains to the north, to the land of darkness and deep night."

"Gee, just that description sounds depressing." High Elf Archer whistled. "But if he wants to go, who am I to deny him?"

The two of them smiled like kids who were in on a joke. Priestess seemed to share their sentiment; she stared at Lizard Priest, whose head was bowed. After what seemed a long time, he exhaled heavily and said, "I suppose I am left without a choice. Nagas, after all, do not flee."

"Is that so?"

"Indeed it is." Lizard Priest nodded without much enthusiasm. Priestess was secretly relieved. *I'm much happier with all of us going together,* she thought. It seemed best to her.

The adventurer called Goblin Slayer, the one she respected and sought to imitate, was certainly...different. But he was also *becoming* different, changing bit by bit. He'd helped run the dungeon exploration contest. He'd suggested they go on a proper adventure. And now he wanted to journey to the far-northern reaches. If helping him do so would repay even a fraction of her debt to him...

But that wasn't all. Of course it wasn't.

"All of us going on an adventure together—this'll be fun!" Priestess said.

"Now you're getting it!" High Elf Archer's eyes sparkled like stars.

This was how adventures were supposed to be.

§

Ahem. However.

"Hrm... Where did I put it...?"

Getting ready for an adventure could be a real struggle. At the moment, Priestess was in her room on the second floor of the Guild building, turning the place upside down.

Failing to prepare for an adventure was no different from preparing to fail—that much, Priestess had learned on her very first quest. To make the same mistake twice would be disrespectful to her first party members. If they'd all survived, if they had all been together now, no doubt they'd be laughing, trading banter, getting ready to go with her.

"No doubt"... Am I sure about that?

It was just a possibility. No matter how vividly she imagined it, it could only ever be a fantasy.

Priestess shook her head, then grabbed her traveling bag from where it sat on the corner of a shelf. "Oof... It's a little dusty..."

Equipment and the like suffered even when it was only left to sit, unused. *Always be prepared* had a nice ring to it, but keeping every single piece of your equipment fighting fit at all times was a tall order.

I've heard that adventurers who travel a lot just buy what they need when they need it and then sell it afterward, Priestess reflected. That sounded like a waste to her, but that choice meant she had to care for her belongings so they would be ready when she needed them.

"I hope it's not bug-eaten or anything..."

She pulled a winter ensemble out of the bag: heavy cloak, tall boots, and so on. She had a sentimental attachment to them; they were nice items she'd bought when she'd wanted to look good for her promotion exam. Once winter was over, there'd been nothing for it but to put them away, but their moment had come again.

"I'll be asking a lot of you," she told them. Then she nodded in satisfaction, gathered up the outfit, and headed downstairs, outside, so she wouldn't be a nuisance. She found a nice, sunny spot behind the Guild in which to set up shop. She spread out a cloth and laid the equipment on it. The cloak, the boots, the rope and hook. She made sure she wouldn't be leaving home without the contents of her Adventurer's Toolkit.

Because they would be going somewhere not only cold but far away, she wanted to make sure she inspected all her equipment, not just the cold-weather gear. The last thing she wanted was to toss the grappling hook only to have the rope snap and send her plunging. To be fair, Dwarf Shaman would probably save her with a Falling Control spell, but still...

Don't let your guard down, act without hesitation, and don't use up your spells. That's what he *would say.*

Fate and Chance between them were impossible to avoid, but one could give oneself the best possible odds.

"Now to air them out... The problem is these thick clothes." Just letting them sit in the sun would be a good start, but it would pay to go the extra mile. Priestess stood and took the back entrance to the kitchen—she had asked for help ahead of time.

"Ah, you're here." As soon as she came to the door, she was welcomed by Padfoot Waitress with a beaming smile.

Even just a quick peek into the kitchen, where the rhea chef bustled busily around, was enough to get her a face full of steam. She smiled—the delicious aroma alone was relaxing—and bowed her head. "Yes, thank you. Sorry for the trouble."

"Aw, don't mention it. I mean, you're a real regular around here, right? I can at least do this much for you." Padfoot Waitress turned toward the chef and shouted, "I'm stepping out for a second, okay?"

©Noboru Kannatuk

before trotting over to the stove. She grabbed a giant stewpot in her arms as if it weighed nothing at all. "Okay, let's go! Outside, right?"

Priestess's eyes briefly went wide, but then she managed, "Oh, yes!" and nodded. "This way, please!" It took her a second; she'd been trying to figure out how she could carry the pot herself or at least help.

She led her friend over to a great communal washbasin set up against the outside wall, which they politely borrowed. They carried it clatteringly back to where Priestess had set up her equipment...

"All right, and...there!"

"Okay, here goes!" said Padfoot Waitress, and then she poured the boiling contents of the stewpot into the washbasin. The murky, gray liquid was lye, made with ash. It smelled, but not like cooking; the girls looked at each other and giggled. "Life is tough for you adventurers. You do this every time you go off somewhere?" Padfoot Waitress asked. Then she added under her breath, "I sure couldn't handle it."

The padfoot looked at the items scattered around the cloth. A grappling hook and pitons, devices that could be strapped to one's shoes to prevent slipping on snowy paths, and many other things one rarely encountered in daily life. She leaned forward, taking a good look; she seemed just like a child eagerly exploring the wares of a shop.

Priestess (dimly aware of Padfoot Waitress's tail wagging in her peripheral vision) nodded. "I'm worried about bugs. The longer you leave things sitting, the more work they need when you take them out."

"Yeah, fleas are so gross."

"I'm concerned about lice, too."

The girls shared a firm nod. Better to put in the effort to clean the items than to take along any unwanted little stowaways. Nobody wanted to be bitten by bugs—but that went double for young ladies at a certain time in their lives.

Thus it was only natural that their conversation should turn in that direction. "Nobles put dark stuff under their eyes, right?" Padfoot Waitress asked, gesturing with a padded paw.

"That's right," Priestess said.

"What's it called again? Eyebrow black? Eye shadow? I hear that face-whitening powder mixed with rouge and pulverized malachite keeps bugs away, too."

"That sounds expensive…"

"Better believe it. I probably couldn't afford that stuff if I worked my whole life."

The cosmetics in question were immaterial to the padfoot girl and her cleric friend. They might be taken with the idea of the stuff, but they would never get their hands on it. Anyway, it wouldn't be very amenable to sweaty kitchen work, and a bit of adventuring would surely take it right off.

Then again, I've heard padfoots don't sweat very much, Priestess thought. Still, any cosmetics would probably run with all the steam in the kitchen. The two of them smiled at each other as if to say, *Oh well*.

"Okay, I'd better be getting back," Padfoot Waitress said.

"Sure thing… And thank you!" Priestess pressed a silver coin she'd had ready into the fuzzy paw that waved at her. Preparing lye took time and effort as well, and it was only fair to compensate the woman for that.

Priestess watched her friend head back to work, then breathed. "Okay!"

She pulled off her boots and socks and rolled up the hem of her robe, then tied up her sleeves, eager to get started. Then she took the winter clothes and tossed them into the barrel of lye. Finally, she hopped into the barrel with her bare feet and started stomping on the laundry.

"Mmmm…" The steaming lye was pleasantly warm, salving her weary toes.

But oops—she didn't have time to stand there. She started working her feet up and down, *sploosh, sploosh*. "Hup! And hup…"

Maybe I should have offered to do everyone else's equipment while I was at it.

Hmm, should she have? She wasn't even sure the other members of her party had winter outfits stashed away. As experienced adventurers, they probably knew how to handle themselves when it came to things like that.

I should ask Goblin Slayer.

Priestess nodded to herself even as she worked her feet; then she glanced up at a window on the second floor of the Guild: High Elf Archer's room, which constantly looked as if a tornado had gone through it. She wasn't sure if any winter preparations were happening in that disaster zone, but... *I should crash the place and find out,* she thought. Then she nodded again, bravely, full of determination, a sense of mission, and a grim resolution. Whereupon...

"Oh, ugh..."

"You can't get careless just because the new adventurers aren't watching. *Sigh...* I thought we were done getting so dirty now that we've left the sewers, but I guess not."

"Aw, can't say as I mind much, y'know?"

Priestess heard three somewhat exasperated but ultimately lively voices. She glanced over and, indeed, saw three of her friends. A boy and a girl dressed in ordinary day clothes, accompanied by someone with a pair of bouncing white ears. They each carried an armload of blood- and mud-stained equipment.

"Another successful day?" Priestess called, smiling, partly teasing but partly sincerely appreciative.

"You know it. I let Masher do the talking...or mashing or whatever!" the boy said, swinging an invisible club. Priestess was well aware that the young man had perfected the art of using both the club and the sword at once. *He's really come a long way,* she thought—but then she chuckled at herself. She wasn't going to let herself get so caught up in being the More Experienced Colleague that she started to act condescending.

"Sorry about this," Priestess said, glancing down at her feet in embarrassment. "I'll be done in a few minutes..." Then she picked up the pace of her stomping.

The girl wearing the sigil of the Supreme God jabbed her friend— who'd gotten a little distracted by Priestess's bare feet—with her elbow and smiled. "Don't worry about it. We're only running late because *somebody* was dragging his feet. We can wait our turn."

"Hoo-ee, those are winter clothes. Goin' back to the mountains, are ye?" the white-furred rabbit-girl asked, peering at Priestess's laundry. It seemed they'd only just been there. Once again, Priestess found herself—without really meaning to—watching the harefolk girl's ears bob up and down.

"The mountains?" Priestess asked. The harefolk girl leaned forward: ears, back, behind, and the round, poofy tail situated right on top of it. "Beyond them, actually."

"Hoo-ee… Nother long trip. Me, I've never been out that far," the girl said easily; it sounded like she didn't know much more about the north than Priestess did. So much for Priestess's (admittedly already slim) hope that the harefolk might be able to give her some information about what to expect. "I heard it was real scary round those parts— I've been told to stay away or the roughnecks might get me."

"R-roughnecks? You mean, like, bad people?"

"I tried to get 'em to tell me, but they'd just go on about gettin' robbed. Point is, well, I guess you oughtta keep your distance."

Apparently, these were strong people of some kind. Priestess blinked, still stuck on the unfamiliar word. It seemed the harefolk had heard this from her grandfather. So had this been a long time ago? But then again, harefolk generations seemed to pass awfully swiftly, so…?

"Damn, you're so lucky. I wanna go somewhere like that," the young man said, gazing up into the blue sky. "I'd love to hit up, you know, like, Neverwinter on the north of the Sword Coast or whatever…"

"I don't think we're going anywhere quite that famous…" Priestess smiled a little at the names, all-but-forgotten realms spoken of in fairy tales. She didn't think they were exactly unexplored lands, even if she'd heard of them only in stories.

"Yeah, but didn't that dark elf ranger do his adventuring up north?" the boy asked.

"Dummy, that's just one of the sagas," the cleric girl said with a sniff. "You very, very rarely encounter a good dark elf."

"I guess not…," Priestess said. She'd encountered dark elves herself at the harvest festival, in the desert, and indirectly in connection with the offertory wine. *Maybe I just don't know that many elves*, she thought. She was getting closer and closer to High Elf Archer, but she didn't know much about the young scout woman.

A good dark elf. The incredible ranger with the two-handed style was just a legend—again, a fairy tale. Yes: It was precisely because he was a fairy-tale character that he was able to go to the places he did. Her, though, she wasn't going anywhere like that—at least, she didn't think so. Maybe she just didn't know it.

"If *we* went anywhere near Icewind Dale, the only thing that would happen is we'd be hit with Horror and die," the cleric girl said, her ruthlessly realistic assessment of the situation crushing the boy's innocent hopes.

"Yeah, but if ye're going at the nation's own behest... Well, that's practically a Gold-level adventure, ain't it?" the harefolk girl said.

The sharp edge of *that* reality brought Priestess to a screeching halt. The water splashed as she froze in mid-stomp on the laundry.

"N-n-no..." Her voice was shaking. "I really d-don't...think so... I don't think..."

It wasn't that she hadn't been aware of the idea. In fact, she had been aware of it and had been trying very hard not to think about it. She, at least, didn't fit the description. She was doing the best she could as a member of her party, but she still had a long way to go with her strength and abilities.

Priestess took a deep breath to calm herself, then silently began working the clothes again. Her friends, however, weren't about to let her get away that easily.

"You're Sapphire, though, aren't you?"

"She sure is!"

"Urgh..." All she could do was stare intently at the ground. She knew the boy and girl were smirking at her, but grumbling about it wouldn't gain her anything.

"Oh, that reminds me!" The harefolk girl, off on her own planet as usual, clapped her furry hands. "As long as you're headin' that way, miss, you think I could ask you to do a little job for me?"

"A job…?" Priestess looked at her even as she continued working the clothes underfoot.

"Uh-huh!" The white ears bobbed again. "I wrote a letter. I'd like to get it, and a bit of cargo, over to the mountains."

"A letter? Okay. But… What's this about cargo?" Priestess didn't necessarily object—in fact, she was perfectly happy to take the job— but what was this about? She cocked her head, and Harefolk Hunter chuckled, almost with embarrassment, before riffling through her belongings. And why did the girl and boy with her look so happy?

"Here! This is it!" the hunter exclaimed, proudly displaying the item she'd finally come up with: a troll fang.

§

"…So you'll be going away again, then."

"Yes, sir." Goblin Slayer nodded ambivalently. "I believe it will be quite a distance."

"I see," was all the owner of the farm, seated across from him, said; then he nodded—more firmly and confidently than Goblin Slayer— and let out a breath.

They were in the dining room of the farm's main house. It was a little too early to use the word *evening*, but it felt a bit late for *afternoon*. When Goblin Slayer had gotten back from town, he'd found the owner of the farm before his friend. He was sitting in a chair, evidently resting after having done his work in the fields.

Goblin Slayer had pulled out a chair for himself as well, but when he sat down, the other man greeted him with only, "You're back?" That was the attitude he always took with Goblin Slayer, but that was exactly why Goblin Slayer was a little concerned by it. He wasn't sure what to say. Or rather, what the owner was trying to say.

Ultimately, still not sure himself, Goblin Slayer had told the owner about the new quest. And the result…

"Well, it's not my job to tell you what to do."

...had been those few simple words. Goblin Slayer grunted behind the visor of his helmet, not quite sure how to take them.

The owner glanced at him, although he probably didn't register Goblin Slayer's discomfort. "It's your work. And when a man starts a job, it's irresponsible to object."

"I see... You think so, sir?"

"I sure do," the farm owner said quietly, nodding. "It's up to you to take care of it and do the best you can with it."

"...Yes, sir."

"But make sure you tell the girl what you're up to."

"I intend to."

"Thought so." The owner smiled faintly, then got slowly to his feet. As a yeoman, an independent farmer, his legs were still strong, and his step was still sprightly. Nonetheless, the shadow of old age seemed to hover around him; he looked tired somehow.

He departed the dining area, going somewhere else in the house and leaving Goblin Slayer by himself. Goblin Slayer, who had never once fully understood all the emotions accumulated within himself.

Think. That was all he could do.

The girl...

She would probably be bringing the cows back to the barn about now. And taking care of the camel, perhaps. Whatever she was doing, he should go and talk to her. Very few things got better for being put off.

Goblin Slayer's chair clattered as he stood. As he left the house, he could hear the canary chirping behind him. He shut the door, blocking out the sound, then took a breath.

The world was a gruesome red-black, the color of deep twilight. It was already getting quite cold. When he exhaled, the breath fogged as it escaped through the slats of his visor.

Ah...

A year already. A year since he had gotten that young woman caught up in a goblin hunt. How much had he really moved forward in that time?

He followed the white fog of his breath with his eyes as it drifted into the sky shimmering against the darkening blue. Flying above, higher than the clouds but lower than the stars, was a single sparrowhawk.

How long ago had it been since his heart had last raced to the stories of that great sage? He couldn't quite remember now whether he'd heard them from his sister or sung by a bard. So many of the stories he'd heard and imagined again and again in his youth were ancient, patchy.

He'd been to the elf village. Visited the capital. Delved the Dungeon of the Dead. Braved the eastern desert. And now he was going to go beyond the mountains to the north. He'd always wanted to. Always assumed he never would. Always, from his youth. He'd understood even then that he would live out his whole life in that tiny speck of a village. Had he even once imagined that things might turn out like this? He wasn't—

"Huh? When'd you get back?" His old friend came walking toward him, her smile obscured by her own fogging breath. "Welcome home!" she said with an energy that belied how tired she must have felt after doing her day's work.

"Yes," he said, nodding. "I'm back."

The two of them weren't quick to return to the main house. Instead, they stood for a moment in silence, their shadows stretching out in the red light of dusk, and then they started walking.

They were heading for the fence that surrounded the farm. Cow Girl leaned on it, as she'd done once long before, in a place that was not here. It had seemed so easy to hop over when she was small, yet somehow as an adult, she found she couldn't do it.

"I wonder why," she said.

"I don't know." Goblin Slayer shook his head. He really didn't know. When he was a child, he'd assumed adults could do anything, and yet...

What can *I do?*

Just looking at the sun as it sank beyond the horizon on the far side of the square put the thought in his head. The fact that just a few months before, he'd been headed beyond that horizon seemed impossible...

No. The sun sets in the west.

The exact opposite of the direction he'd gone. Behind his visor, he very nearly smiled at his own stupidity. It gave him the push he needed to speak.

"I'll be traveling far away again."

"On an adventure?"

"That's how it seems to me." He nodded—she was almost looking up into his visor—and then he peered once more toward the horizon. The very edge of the Four-Cornered World. He'd once gone to a tower that had nearly allowed him to touch it. But so what? It wasn't as if doing so would have unveiled to him all the secrets of the world.

And anyway, that hadn't been *his* adventure. This one would be. Even if he still felt a substantial internal resistance to calling it so.

"It'll be beyond the mountains to the north," he said.

"Hmm!" His old friend kicked the air. Then, suddenly, she turned to him, and her red hair in the dying sunlight made her appear to be wreathed in flames. Her eyes, shining like jewels, focused keenly on him through his visor. How many times had he looked her right in the eye like this? Even though he thought he lacked the courage.

"Are you waiting for me to give you permission to go again?"

"…"

She certainly wasted no time. And when had she started doing that? He felt as if she'd been that way since they were young… And certainly since they had been reunited. It was she who understood him, better than anyone else, better than he understood himself. He could hide nothing from her, nor did he wish to.

"Yes," he said with a nod. The honest answer. He'd tried to look big once already and had regretted it. Once was enough. "I know I'm pathetic."

"I guess so…"

She refused to deny it, but she smiled a little uneasily and repeated, "I guess so. Pathetic, and troublesome, and maybe not very cool-looking."

"…"

"But... Mm. I like that, I think. I like you."

He had to inhale deeply to get himself breathing again. "Is that...so?"

"It sure is." His old friend gave a gentle kick—the way she began so many of her movements—and hopped down from the fence. She landed lightly next to him and placed her hand over his own gloved one. He turned his helmet and found her looking at him from so close that he was afraid he might bump into her with his visor.

"*See you real soon.* Is that good enough?"

"..."

Her eyes were so close. Her breath seemed like it might float past his visor and into his helmet. Her cheeks were red.

"Yes... I think so."

"Good!"

The sun in the sky was sinking past twilight, but the smile on her face was as bright as the dawn as she nodded at him. "Don't forget a souvenir, okay? I'll be looking forward to finding out what you bring me. But, uh, no animals this time, all right?"

"A souvenir?"

"I guess we'd better eat dinner first, huh? Ha-ha, gotta do things in the right order."

She was already trotting toward the main house, pulling him along. Wanting to be sure he kept up with her, Goblin Slayer took the first of many steps forward.

CHAPTER 2

OVER THE MISTY MOUNTAINS

"All right, then—have a safe trip!"

It had been three days since the good-natured hare-wife had sent them on their way with those words, and Goblin Slayer's party was now in the middle of a blizzard. Or, to be more precise, they were working their way along a most unwelcoming mountain path carved into the craggy cliffside of a peak beset with ice and snow.

The path was so narrow that they had to cling to the mountainside as they went. The wind gusted mercilessly, assailing them with such clouds of debris that they didn't know if they were in a blizzard or a dust storm.

They went along, all but sliding their feet, unwilling to look down but unable to see anything ahead of them on account of the elements. It seemed as if the breath froze the moment it left their mouths— though they couldn't quite be sure if it was really happening or if it only felt like it was.

If we aren't careful, we could die here...! Priestess found herself thinking, and the other members of the party were likely contemplating something similar. After all, what they were walking on hardly qualified as a road; it was more of a narrow track across the top of a cliff, with only a bottomless drop waiting below. It couldn't be perfectly vertical, but the fact that there were times when it seemed like it was spoke to how difficult the going was. If one was to slip, one would be assaulted by rocks and snow and ice, and it would only be a question of how long life and limb lasted after that. But the horror of falling could stop you only if you didn't start; once you began putting one foot in front of the other, it was impossible not to carry on. In fact, Priestess was learning that it was stopping that posed the greatest risk of causing a fall.

"You doing okay?" She could just barely hear High Elf Archer's voice. The elf was wearing a hat that covered her ears.

Priestess finally managed to tear herself away from the fond thought of the hare-wife's home-cooked meal long enough to answer, "I... I'm okay!" She wasn't sure whether her voice would reach High Elf Archer. Then again, it was probably fine. Her cherished friend *was* a high elf, after all.

She saw High Elf Archer respond with a big wave of her hand. She walked along the mountain path as if it were a branch of a tree. "How about the rest of you?" she called. "Still there, or did you fall down?"

"We ain't fallin' anywhere! C'mon, Scaly, steady now!"

"Mm...!"

Priestess heard Dwarf Shaman and Lizard Priest behind her. The dwarf was supporting the lizardman, who looked like he'd become a ball of fluffy down. ("Even my forefathers might have smiled to have had one of these," he'd announced when he showed them the cloak.) The brightly colored feathers warded off the snow and wind, repelled water, and made Priestess feel warmer just looking at them. But...

"This is proving...quite the trial, I'd say...!"

...the path, which crawled around the mountainside like a centipede, seemed even smaller under Lizard Priest's huge bulk. His claws dug into the ground with every step, so he wasn't likely to fall, but he still had to deal with the cold on top of everything else. Dwarf Shaman had provided warm stones, but the situation remained a challenge. Admittedly, the sight of the lizardman struggling along was somewhat comical, but Priestess felt concern more acutely than amusement. Or she would have, if she'd had the free resources in her mind to worry about her companions...

"Hey, Orcbolg. I know it's a little late to be asking, but are you *sure* we can do this?"

"I had heard the stories, but I admit, this is hard."

How can the two of them up there sound so...used to this? Priestess wondered. There wasn't so much as a rope strung along the side of the path; a couple of wrong steps would send them plummeting into the abyss. Granted, they weren't likely to take that many wrong steps, but even so...

Goblin Slayer, wrapped in a cloak evidently given to him by the owner of the farm, proceeded as if nothing was the matter. Priestess, laboring for every step, watched him with equal parts envy and resentment. It didn't matter that she knew perfectly well that his ease was born of experience as both a scout and a ranger.

The world around them was a single, barely differentiated gray, a swirl of black and white. The only thing they could hear was the roaring of the wind. Mountains, Priestess reflected, truly weren't suited to human habitation.

"Isn't there at least somewhere we can take a rest?" Priestess called to Goblin Slayer.

"I've heard there's a cave just up ahead."

"He says there's a cave!" Priestess shouted to the two behind her, rewarded with an "a'right!" from Dwarf Shaman.

Just have to keep pushing...! Priestess thought. As was her habit at moments like this, she clenched her fists in resolve—then quickly put her hands back on the cliffside when she felt like she might lose her footing. She'd strapped her sounding staff to her back, and even if she slipped, she wouldn't immediately go right over the edge, but even so. *If I dropped my staff...* She knew she would never get it back, and the thought was terrifying.

And so they worked their way carefully along, but Goblin Slayer never slowed and never stopped. He moved with one hand on the cliffside, clutching the rocks, his hips low—but he moved methodically, decisively. Though of course his movements couldn't compare to the lithe hopping and skipping of High Elf Archer, who looked like she was jumping from stone to stone across a river.

"You're pretty good at this," Priestess heard the high elf remark. "I knew you had a lot of talents, Orcbolg, but I didn't realize this was one of them."

"As far as it goes," he replied, even as he carefully picked his next step. Then he stopped, brushed the dirt off his cloak, and said, "However, there are fifty thousand who are better at it than I am."

"Such as?"

"There are many stories of the people called ninjas." He abruptly fell quiet, then grunted, and then said as if recollecting: "My master once told me of people who were so good at climbing that they could scale a sheer cliffside free solo, with no rope or tools."

"You'd fall to your death if you slipped!"

"Of course you would," he said, the helmet nodding. "That's why I could never do it."

"Aw, man..." High Elf Archer sounded absolutely exasperated. "I can't believe anyone actually did it. I can't believe anyone even *tried* it."

"I see." Almost disinterestedly, he murmured something about how there were humans who had powers even he could not imagine. Then he went silently on.

Priestess was so busy trying to keep up that she wasn't sure she'd caught the entire conversation correctly. And keeping up wasn't the only thing she was busy with. Even as she worked her way forward, she glanced back, calling, "Are you okay?" to the other two members of the party.

Being in the middle of the formation was something she'd had bad memories of ever since her first adventure. At the same time, she was the only one who could see everything that was going on and notice everything around them at once. She'd done this several times now...

Because they asked me to.

The thought didn't inspire self-confidence so much as something akin to pride.

"There *must* have been another path, right?" High Elf Archer said calmly. Even if this had seemed the fastest way. It was strange how the high elf's melodic voice could reach them clearly even in the midst of the snowstorm. "What made you pick this one?"

Goblin Slayer didn't answer right away. Instead, the strange, stubborn adventurer continued as he had been: walking silently, one hand on the wall, leading them all ahead. Thankfully, before High Elf Archer's hands started to go numb, they spotted the dark opening of a cave.

At about the same time, Goblin Slayer said, "I wanted to try it."

Priestess steeled herself: Clearly, this adventure had a lot in store.

§

The cave entrance was marked by a tall, yellowish-green boot. It was still attached to the foot of someone buried in a snowbank. Presumably, an adventurer who had made it here at some point before them— whether on their way up the mountain or down, it was impossible to tell. Priestess prayed silently to the Earth Mother that this anonymous person would be blessed in the next life.

Attempting to carry a body, whether ascending or descending the mountain, would put everyone's lives at risk. Hence why this person had remained, welcoming many an adventurer and seeing them off again.

"My teacher told me stone giants sometimes fight around here," Goblin Slayer said, setting his baggage down heavily.

"Gee, sorry we missed them," High Elf Archer teased, sticking out her tongue. She sounded sarcastic, but it was a sight that not even a high elf was likely to see very often in her life. So perhaps she really was sorry to an extent—but that's neither here nor there.

The snowstorm had done a number on her, but simply by dusting herself off, she regained the beauty one expected of a high elf. It indeed showed her to be a separate form of life from mortal humans. Priestess took off her sodden cloak, looking around at the others as she wrung it out so it wouldn't freeze. Goblin Slayer was carefully clean-ing his cloak, folding it, and looking deeper into the cave. In any case, there was someone who worried her more than him.

"Are...are you all right...?"

"Mmmm..." Lizard Priest's voice was lethargic as he removed his down cloak. "I am, somehow."

"Here—you'll be wantin' a sip o' this. Need to warm yourself up before you drop dead, since that wouldn't be any fun."

Dwarf Shaman tossed Lizard Priest his gourd. "My thanks," he said as he caught it and undid the stopper with shaking hands. Meanwhile, Priestess started gathering twigs and leaves that had been blown into the cave, thinking she could get a fire going.

"Oh... They're all soaked..."

Well, it wasn't that surprising. Branches, leaves—and if not those, then at least moss: There was plenty of fuel for a fire. But it had all been soaked by the snow and was now drenched through. It didn't look fit to serve as kindling.

So what to do? Once, Priestess might have been depressed by this turn, but now she put a finger to her lips and thought. "Hmm..."

Maybe Goblin Slayer heard her mumbling to herself, because he turned from his contemplation of the interior of the cave and asked, "Do you have a torch?"

"Oh, yes." But of course. Priestess nodded. The Adventurer's Tool-kit. (Never leave home without it!)

"The torch will light even if it's slightly damp. Use that to dry out the rest of the fuel."

"Oh!"

Yes, that made sense. Priestess clapped her hands. It was so simple. And now that she knew what to do, she was used to all the rest. She got together everything she needed readily, then lit it from the torch, and the fuel began to dry out even as it burned. After being an adventurer for several years, this sort of thing was old hat, and the heat and light of the fire were very calming.

"Wow," someone said, and Goblin Slayer nodded.

"Even if you don't have a torch, you can make do so long as you have green wood. Even damp, fire will catch easily on it."

"You've got some nerve, talking about burning living wood in front of an elf." High Elf Archer had removed her gloves and was massaging her fingers, toes, and ears, but she found time to spare a sharp look at Goblin Slayer, her lips pursed.

A living human body could freeze and even begin rotting if exposed to the cold for too long. Priestess, almost fondly remembering being threatened with as much on the snowy mountain, imitated her elf companion. This time, she'd even thought to bring a change of socks, for her original pair was now soaked through with sweat.

"Brrrr... Many pardons, but if I may..."

Everyone naturally gave the place closest to the fire to Lizard Priest. His down cloak didn't change the fact that he was a lizardman and sensitive to the cold. But then, the fact that he hadn't voiced a single complaint once this path had been chosen and set out on was also very much the way of a lizardman. "Might I request the miracle that was mentioned prior to our departure?"

"Oh! Certainly!" Priestess nodded vigorously. "Just as soon as my clothes are dry!"

"A'right, first, everyone drink up." Dwarf Shaman laughed and shook the gourd full of alcohol, which he had retrieved from Lizard Priest. "This is good fire wine. Just a tipple on yer tongue'll warm yeh all the way through."

"I think it's more likely to make my head explode," High Elf Archer said, but she still took the gourd and had a delicate sip. She frowned expansively at the way the stuff burned, but then after a breath, she said, "Here, you too."

"Th-thank you..." Priestess took the gourd from High Elf Archer, whose cheeks were flushing with the drink. Everyone in the party knew how delicate their high elf was when it came to alcohol—was it being a high elf that made her look even more beautiful nonetheless? Priestess always found herself enraptured by the archer's lithe movements.

"What about you, Orcbolg? Want some?"

"Yes," he said after a moment's quiet. "Just a sip."

Snow, water, sweat. Get soaked through and the chill would sap your strength; then when you went outside, the liquid would freeze, and you would only get colder. Thus, on a snowy mountain, it was crucial to have warmth, a change of clothes, and to rub your arms and legs.

In the picture scrolls and sagas, the heroes—well, they rarely did things like this. In the stories, they always appeared like they normally did and adventured as if nothing was different. One never saw a hero slipping on a patch of snowy ground or gathering kindling to build a fire. If Priestess hadn't become an adventurer herself, she would probably never have known.

"...Do you think we should have tied ourselves together with a rope or something as we walked?" Priestess asked.

"There's a time and place for that," was Goblin Slayer's estimation.

"I'm rather concerned that if I was to miss my step, I would drag you all into the void with me...," Lizard Priest said.

"Yeah, and the dwarf would have the same problem, so that's twice the danger!"

"I suppose no one can best a high elf when it comes to a discussion about weight!"

At length, with her clothing and equipment starting to dry and the alcohol warming her insides, Priestess said, "All right, I'm going to give it a try." She held up her sounding staff with a clear ringing and stood tall. She took a deep breath and clutched her staff with both hands, sending her consciousness high up to the far heights of the heavens. It was a connection of the soul. A prayer but also a supplication, as if she was prostrating herself, the better to send every sign of her love and respect to the gods above.

"O Earth Mother, abounding in mercy, please, by your revered hand, cleanse this land."

This was indeed precisely why the miracle occurred. One does not pray in hopes of being rewarded with a miracle. Neither are miracles granted as a reward for faith.

There was a breath of warmth as the Earth Mother's unseen fingers brushed the cave. Her very hand blocked the snow and wind that howled in from the entrance. This was the Sanctuary miracle.

"Ah, ahhh… I am most grateful indeed for this…!" Lizard Priest regained so much of his strength that he was even able to slap the floor of the cave with his tail—the miracle was showing its effectiveness. "Were I not bound in service to my ancestors, I might be moved to dedicate myself to your Earth Mother."

"I can just see it—you making cheese in her service!" High Elf Archer, who, like the Earth Mother, had an intimate connection to nature, laughed easily and loudly. She had kicked out her legs as if she were in her own room and was relaxing with a smile. "Divine miracles, huh? I've seen you do it a bunch of times now, but it always feels strange. It's not like hearing someone's voice, is it?"

"I can tell yeh, sprites aren't like gods—that much is certain," Dwarf Shaman offered.

"I'm afraid I can't really put it into words, either," Priestess said, smiling with some embarrassment. Then she sat down squarely on a rock.

To be fair, anyone who could explain it would have to be beloved of the gods indeed—a virtuous priest, perhaps. Then again, maybe such a person would refrain from speaking definitively about the gods precisely because of their virtue. Whatever the case, such explanations were certainly beyond the inexperienced, young Priestess…

"Excellent work," said someone close to her. "Can it be used for defense?"

"No, it isn't like Protection." You see, Priestess had her hands full even trying to answer Goblin Slayer's brusque question. "It's not defense so much as it's… Hmm… A secure purification, I guess…?"

"Whatever it is, we're grateful for it, and that's enough," High Elf Archer said. She was already digging through their supplies for the provisions, apparently ready to eat.

Marching along a snowy mountain took real energy. Rest was important—even for a high elf. High Elf Archer waved a leaf-wrapped bundle at Goblin Slayer. "You need to be more grateful for amazing gifts like this, Orcbolg," she said like an older sister chastising her younger brother.

"Hmm," the helmet responded, and then there was a moment of silence. At length, he nodded earnestly. "You're right. I'm grateful for it." That much was certain.

"Good!" High Elf Archer replied jovially, and started chowing down. She was eating elven baked rations. Priestess had become rather fond of them and wanted to ask for a bite, but…

I'm a bit embarrassed…

After all this talk of gratitude…and immediately after she had been praying, as if the effulgence of heaven still shone around her. She sighed. The way she looked enviously at the snacks was almost childlike.

Dwarf Shaman pulled out some cheese, followed by Lizard Priest, crying, "Sweet nectar!"

I need to eat something, too. Priestess was just reaching into her bag when her eyes happened to meet those of High Elf Archer, whose mouth was stuffed full of the baked goods.

"Wanth thome?" she asked.

"…Yes, please." Priestess looked shyly down at the ground, but she could feel the Earth Mother smiling.

Thus the entire party sat in a circle, enjoying their modest but satisfying meal. They ate dried meat and hardtack, then they melted snow in a pan over the fire so there was plenty of water to drink. It didn't feel like any goblin hunt. It didn't even feel as if they were in a hurry.

No, they were on a journey north, over the towering mountains covered with snow and mist. To a place they'd never been, a land they'd never seen—this was a true adventure.

On a journey, one must stop on the road and enjoy the showers that pass as one goes...

Was it the famous burglar who'd sung that song or perhaps the renowned spell caster? Whichever it was, Priestess thought truer words had never been spoken.

"Don't you think it'll be a pretty tough trip if the weather keeps up like this?" High Elf Archer asked, grabbing a piece of toasted cheese from Lizard Priest.

"Ah!" he exclaimed; she pressed some of her elven baked goods on him as she ate her cheese. "It'd be great with cheese. Probably."

"Indeed...!"

True. Definitely not an argument.

Priestess, watching Lizard Priest tear open the baked good and gleefully stuff some cheese inside it, shifted in her seat. "We could wait until the snow calms down... But we have no idea how long that might take."

Mountain weather could be capricious. More to the point, people simply didn't belong in the mountains. It already felt as if they were in some other world.

The mountains treated all equally—and mercilessly. Passable roads, edible food, water—all were found only where they belonged. Surviving a trip through the mountains required knowledge, experience, and skill, along with Fate and Chance. No living thing could expect a helping hand from the mountain itself.

That's the teaching of the Earth Mother anyway.

Priestess was starting to think she understood it...a little. She'd started to think she understood more and more things (a little) recently. She need only think of "The Many Colored Death" that had attacked them in the desert to remind herself of the truth of her religion's teachings that nature was a harsh thing.

"We have food and water, so I think we should be able to make it off the mountain even if it takes a few days...," she said.

"Discretion might be the better part of valor, but I have to admit, I'd like to see this through. You know, as an adventurer." High Elf

Archer smiled, gently and easily, full of the pride of a Silver-ranked adventurer.

Cocksureness and sagacity. Cowardice and care. These things looked similar, but the line between them was fuzzy. Anyone could see the dangers, come up with perfectly logical reasons to avoid them, and walk away from the adventure. Being willing to take on the challenge, even though they knew the risks, and still prevail was what made this an adventure—and what made them adventurers.

"But we have to be careful not to do anything heedless, ridiculous, or outrageous," Priestess said.

"Sure—even knights errant are careful about those pitfalls." It was that sort of awareness that made her elder friend so effective.

"Right," Priestess replied to her wink; Goblin Slayer grunted.

"Hmm. In that case, we should pick a different path," he said.

"Pick a different path? From here?" Dwarf Shaman asked, taking a swig of wine. "Ah...I see."

"You know it?"

"Well, I'm a dwarf. Frankly, I'm surprised that *you* know about it. Awfully old story, that."

"My teacher... I mean, my master taught it to me."

That seemed to satisfy Dwarf Shaman, but Priestess and High Elf Archer were left looking at each other. (Lizard Priest was too busy getting warm and fawning over cheese to notice anything.) High Elf Archer flicked her ears. "What? You know a shortcut?"

"Yes," Goblin Slayer said with a nod. "There's a subterranean passage in here."

§

It was a mossy, old, seemingly forgotten passageway. A narrow path led down from a crack in the interior of the cave that looked like it had been hewn with an ax. Indeed, the rent looked almost natural, but there was undeniably a path there. There were handholds and footholds, and the farther one went, the easier the passage was. At the same time, the path branched out in places, twisted back on itself, and became something of a maze. It seemed likely that someone had capitalized on naturally occurring caverns to create a tunnel system.

Priestess thought she recognized the traces of the craftspeople on the rock walls by the gloomy light of her torch. Perhaps that was what put her in mind of those old fairy tales. Many knew the stories of the adventures of the dwarves and the rhea or of the human, elf, dwarf, and rheas. As well as the tales of the barbarians who had emerged from the north, beyond these very tunnels…

"S'posed to be loads of battlefields left over from the Age of the Gods around here. Lots of ruins," Dwarf Shaman said, interrupting Priestess's thoughts. He didn't need light, so he walked at the back of the formation, studying the rock walls intently, running his fingers over them. "There are elven strongholds and dwarven fortresses. And if there are dwarven fortresses—"

"—then there must be underground passageways," High Elf Archer said knowledgeably. She, likewise, needed no light to see perfectly well. For elves were themselves beings like starlight—or so the poets said. Indeed, Priestess sometimes caught the flash of High Elf Archer's hair in the dark. Most mysterious.

"If there's *one* thing I'll admit dwarves are good at, it's digging holes," High Elf Archer went on. "Even if dark elves are better at it."

"I'd agree with yeh, right up to the part about dark elves." Dwarf Shaman snorted, but he didn't actually sound like he thought it was much of a compliment. Elves and dwarves hardly got along with each other, let alone with dark elves—even children knew that.

But only they know the deeper truths about themselves, Priestess thought. A human like her probably couldn't imagine.

As she walked along with the flickering flame in her hand, she tried paying attention to the walls and floor.

Imagine if I'd come here alone.

She was sure she would have gotten completely lost and never found her way out again. She wasn't sure she remembered which way they'd come or how. A dwarven tunnel this may have been, but to a human, it was just another cave. It was nice and wide, but the ceiling height left something to be desired.

"It's rather warmer here than on the surface. Now I see why those who drink milk fled underground to escape trouble…" Evidently, low ceiling or no, Lizard Priest was happier here than up above. The way he kept his long neck and head down, all but crawling along, very much made him look like the lizardman he was. "Perhaps my own forebears might have succeeded in establishing a naga kingdom or two, had they done the same."

"I wish there had been time at that other fortress to search for underground passages," Goblin Slayer said. He was talking about the adventure on which Priestess had met Noble Fencer—that is to say, Female Merchant. Indeed, Priestess remembered—that terrible goblin stronghold had once been the remains of a dwarven fortress.

If the weather was clear…

If the weather was clear, might it have been possible to see that structure from the top of this mountain? Or would it have been buried in snow?

"Your Tunnel spell saved us."

"Aw, don't mention it. That was all thanks to the power of the sprites."

"I'm not sure that avalanche was such a good thing, though," Priestess (with the aforementioned thought in her head) said with a pointed frown.

Goblin Slayer fell into a sullen silence, and High Elf Archer giggled. In spite of her laugh, she said, "Not that I care that much, but you *do* know where we're going, don't you?" That was what passed for concern with her, apparently. Perhaps even a high elf's senses were dulled so far underground, for her ears twitched restlessly.

From behind, Priestess heard the jocular voice of Dwarf Shaman, who seemed to have picked up on the elf's body language. "Believe me, we'll be out of here long before an elf's life span would be up."

"Ugh. When I think about spending thousands of years down here…" High Elf Archer gave a frustrated wave of her hand. She added under her breath that it would be no joke. "I might turn into a dark elf. And you only find the weirdest monsters underground."

"You could grow a little moss. Start a mushroom collection."

"Yeah, well, they do say dwarves are kin to rocks."

It was the usual banter. Lively and calming.

Priestess was always nervous when they were underground, such as when they were delving into a dungeon. She always had been, ever since her very first time—she suspected she always would be.

And yet...

She also thought she had gotten used to it. Yes, she was nervous. But she was used to the nervousness. And it was such a help when her party members were chatting amiably around her.

"As I said, the place used to be a battlefield long, long ago. So if there was anything here—" Suddenly, Dwarf Shaman stopped talking, and then he stopped in his tracks. In the cramped confines of the underground space, crisscrossed by tunnels like an anthill, the party formed up.

Before, Priestess in her incomprehension might have simply felt panicked, might have cried out or asked questions. But now, she knew. She recognized the way the hair on the back of her neck stood up. The way her heart beat faster inside her little chest. She gripped her sounding staff firmly, peering into the seemingly endless darkness.

"If there was anything here...," Goblin Slayer said, drawing his sword with its strange length from its place at his hip, "...it would be a remnant from that time."

From the darkness, Priestess felt a sensation coming closer, an aura she knew very, very well.

"GOOROGGBBB...!!"

They're coming.

§

"I can't believe there are goblins here of all places!" High Elf Archer cried, her complaint piercing the darkness in the form of an arrow that lodged itself in a goblin's skull and brain. The monster fell back without even a cry, and his companions paid him no more attention than a stone on the roadside.

"GOROGBB!!"

"GBBG! GROGB!!"

Maybe the creature even survived the shot—but it didn't matter; he was promptly trampled underfoot.

"Why does it turn out like this every time I go on an adventure with you, Orcbolg? You need to take some responsibility for these things!"

"No, I do not," Goblin Slayer said simply as he charged the group of goblins head-on.

"GOROG?!"

First he bashed one of them in the torso with his shield, then immediately lashed out with the sword in a reverse grip in his left hand. "This makes two!"

"GRGGOOB?!" A goblin trying to slip past his companion found his throat pierced from the side, bloody froth bubbling up. Goblin Slayer twisted the blade to make sure the creature was dead, then lifted one foot and planted it firmly between the legs of another goblin.

"GBBORGB?!"

"And this is three."

The sensation was soft and unpleasant but exhilarating. The goblin somersaulted backward and rolled on the ground, knocked clean out. Almost mechanically, Goblin Slayer pulled out his sword and thrust it into the monster's throat, killing him.

One round—hardly a breath—three goblins. Seeing the fools in the vanguard cut down in virtually the blink of an eye set the other creatures back on their heels; they stopped moving.

"GOROGG...?!"

"GORG! GOBBGRRGB!!"

They're well-built. Goblin Slayer grunted to himself as creatures in front of him pushed and shoved, trying to induce someone else to go ahead of them. Normally, goblins came up to no more than waist height on a human, but these reached almost to his chest. Their arms and legs were thick. That is, strictly in comparison to the average goblin, of course, but still...

There's no problem.

So they were a little large—they were still nowhere near being hobgoblins. And above all, the nasty little glint in their eyes as they held back, looking for their chance, was entirely the look of goblins.

So there was no problem, then. Goblin Slayer brought up the sword in his hand and let it fly.

"GBBORGB?!"

"Four. Can't tell how many there are—we'll have to charge through. Which path is it?"

"Sure, sure!" Dwarf Shaman shouted. "Run for the next branch, then down to the right!"

The adventurers were off and running even before the goblin with a sword in his neck could expire. The goblins were thrown into confusion by the forceful advance; the party peppered them with arrows while the front row grabbed weapons from the corpses and pushed farther forward still. Priestess jumped over the corpses that seemed to materialize in front of her, while Lizard Priest made extra sure they were dead. If they simply followed Dwarf Shaman's instructions as they headed deeper into the depths...

"GORGGBB!!"

"GBBG! GBOGGB!!"

"Guess they're coming after us," High Elf Archer said. She didn't sound the least bit winded despite the run, and in the dim torchlight, her ears could be seen to give a less-than-pleased flick.

They could hardly have expected there would conveniently be no pursuit. The cackling, caterwauling voices of goblins came from everywhere in the maze of tunnels. That much, at least, was familiar to this party.

"There are ten of them... No, a little more. Less than twenty. All the echoes are making it hard to tell," High Elf Archer said.

"But...they're not...hobgoblins, are they?" Priestess asked. She was huffing and puffing along, but there was no sign of nervousness on her face. Her expression was firm, and she was looking around vigilantly, but she betrayed no fear or hesitation.

High Elf Archer glanced out of the corner of her eye and bit back a laugh so Priestess wouldn't know she had looked. Goblin hunting was by no means funny—but watching a human grow and mature was always a joyous thing.

"Aren't they?"

"They're...a bit bigger than normal. But not that much...bigger." Priestess was paying unusual attention to her own shoulders as she ran along. She remembered all too well an adventure on which that soft flesh had been bitten into.

Now, that was one big opponent, though.

If it hadn't traumatized her, that was what counted. High Elf Archer, remembering that she herself had been thoroughly abused on one of these quests, nodded. "Eh, just a little more trouble... That's all they are."

"One might point out that our classifications of creatures are purely arbitrary and artificial."

"There may not be real differences... Ah." Goblin Slayer's response to Lizard Priest, already in his usual laconic style, was cut even shorter as they emerged from the cramped, narrow tunnel into a vast cavern.

How to describe this place? One hesitates to say it was the ruins of a dwarven village. There was no longer any trace of the breathtaking metal-work that characterized the output of their craftspeople, who seemed to have the blessing of the smithy god in their very hands. Dilapidated, collapsing buildings, the wood rotting away, were haphazardly connected in a sort of pile. Hallways were everywhere, looking like they might fall down at any moment—yet holding one another up. It was as if someone had shoved a slum underground and then shaken it violently. It made High Elf Archer think of an anthill—as if it might be the dwelling of something very strange.

The king of the shacks, she thought. It hurt to think it, but the small handful of dwarven fortresses left on the surface were now old ruins.

If it weren't for this thing, and the goblins, she might have seen fit to spare some time sightseeing—for an elf, it would have been very little time indeed.

When Goblin Slayer came to a halt, however, it wasn't for the tourist opportunities. "A town?"

"Living quarters, more like. For the fortress," Dwarf Shaman spat; he steadied his breathing and then took a swig of wine as if to wash out his mouth. "Everyone probably died defending the castle against the demons, and then an army of Chaos took up residence here…"

"And in time they, too, abandoned it, or perhaps were driven out. I suppose such is the story…" Perhaps once upon a time, this place had been the setting for an adventure.

At Lizard Priest's words, Priestess quickly knelt down and formed a holy sigil in the air with her fingers. While he waited for this brief but heartfelt silent prayer to conclude, Goblin Slayer turned his helmet.

"What do you think?" he asked, his breath perfectly calm. "Will the goblins be able to get out of the tunnels?"

"Without anyone to show 'em where to go, I doubt they'd make it up top." Dwarf Shaman narrowed his eyes and glared around at the profusion of galleries.

"Hmm," Goblin Slayer grunted. "Only any who followed us, then."

"If there should be any, we simply kill them, make our escape, and let the rest of them tear one another apart," Lizard Priest said.

Goblin Slayer nodded. It didn't matter where they had come in from. Then he grunted again. "Large goblins. I heard long ago that animals that live in cold regions grow larger."

"Not that I really care," High Elf Archer began, her ears trained for any sound of goblin footsteps, "but there aren't some awful blind monsters keeping them down here, are there?"

"If you mean Flying Polyps, they're farther down," Dwarf Shaman said.

"Po-lyp?" Priestess asked, getting to her feet.

"There are a lot of ancient creatures left over around here," High

Elf Archer explained, and Priestess thought she understood. She dusted herself off, then picked up her sounding staff, which made a pleasant ringing.

"I'm sorry for keeping us," she said.

"Think nothing of it. I must say, however, that escape would be quite simple if one were to go through the walls or ceiling," Lizard Priest remarked.

"This is dwarven make. Don't think the likes of goblins could get through it, and if they tried, it would come down on their ugly heads. The ruins notwithstanding," Dwarf Shaman replied.

"Hmm?" Priestess put a finger to her lips. After a moment, she added: "I don't think goblins would think that far ahead, do you?"

"Okay, I think it's time to leave!" High Elf Archer shouted.

"Agreed." Goblin Slayer nodded.

"GOROGBB!"

"GRGBB!!"

The adventurers launched themselves into the ghost town at almost the same moment as the goblins came piling in like an avalanche.

"I'll take the rear guard," Goblin Slayer said.

"And I shall accompany you!" offered Lizard Priest.

Their feet could be heard sliding as they dropped their speed and worked their way to the back. At a moment like this, they were in perfect harmony. Likewise the other party members, who nodded to them as they ran past and sped up.

But then, that's perfectly ordinary for us, thought Priestess.

As they went by, High Elf Archer stuck out her tongue a little, then twisted her torso toward the back. "Take this!"

"GBBBORG...?!"

Did the goblin's scream trail off because of the pain, or the pierced lung, or was it both? High Elf Archer's hand moved so fast, it couldn't be seen, but her arrow flew clear through the goblin in the vanguard.

"Wow...," Priestess breathed out at this shot—taken with hardly the time to aim. High Elf Archer's archery was always astonishing to her, no matter how many times she saw it.

"Hee-hee!"

"If yeh've got time to be proud of yourself, yeh've got time to work!"

"You just make sure you don't take us down a wrong turn! It makes my head hurt, knowing we're in dwarven tunnels!"

"Ha-ha…" Priestess managed a small laugh between measured breaths.

The cramped confines of the cave. The onrushing goblins. The desperate running. The darkness. All of them could easily provoke terrible memories for her, and yet…

Right now, I'm not afraid… I'm really not.

In fact, she had the wherewithal to be slightly annoyed that she couldn't be more helpful at this particular moment. She could hardly engage with the goblins in melee combat—not of the kind she could hear in the clangor behind her. There was the *whoosh* of a dagger, the thumping of claws and teeth and tail, a goblin death rattle, and the smell of blood.

I'll never be quite like them, she thought. Even if she did feel a certain admiration for that female knight and her ancient, forgotten sword technique.

At the same time, she wasn't good enough at slinging yet to do it while running. She'd already used a miracle earlier and wanted to save her others…

And the only torch I have is the one for myself—these two don't need one.

Round human ears would never best an elf's hearing when it came to ferreting out enemies.

Considering all this, really the only thing for Priestess to do was to run as mindfully as she could, being careful not to stumble. The thought brought a smile to her face. *I guess I am getting used to this.* Imagine: her worried about things like that in the middle of a goblin hunt! She almost wasn't nervous *enough.*

A time and place for everything. This wasn't her turn, her moment. She would do what she had to; thinking could come later.

"There's no end to them—as if there ever is."

"Eep!" Priestess yelped. The words had come at her just as she was about to refocus herself on the task at hand. Of course, the owner of the voice *always* talked about goblins, so that was no surprise. But she felt like she had when the Mother Superior called on her right when she hadn't been paying attention during lessons.

Priestess took a deep breath to steady her pounding heart. She spared a glance over her shoulder to see a figure in gore-spattered armor coming toward her. He had a brand-new rusty sword in his hand. Given that his shield was also streaked with blood, she assumed he'd bludgeoned a goblin with it and then stolen his weapon. Behind him, she could see Lizard Priest's lithe form. He spun his eyes around in his head, then winked at her.

Phew!

"They're both safe!" she called to the two in front of her, letting out a sigh of relief. High Elf Archer, with her hearing, would certainly have picked up on the fact without Priestess telling her, but communication, she believed, was important. As if in proof, the elf waved back at her, and Priestess nodded.

Very well—the next thing to do was to ascertain the situation.

"Are there many of them?" she asked.

"For wanderers, yes." Despite the fact that he had just finished a pitched battle, Goblin Slayer was able to answer Priestess's question immediately. "But there's not enough of them to be a separate tribe."

"Is there a horde somewhere, then…?" If so, they would have to finish it off… But where were they? To find them, the party would have to… No. "First we have to deal with the goblins right in front of us and then get out of these passageways, right?"

"Yes," Goblin Slayer said with a nod. Then he added: "That's right."

"Ha-ha-ha! If we simply planted our feet and made ourselves immovable objects, I believe we would find a way to prevail!" Lizard Priest exclaimed, scraping his claws noisily along the floor, his breath reeking of blood and innards. "Even my heart has finally begun to grow warm!"

"I'm afraid it might cool right down again when we get outside," Priestess said. That was why they couldn't overdo it.

She felt a little nervous offering this advice, but "Yes, indeed!" was Lizard Priest's response. "I see you've learned to say quite the right thing. Goodness gracious, I must not neglect my own study!"

"O-oh, really, I…" Priestess felt her cheeks softening into a smile at Lizard Priest's teasing, but she forced herself to keep a straight face. This was no time for either modesty or embarrassment.

"Whatever the case, we need to clean this up quickly," Goblin Slayer said.

And then there's…

Goblin Slayer—something seemed off about him, as if he wasn't quite focused.

"Watch your heads, everybody!" Dwarf Shaman shouted.

Priestess didn't have the time at the moment to be lost in such thoughts. They were barreling toward a tunnel with a shockingly low ceiling. A perfectly ordinary passageway—but it was effectively a deadly trap for humans, elves, and lizardmen.

"These dwarven towns, always so cramped…!" The high elf was the only one to go flying into the tunnel like an arrow without slowing down at all. Leaning so far forward that she was almost on the ground, she looked like a gust of green wind rushing along. All Priestess could do was crouch down likewise and try her best to follow her. She held her staff up near the top so she wouldn't drop it. Her willowy body might not have looked like much compared to Witch or Sword Maiden, but at times like this, it proved very useful…

"Well, my goodness! Quite a thing, this…!" Even Lizard Priest, who indeed looked like a lizard slithering along the ground, was having trouble.

Priestess slowed her pace to match Goblin Slayer's, raising her voice in hopes of being able to communicate the situation. "Goblin Slayer, sir!"

"Give me a torch."

"Yes, sir!"

They were in perfect sync. He reached toward her; she passed him the burning torch—it hardly took a second. Then she could hear his feet sliding again as he returned to the back of the formation.

A low ceiling was no obstacle for goblins.

"GOROGGBB!!"

"GBB!! GOROOGBB!!"

Goblins—whose numbers might diminish but whose momentum never did—interpreted everything in the most congenial possible way. What's that they say about big heads and little wit? The huge simpleton was obviously an idiot. Push him down. Kill him. Make him pay for all that he's done. And while you're dealing with him, I'll take the human girl or maybe the elf maiden.

Perhaps that's what they were thinking.

"We're lucky they have no archers." Goblin Slayer took aim at the monster at the front of the enemy formation (there because he was stupid, not because he was brave) and slammed him with his shield.

"GOROGB?!"

The creature tumbled backward, filthy blood spraying from his shattered nose, taking several of the goblins behind him with him as he fell to the ground. He might be one of their own, clutching his face and writhing in pain, but to the other goblins, he was nothing more than an obstacle. They kicked him, taunted him, punched him—in other words, for several seconds, the adventurers ahead of them completely disappeared from their minds.

And that was as good a diversion as any.

"See you in hell." Goblin Slayer pitched a bottle of flaming liquid along with the torch, then made tracks down the tunnel. Behind them, they could hear the glass shattering—followed by goblins screaming and a rush of heat.

"I wish you wouldn't throw explosives around so casually!" High Elf Archer groused, greeting his arrival with her hands on her hips.

Underneath his helmet, Goblin Slayer was looking left and then right, checking on Priestess, Lizard Priest, and Dwarf Shaman. They were out of the tunnel but apparently not out of the dwarven city. Even in the gloomy light, the silhouettes of a wild array of ruins could be plainly seen. Priestess was lighting her next torch as she thought: *I can't believe I'm actually used to this…*

Goblin Slayer was standing silently; one might have taken him to be doing nothing at all—but High Elf Archer twitched her ears at him in an annoyed motion. "There's not many wind sprites down here. I think we might suffocate."

"…No, I doubt it," Goblin Slayer replied, simply and with a long exhalation. "Although it might be a different matter if one was to launch Fire Bolt seventy times."

High Elf Archer pursed her lips and could be heard wondering what that was supposed to mean, but she quickly said something else altogether: "There's more of them! We'd better hurry!"

"GROOROOGB…!"

Be they dragons or goblins, green-skinned monsters never seemed to know when to give up. Why was that?

Some of the goblins had pushed or jumped their way through the flames, even as the tongues of fire licked at their own skin. This, too, was not bravery—it was simple rage or, again, perhaps they felt they were different from those other fools. (One might forgive a dragon for using its breath weapon on anyone who actually dared to put it in the same category as these creatures.)

The Chaos horde came on, crushing their companions underfoot. Goblin Slayer grunted. "Let's go."

"Don't have to tell me twice—this way!" Dwarf Shaman called, and then the adventurers were running again without a moment to catch their breath.

In terms of comparative prowess in battle, it was a simple matter: Goblin Slayer and his party held the advantage. But they didn't know how many enemies there were. And the adventurers' strength and stamina would have to last against all those goblins.

They would have to kill any goblins they encountered on their way to the surface, but they couldn't afford to dally. If only they'd had something. Anything—yes, anything other than just knowledge of the right path.

That thing arrived in the shape of a huge cliffside that appeared before them.

Of course, Dwarf Shaman was leading them—it wasn't possible that this was a mistake. There must have been some significance to it, some reason the dwarves had cut this giant rift in the land—a water channel, perhaps. If any of the adventurers had peered down into the abyss, they might have seen a faint, cold glimmer, as of a dark metal. It was a river of molten steel, from those ancient days when the fires of the dwarven forges had not yet cooled.

And where you had a river and you had a town, then you must have something else, too.

A low railing and nice, wide slats. It creaked in the subterranean wind, but it was unmistakably a metal—

Bridge!

"Let's bring it down!" Priestess cried, knowing that they now had the advantage of terrain.

"Oh, for—!" High Elf Archer exclaimed beside her, looking up at the ceiling and wasting a turn on a gesture of futility.

"This calls for a spell," Goblin Slayer said, and, as ever, his judgment was just right.

"My ancestors aren't going to like this one bit…!"

"It won't be any worse than the day goblins invaded their home!"

"I daresay milady ranger is correct!" The ancient dwarves would not have been pleased to see the goblins who now pursued the party.

Dwarf Shaman, still frowning, crossed the hanging bridge, pumping his short arms and legs. High Elf Archer leaped ahead of him—at this point, they needed no one to tell them where to go. "If we're going to drop this bridge, we want as many of them on it as possible…!" she said.

"Agreed," Goblin Slayer responded.

"Yes, exactly!" Lizard Priest crowed.

This meant that the two frontline fighters would become the

Noboru Kannatuki

knights on the bridge, blocking the goblins' advance for as long as they could.

"GOBGOB!"

"GRG! GOBG!!"

The horde of goblins came on, armed with a motley assortment of weapons. The bridge began to shake violently; even with its redoubtable metal construction, it wasn't built to be a battlefield.

The monsters' footsteps rumbled, the bridge groaned, and the adventurers' shields and claws added to the cacophony.

"GRROGOB?!"

"GROB?!"

"Feh!" Goblin Slayer clucked his tongue, confronted by one goblin torn clean in two by claws and another with its throat crushed. Maybe he'd been a little too enthusiastic with his rusted sword, for the blade gave up the ghost, cracking under the assault. An ugly hit.

I didn't think I was that attached to it.

Without hesitation, he flicked the hilt, the sword rotating to an ice-pick grip, and slammed the shortened blade directly down.

"GGOBGRGG?!"

Even a broken sword could take a life when driven with sufficient force.

Goblin Slayer left the weapon lodged in the monster's throat, crushed the monster's fingers with his foot, and took his club instead.

"Shaaa!"

"GOROOGBB?!"

It was Lizard Priest's whirling tail that protected him at that moment, flying overhead. The mass of muscle and bone became a fearsome whip, slamming a goblin in the sternum so hard, it burst the monster's internal organs and sent him flying backward.

"GOBOBRG?!"

"GRRG! GOBRO!!"

The object of Lizard Priest's aggression was already dead, and the momentum of his corpse now made it a weapon in its own right. Spewing guts and filth, the goblin went tumbling off the bridge, taking several of his erstwhile companions with him. And it is the way of goblins, when someone interferes with them, to take their eye off their goal and abuse the interloper instead.

"Ha-ha-ha! And have you become more careful with your weapons, milord Goblin Slayer?"

"Even I don't *constantly* throw my possessions away."

"GBBORGB?!"

Goblin Slayer flung the club with a casual motion, adding another obstacle—read: *corpse*—for the pursuers.

"Only when necessary."

"Most enlightening." Lizard Priest laughed so hard, his fangs showed. Goblin Slayer's helmet nodded up and down. It was time.

The two adventurers fled from the goblins who had packed themselves onto the bridge. At the exact same moment...

"O Earth Mother, abounding in mercy, grant your sacred light to we who are lost in darkness!"

A prayer rang out, working its way from the depths of the earth up toward the heavens—and a radiant light scattered the forces of Chaos.

Priestess hadn't needed anyone's permission; she'd seen that this was the moment, and she hadn't hesitated. The light granted by the Earth Mother shone from her sounding staff, pouring down equally upon all the goblins.

"GOBOB?!"

"GBGRR?!?!"

The goblins hid their faces from the light, yelling and writhing. Filthy tears flowed from their eyes—a pitiful sight, yet not one deserving of pity.

The moment a hand stretched out in the direction of one of the goblins, everyone there knew that his head would be crushed by a stone.

The goblins had been drawn along, held in place, and then blinded by Holy Light in the middle of the bridge.

"Right where I want 'em...!!"

When Dwarf Shaman saw that his companions were safely off the bridge, he gave it an almighty whack with the palm of his hand. The metal span, which must have been built in the days of his ancient forebears, creaked loudly.

"Come out, you gnomes, and let it go! Here it comes—look out below! Turn those buckets upside down—empty all upon the ground!"

The screws popped. The metal buckled. The chains stretched—and then, with a cracking sound, they gave way. One of the most powerful forces in the Four-Cornered World—gravity—grabbed hold of the bridge, goblins and all.

"GOBRG?!"

"GOBOBROR?!?!"

They could panic, but it wouldn't save them. Would it have been better for them had this still been the time when a great stream of glittering molten metal heaved below? The goblins were dragged into the abyss in the blink of an eye; even their screams didn't last long. For their collective death rattle was drowned out by the sound of the dwarven bridge annihilating its old enemies.

The roar as the bridge collapsed against the dark, frozen metal below was like a thunderclap. The floor shook, and pebbles danced, and dust even came raining down from the ceiling far above.

"Eep!" Priestess exclaimed without meaning to and huddled down; even High Elf Archer covered her ears and curled up. Lizard Priest and Goblin Slayer, meanwhile, were busy receiving Dwarf Shaman, who sniffed proudly.

"'I am a servant of the Secret Fire,' as they say. Startin' to think maybe I should've gone into the world-creation business!"

"...Gosh, you almost sound like an elf," High Elf Archer said.

"Quiet, yeh..."

High Elf Archer mumbled that the shaman would invite a punishment from the smithy god, but he only laughed. Dwarf Shaman seemed downright impressed with the grand ending of the great bridge his ancestors had built.

He shook a ninepin bottle, made from a plant from the east, and there was a simple *splish* of liquid. Dwarf Shaman undid the stopper, turned toward the bridge that now ran across the floor of the valley, and scattered the alcohol in a spray.

"Doesn't matter if it's mead, cider, or the potato stuff… If yeh don't have the water of life, ye've got nothing at all." With those words, he drank down the remaining mouthful of alcohol. It wasn't exactly drowning his sorrows in drink—more like an excellent excuse. Priestess let out a breath.

Nothing to worry about, then. Drinking wine was what dwarves did; a dwarf who didn't drink wine was hardly a dwarf at all.

"Is there still a way home?" Priestess asked. "I hope we didn't need that bridge."

"They say it takes one to know one—well, this place was made by dwarves, and I'm a dwarf!" Dwarf Shaman said, wine dribbling into his beard. If he said so, then there was nothing to fear. Priestess would have been in serious trouble if she'd been tossed in here all alone—but thankfully, she had friends.

And as one of them, she would watch for enemies, judge when to use her miracle, and keep everyone safe. Priestess nodded to herself, counting off on her fingers one at a time; she seemed to have acknowledged something in her heart…

"All right!" She made a fist—recognizing, first of all, that she had done her job. She didn't notice Lizard Priest watching her, his eyes narrowed in a smile at this habit she'd recently adopted. He didn't say anything about it, either, for if she realized he had seen her, she would probably have shrunk into herself with embarrassment.

Instead, he stuck out his tongue merrily at Goblin Slayer. "I suppose this means the road home will be rather more circuitous."

"It makes no difference to me," was Goblin Slayer's brief but unambiguous answer. "Going there and back again isn't such an urgent journey."

He then added under his breath, "It isn't as if *my* possessions are going to be sold off." Priestess heard him, but she didn't understand what he meant.

§

It was only now that Priestess truly appreciated how light could be bright enough to bring tears to one's eyes. As they emerged from the underground dwarven city, at first all she could see was white. She didn't know if the glow was that of the morning sun or of twilight; it was as if a shard of ice had gotten stuck in her eye.

She covered her face with her arms to protect her stinging, bleary eyes and blinked several times. For some reason, she saw a strange, hazy rainbow wavering in front of her, and even after the focus returned to her vision, it was difficult to make anything out.

If any of those goblins had still been alive…

Things could have been very bad indeed—she cursed her own carelessness, and finally, the outside world began to come into view…

"Is this light…from the snow?"

As far as she could see, the world was a silvery white, glittering like the sparks of flames. Even Goblin Slayer could be heard to grunt "Hrm"—maybe he hadn't expected this, either.

"Goodness gracious," said Lizard Priest, who had closed his second eyelid and was now holding himself and shivering. It couldn't have been pleasant for him. "This is quite something. Cold that pierces to the bone, yet a light that shines as if we were in the desert…"

"Heh!" High Elf Archer scoffed and took out what appeared to be a leather bandage with small slits cut in it. She tied it with a string around her head, being mindful of her long ears, then turned proudly to Priestess. "What do you think of my snow goggles?"

"When exactly did you buy those…?"

"A friend told me about them before we left. Looks like their moment has come! Neat, huh?" She puffed out her modest chest—but did a high elf really need such a device?

It sure seems like it would constrict your field of vision…

Then again, Goblin Slayer's helmet had a very constricted field of vision, as she remembered from when she had tried on its cousin once. So then maybe there was no problem... But then again, it really *didn't* seem like a high elf needed such a thing. *Maybe it's those kinds of purchases*, Priestess thought, *that leave her room in such a state...*

At least she looks like she's having fun, I guess. There was no need to be condescending about it. Besides, Priestess was interested in them, too.

"Could I try them later?" she asked.

"Sure! I think they might constrict a human's field of vision, though..."

Goblin Slayer, with just a glance at the bantering girls, grunted quietly. "Do you smell fire?"

"Hrm?" Dwarf Shaman was using his sleeve to wipe wine out of his beard before it froze. "Sure your nose isn't playing tricks on you? We did just come out of those ruins."

"...Perhaps," Goblin Slayer said. "You."

"Yeah? What?" High Elf Archer bounded across the field so lightly, she didn't leave footprints in the snow. "Need me to check for enemies?" She flicked her ears, thoroughly pleased to realize that Orcbolg couldn't see for the brightness, either, and then peered into the distance. In spite of the fact that she was wearing snow goggles already, she put a hand to her forehead to shade her eyes. Priestess wondered if there was really any point to that.

At least she looks like she's having fun, I guess, she thought again. She nodded to herself. She was definitely going to try those shades.

"Something's burning."

High Elf Archer's report made Priestess abandon her lighthearted thoughts in an instant. The elf, still squinting into the distance and obviously listening carefully, continued calmly but sharply: "I don't know if humans would be able to see it, but there's smoke. And the sounds of battle."

"Goblins?" Priestess asked.

"N—" High Elf Archer began, but then she looked over at Priestess through her goggles and sighed. "No, it's not goblins. I don't think."

"So it's not goblins." Goblin Slayer glanced back at the iron door set into the rock face, a massive construction considering the size of the dwarves who had built it. Was this somehow connected to the goblins who milled about under the earth? In this world, there was nothing trivial. The flap of a butterfly's wings could cause a storm elsewhere, and from a village burned for amusement, there might arise a hero.

Hmph. They were his own thoughts, yet he felt them hardly accurate. Well, he didn't plan to rely on them anyway. Do or do not. In this world, that was everything.

"Let's go." Goblin Slayer took the sword, presumably of dwarven make, that he had picked up after dropping his club (without hesitation, of course) and put it into his scabbard. Dwarven swords were likely to seem a strange length for a blade to most humans, but Goblin Slayer was quite accustomed to weapons of this size.

"...?"

Speaking of size... This weapon looked like it must have been commissioned long ago by someone who lived in the north. Goblin Slayer had picked up a very thick, very long, very heavy blade, practically a greatsword. Priestess found it somewhat—indeed, *very*—strange, but Goblin Slayer voiced no complaint, only stashed it at his hip. Without really thinking about it, she cocked her head and blinked at him, and who could blame her?

"From the position of the sun and the shape of the mountain," Lizard Priest said, sticking out his tongue, "I believe the village we're after should be nearby."

"Yeah, but I bet it'll all be over by the time we get there." High Elf Archer pushed the snow goggles up to her forehead.

"Whatever the case," Goblin Slayer said decisively, "not going is not an option."

None of the adventurers argued otherwise. They nodded to one another, then set off with a hush of snow under their boots, angling across the field. As they ran along at full tilt, Priestess realized it was evening, and the burning shimmer was the glow of twilight.

She followed closely in High Elf Archer's footprints (well, figuratively; the high elf didn't leave footprints in the snow), her breath fogging in front of her. She kept one eye on Goblin Slayer, who jogged along silently, and watched vigilantly to her right and left, as well as behind, where Lizard Priest was trying to keep up the rear.

As they went along, they reached a point where even Priestess could make out several pillars of smoke. They were coming from…a town. A city built hard against the mountain they were now descending, surrounded by snow and trees and sea.

A port.

This was the first time in her life Priestess had seen such a thing. It was nothing like the water town or any fishing villages she had seen. There was a great stone hall built on a small swell of a hill and houses with triangular roofs, looking like overturned boats. A wooden quay extended into the bay, with several long wooden sailing ships, the likes of which Priestess had also never seen, at rest around it.

Unfortunately, Priestess didn't have the time to be taken by the exotic scenery. In addition to the long ships sitting calmly at port were several more vessels jammed haphazardly among them, disgorging warriors in gear the likes of which—yes—Priestess had never seen. They were attacking the town. They wielded axes and swords; they stole barrels and chests, and some of them could be seen heading back to their boats with young women slung over their shoulders.

"They're kidnapping those people…!" Priestess said, and then blinked. This was theft, plain and simple. She'd seen goblins do it. She knew what it looked like.

And yet… And yet, she'd never seen women shout and cling to the necks of their kidnappers, almost as if they were excited by it. She'd never imagined they would blush, a color visible even against the twilight.

"Wha…? Wha…? Whaaaaaat?!" Despite the confusion and embarrassment that colored her cheeks, she didn't stop running—that much, perhaps, was praiseworthy.

As the town got closer, they could hear the triumphant yawps of the kidnappers, the pained shouting of the men, and the yelling of the women.

"...The heck is that? Do those women sound, like, really, really *happy* to you?" High Elf Archer asked.

Yes. Yes, they do.

High Elf Archer's face said *I don't understand* better than any words ever could have.

The women were yammering ecstatically and holding fast to the men who were kidnapping them, obviously transported with joy. What the kidnappers were doing was so obviously barbaric—and yet, it seemed to be entirely different from when goblins did it.

"Ahhh... They are taking wives for themselves, I believe." Lizard Priest stretched his long neck, his voice made profoundly languorous by the cold.

"Wives?" Priestess asked, a question mark practically hovering over her head. Maybe her voice scratched a little as she said the word. Then again, maybe it didn't.

She could barely follow what she was learning of the situation. Taking wives. Wives? So was this a wedding ceremony?

"Such a tradition existed in our village as well—when a woman was abducted, she was perforce recognized as married."

"'Perforce'...?"

High Elf Archer shot Lizard Priest a deeply exasperated look, but he simply nodded and replied, "Indeed. For it is proof that they have the intelligence, goodwill, and martial valor to steal themselves a bride. Could there be anything to inspire greater confidence?"

"In other words," High Elf Archer said, her tone tart, "your wives are all abductees?"

"Not all, no. But it only goes to show how desired a bride is—so most couples are harmonious."

"Talk about yer cultural differences..." Dwarf Shaman couldn't help laughing aloud at the way High Elf Archer hung her head.

Priestess, unsure what to do, looked desperately at Goblin Slayer. It was... How to put this? She'd been anxious, then managed to relax, then suddenly grown anxious again... And now this.

I know they say adventures can run the gamut of emotions, but this is ridiculous...! She had no idea whether to treat this situation as grim or carefree.

"What should we do...?" she asked.

"...We'll have to talk to them," Goblin Slayer said after a few seconds' silence.

"No matter what's going on?"

"No matter what's going on."

They worked their way down the mountain, and just as High Elf Archer had predicted, everything was over by the time they arrived at the foot. The vessels were drifting away from the port, and the people left behind appeared rueful but not particularly bereaved. Their attitude felt out of place among the flames, blood, and hovering smell of battle, the smashed houses and hewn limbs everywhere.

Priestess felt something akin to drunkenness threaten to overtake her, and she took several breaths to steady herself. They weren't the only ones who had noticed something, after all. The people of the town had spotted the unfamiliar group coming down the slope during the battle. A motley crew consisting of a warrior in grimy armor, a priestess of a foreign religion, an elf, a dwarf, and a lizardman.

Muscle-bound men dressed in pelts and carrying axes stared Priestess down; she felt their gazes piercing her small body.

My rank tag...

That wouldn't help. There were no Adventurers Guilds in this part of the world yet. Adventurers were just drifters; no one knew who they were or if they might be trustworthy. Priestess felt anxiety very much like she remembered from the desert, and her hand clenched by her chest. Even that slight motion earned her looks of suspicion.

So the armed populace and the five outlanders faced each other. Nobody knew what might send everything spiraling off in the wrong direction. The gods, quite rightly, swallowed anxiously as they rolled the dice.

Fate and Chance are inscrutable to all—as are the consequences of the wills and choices of Pray-er Characters.

High Elf Archer asked sotto voce what they should do. Lizard Priest held his peace, and Dwarf Shaman only shrugged.

It was Goblin Slayer who, after a long moment, snuffed out the fuse: "......We have come from the kingdom to the south." That was all he said at first, as if he thought this single sentence was a perfectly sufficient explanation—then he hesitated for a beat before adding, "We are adventurers."

There was no answer. The men, still redolent with the excitement of battle, began murmuring to one another, creating a low buzz.

Priestess slid her hands along her sounding staff, holding it tight. She wanted to be ready to react, whatever happened. She couldn't spare a second to look to either side, but she knew her party members were doing the same.

After another long moment, there was a clank as of metal against metal, and the crowd parted, revealing a young woman. She wore beautiful black mail that went down to her knees and carried a shield as well as a spear with a broad metal tip. None of this concealed the generous lines of her chest and hips, around which ran a tightly bound belt. The belt bore a bunch of keys that jangled as she moved—it seemed these were the true emblem of her office.

Her face, slim and paler than the snow, was the finishing touch on this statuesque body. Her braided hair seemed to shine gold, but Priestess thought it was probably in fact a very light brown. The woman's eyes were deep green like the depths of a lake. One of them was covered by a cloth bandage—but it did nothing to detract from her beauty.

Priestess swallowed the "wow" that almost came to her lips. One could say she was quite smitten. After all, she hadn't seen anyone this beautiful (other than a high elf) since meeting the Archbishop of the Supreme God. She looked the very picture of the Valkyrie, the goddess of battle, though perhaps in slightly different equipment. The tiara that could be glimpsed in her hair showed that she must be a person of no mean status.

©Noboru Kannatuki

This lovely woman looked at the party, and her rose-colored lips softened. Priestess swallowed hard and straightened up, trying to look proper.

"From fair far you've come, hale, hardy ones, and many a trial endured. I urge, beg, and invite you to please repose yourselves in our halls."

"...*What?*"

This time, Priestess was too late to swallow the word.

CHAPTER 3

THE FARAWAY PRINCESS

"Ah, I heard of you from my *husbondi*; he was *þverted* in greeting you by a sudden visit from his family."

"Husbondi"? And "þverted"? Priestess was completely at a loss as to what these things meant. From the way the beautiful woman was scratching her cheek, Priestess surmised that she was embarrassed. It seemed this was the *húsfreya*, the housewife, of the man who ruled this area. Her tone seemed to prove that the battle they'd just observed was nothing to get upset over.

Maybe it happens all the time...

Priestess couldn't hide her hesitation as she worked her way over the hardened ground. And not because of how strange the town, which might have passed for a giant farm, looked. Nor because of the scattered limbs, bloodstains, corpses, and wounded men everywhere. It was because everyone was just cheerfully cleaning up, as if it was a delightful festival and not a major battle that had just occurred.

The words that the *húsfreya* had spoken unsettled her, too. Myths held that the Trade God, who is the wind, had created words, and the god of knowledge had created writing. These had been, the myths said, a shared language among all in the Four-Cornered World.

Meaning language has existed ever since then. Be it elvish, dwarven, or the speech of northerners like these. Despite being born and raised on the frontier, Priestess was familiar with a smattering of dialects and could understand them. But she'd never heard such a distended form of the common tongue—perhaps the desert people had been more blessed by the Trade God than she'd realized.

The people were whispering:

"Foreigners…"

"Behold their leader—an unpleasant-looking lad is he…"

"Don't be foolish. Be a warrior strong of heart; it matters not how he looks."

"That sword—it's old but of the *dvergr*. A fine piece of work."

"From the high mountain they climbed down, of that there's no mistake."

"They come of the same homeland as the *goði*."

"Sooth!"

"Think the young lass there be a *gyðja*?"

"A mannish lass, nothing like ours, is she?"

Priestess was further discomfited by the warriors' unfamiliar language and their unrestrained stares. The *"lass"* who had just been called *"mannish"*—that is, Priestess—snapped "Hey!" and the warriors all pointedly averted their eyes.

It seemed that they were the subject of some friendly teasing, but Priestess could barely follow what was being said. Including what was being said to her party. Maybe the northerners found her strange because she was a follower of a foreign cult—or maybe they looked down upon her for being a willowy-looking woman.

The warriors in their teardrop-shaped helmets looked like dwarves who had simply been stretched to human height, their girth remaining unchanged. They were well-muscled and strong, bearded, looking altogether like boulders that had come to life. Priestess was surprised only that none of them had horns on their helmets. Illustrated stories about the northern barbarians always depicted them that way…

"A dragon!"

"A lizardman, that be."

"A terrifying countenance has he!"

"Behold the *freya* there. Gods, is she an *álfr*?"

"Hoh, there's an *álfr*!"

"She's lovely as a celestial maiden…"

"Beautiful indeed. Merely to look at her is to be taken by gooseflesh…"

The warriors—to say nothing of the townspeople cleaning up the charred parts of their home—naturally took an interest in another member of Priestess's party.

"Ah, I believe I feel the chill abating…"

"Oh, act decent. They're watching us."

Lizard Priest plodded heavily along—while beside him, the high elf was practically dancing. She looked this way and that, her gorgeous hair blowing in the breeze, truly a stunning sight.

What was more striking still was that the princess of this land suffered nothing in the comparison. "My apologies. They're younglings."

"Well, they probably don't see many like me. The high elves are pretty much a thing of the past up here, right?"

Those of High Elf Archer's kindred who remained in these lands either kept clear of human dwellings or else had disappeared seamlessly into human society. Meanwhile, the elf in question was drinking in the attention. Priestess, feeling a touch of jealousy, hid in the elf's shadow to keep herself out of sight. She'd always thought her friend was beautiful—an otherworldly beauty.

"Looks like they don't pay much attention to dwarves, though," High Elf Archer said.

"Well, that'd be because we've provided weapons around here, ourselves." The dwarf, walking quite easily along the dirt path, looked as much at home as if he was in his own town. He might be considered the most grown-up of the party members, in the sense that he had the widest experience of the world. Priestess thought maybe he'd even been up to the north before, but he merely laughed. "Goodness, no. But we worship the same deity of iron. Humans and dwarves are cousins… Well, perhaps second cousins."

"Ah, the smithy god." Priestess nodded. One of the deities she'd learned about as a cleric. She didn't know much about him, though. Only that he was ancient, and terrible, and an enigma…

As for Goblin Slayer…

Wondering what he was up to, she let her gaze wander in search of the cheap-looking metal helmet. She found him standing directly behind the *húsfreya*; from the moment introductions had been made, it seemed he had been understood to be the leader of the party. He walked along at his usual bold stride, giving no indication that he noticed the whispering…

Huh?

Priestess involuntarily cocked her head, surprised. The tattered tassel that hung from Goblin Slayer's helmet was shaking more than usual. Or rather, the helmet itself seemed to be turning this way and that. He was taking it all in: the burned houses, the buildings that were still standing, and the towering hall toward which they were headed. He was being vigilant, Priestess suspected, feeling herself stiffen.

"…I thought it was simply rubble, but it seems I was mistaken," he said.

"Are such things of interest to you?" the *húsfreya* asked. A beatific smile added itself to the already radiant beauty of her face, and her rosy lips formed the musical sounds of her words. "'Tis but peat. Nothing to warrant your surprise."

"I see," Goblin Slayer said and nodded as if this answer truly satisfied him. "Peat." Then he could be heard to mutter inside his helmet: "Hearing of it and seeing it are such different things." Priestess blinked to realize that while his voice was soft, it was neither mechanical nor nonchalant.

"What about that, then?" Goblin Slayer asked, pointing to a silhouette that rose on the far side of town. In the direction of the port, if Priestess remembered correctly. Whatever it was, it was massive, vaulting up into the air, too small to be a wooden strong tower and yet too slender to be a watchtower. In Priestess's eyes, it looked like nothing more than a giant arm.

"Ah, most interesting, is it not? It is a heavy lifting device we call a crane." The *húsfreya* smiled broadly and clapped her hands, as pleased as if Goblin Slayer had been impressed by her own self. "To help load cargo on the boats, it is—my *husbondi* tells me they have quite the same thing in the capital." According to him, she explained, even the largest of objects could be lifted without the need for so much as a harness—it was very easy.

As she spoke, the *húsfreya* touched the keys that dangled at her hip, moving her hands and even her whole body up and down so that despite her accent, even Priestess grasped that the thing at the port was a device for lifting cargo.

"Wow," she breathed to herself as she imagined the great wooden arm hoisting a load of cargo. The image seemed unreal to her, and she couldn't let go of the thought that magic must be involved somehow. Then again, for the life of her, she just couldn't follow exactly what the *húsfreya* was saying, so maybe there was something she was missing...

"I see," Goblin Slayer said, then repeated the words under his breath along with a nod: "I see. Extremely interesting. In that case—"

Priestess steeled herself, clutched her sounding staff, and piped up: "Um, uh, Goblin Slayer, sir...?"

"What is it?"

"Are you...curious about it?"

"Yes." The helmet bobbed up and down, distinctly and immediately. "Very curious." Priestess had never heard him speak in this tone before; she almost wasn't sure how to respond to it.

The *húsfreya*, meanwhile, smiled as compassionately as a goddess and said, "If your curiosity is so great, perhaps you'd like to go and see it later?"

"Absolutely." Goblin Slayer's response was as decisive as ever. Priestess was left blinking. "However, we must first offer our greetings."

Happily, Priestess's confusion was soon relieved—or perhaps one should say, the need for it disappeared. The *húsfreya* and then Goblin Slayer stopped before the great gate of the hall.

"This is the portal of my *husbondi*'s *skáli*, his longhouse."

So on the other side of this gate...

On the other side resided the man who oversaw this territory. Priestess swallowed.

The *húsfreya* seemed to perceive her nervousness; her eyes glinted with playful mischief. "Adventurers, we bid you welcome."

Priestess felt herself tense up again.

§

"Pardon us, *husbondi*. I have brought the honored adventurers."

"Hoh! Have you indeed, my wife? Excellent, excellent."

"'Twere nothing."

"My thanks. Now, come here and warm yourself at the hearth. 'Tis cold, and for a young *freya* to let herself freeze is bad for the health."

"But of course..." The *húsfreya* bowed her head and blushed, mumbling a few words of protest at her demonstrative husband. The way she let her fingers brush the keys at her hip, though, suggested she felt comforted. *Apparently, this husband and wife get along very well...I think*, Priestess mused. Even inside the gloomy building, she was still tense, her breath coming in short gasps.

So this was the king of the northern barbarians. Or no, maybe their governor? Or chieftain? Maybe that would be the most appropriate term...

"I've been told to stay away or the roughnecks might get me... They'd just go on about gettin' robbed."

In Priestess's mind, he appeared as a great, rough man with a beard, huge and terrifying. Surely the king, at least, would wear a horned helmet. And armor, no doubt...

Almost before her hazy imagination could take the form of one of the terrible kings of old, there were brusque footsteps. It was Goblin Slayer, marching forward without a trace of fear.

"Oh—oh!" Everyone else followed him, with Priestess catching up a beat later.

No wonder the longhouse—the *skáli*—was so gloomy. There was not a single window to speak of in the structure, which was built up from piled peat. There was something that arguably amounted to a skylight up in the triangular roof, but…

Is that some kind of…leather?

A thin, semitranslucent animal skin was stretched across the opening.

It wasn't true, though, that there was no light at all inside. Priestess gradually registered that the floor was dirt and that there was a fire glittering in the large central hearth. That would explain the warmth she felt. Meanwhile, long benches ran along the walls on either side of the hearth. They looked somewhat like oblong chests; maybe they concealed storage space.

I've seen plenty like them back on the frontier…

Priestess smiled a little, relieved to see something familiar here in this foreign land. She could easily picture people sitting on these benches, eating dinner together around the fire.

"This way, if you would be so kind."

Priestess found herself with plenty of time to observe the interior of the longhouse as the *húsfreya* guided them along. For Goblin Slayer, though his steps were decisive, was also looking this way and that. It gave Priestess every opportunity to drink in the details of the unusual building.

"…It's like being inside a ship," High Elf Archer whispered to her.

"You're right," Priestess whispered back. "Except the roof would be the bottom…"

At length, they found themselves at the very center of the bench, where one seat, raised above the others, was positioned directly before the hearth. It was wide and deep, such that it looked like even Lizard Priest could have rested comfortably on it.

The party looked at one another, then sat in a row with Goblin Slayer at their center. They sat with a fur blanket over their knees, and when they looked up, they saw two pillars flanking the high seat. Much thicker and more imposing than any of the other pillars, they were carved with images of the gods in stunning, fluid likenesses. One of the pillars depicted a fearsome-looking one-eyed, one-legged deity Priestess took to be the smithy god, but the other…

Is that…a goddess?

It was an unfamiliar deity, neither the Earth Mother nor the Valkyrie, yet one who combined martial prowess with compassion.

"Wife."

"Yes?"

The *húsfreya* bowed her head at this summons from the hearth and shuffled closer. Much later, Priestess would learn that this was the *stofa*, the living room, and the chieftain was seated upon the *öndvegi*, the high seat. Even at that moment, however, she understood the meaning of the seating arrangement.

We're facing the throne, in essence.

She gazed warily at the seat on the far side of the gloom and the fire and the haze of smoke. There was a tapestry depicting the brave deeds of ancient warriors. A powerful man standing upon mountains of corpses and rivers of blood as he sought to steal the robe of the Ice God's Daughter, who ate warriors' souls.

This brave young man, who no doubt would go on one day to be king, subdued the terrible monsters with his bare hands, could be seen breaking their arms. It even showed the dark elf ranger, the man's friend and companion, the fearsome user of a two-sword style whose presence could be just glimpsed in the old stories.

Below this tapestry of this song of ice and fire a huge man sat, as if he embodied the stories themselves. He wore tall fur boots and sheepskin trousers. Lengthy mail of black metal. A pelt around his shoulders. And the buckle on his belt was made of bronze. What's more…

"Ah, welcome, welcome, my adventuring friends. It must be rather colder here than you're used to in the south, eh?" he offered. The young man had a face like a brave gray wolf, and as friendly as his smile was, it still looked like he was baring his fangs.

"Oh…," Priestess said.

He spoke the common tongue. With no accent at all. And he didn't even have a beard, nor were there any horns on the helmet beside him. As he sat there, his left hand resting on the hilt of a sword buried in the earth, he looked less like a chieftain of the northern barbarians and more like...

"Are you a knight?" Goblin Slayer asked, decisive as ever.

"Was once," the young chieftain answered amiably. "I was blessed with great deeds and better fortune. Last year, when these lands were added to the kingdom... Well, I was added as a son to this family by marriage."

"And we, too, by my *husbondi*, were blessed by the loving mother of darkness," said the *húsfreya*, who waited beside the chief. She smiled— Priestess thought she might have blushed, too—and acknowledged him with a nod.

Yes, she had heard of something like that before they set out. Something about a land where adventurers were not yet established. That was why the quest had been largely about observation—but even so, one thing made Priestess absolutely goggle.

"The loving mother of darkness—you don't mean the sadistic god, do you...?!" She wouldn't go so far as to call this god evil. But it was unquestionably a deity aligned with Chaos. A deity of Chaos worshipped by the dark elves, who venerated pain and hurting people. A name to curse by.

The *húsfreya* looked at Priestess, perplexed, and Priestess realized that the woman wasn't that much older than she was. But while she didn't seem to understand the source of Priestess's shock, the chieftain laughed merrily.

"Ha-ha-ha! I labored under the same misimpression at first. But in a land as harsh as this one, she's a beneficent deity."

"Sooth. Is it not said that the Valkyrie herself once served the loving mother of darkness?"

"Wh-what?"

Priestess blinked, not hiding her amazement. She'd thought that myth had to do with the smithy god. First the tranquility in the face of murder committed in the name of...taking wives or some such, and now this… Priestess felt dizzy, her head spinning as if she'd had some less-than-high-quality alcohol.

She seemed to recall that the runners had a saying: *Don't let the culture shock kill you.*

"My own father was a friend of the chieftain here—the last one, I mean—and so when there was word that demons had appeared in this land, I came to help." He'd meant to go straight home after that. "But it was not to be!" he said with a laugh. "Even the strongest warrior may be overcome by love. And ahhh, love captured me completely!"

"Gracious, *husbondi*…!"

Yes, indeed; they got along very well. The *húsfreya* tugged on her husband's sleeve and glanced shyly at the ground.

"You do not mind us looking around?" asked Goblin Slayer. "It seems you have much going on."

"You mean the *brúðrav*, the bride-taking? Oh, that happens all the time. Surprised me at first, too."

Was that what the chief figured Goblin Slayer meant by *"much going on"*?

"Anyhow, we were the ones who asked His Majesty to send a survey. Not that winter is quite over yet." The chieftain grinned and reached out with his right hand for a stick with which to stir the fire, but the *húsfreya* stopped him and attended the flames instead. There was crackling and sparking, and the chieftain whispered something to the *húsfreya*, who nodded.

Then he said, "I admit, one thing we weren't told was that there would be a lizardman. Before anything else, you must warm yourself."

"Ahhh, for that, I am most grateful…!" Lizard Priest with his down cloak leaned almost hungrily toward the hearth. High Elf Archer, beside him, smiled hopelessly and made room. Closer to the fire would certainly be more comfortable for him.

"We have no inns around here, but we've prepared a house for you to sleep in. Please, use it as you like."

"And what might we do about, *ahem*, victuals?" Dwarf Shaman inquired.

The young man grinned. "There's nowhere in the world the radiance of the god of wine doesn't illuminate, and no land that's ignorant of *drekka*."

"This *drekka* you speak of," Dwarf Shaman said, stroking his beard. "Would it be the name of a wine?"

"It means to drink alcohol. And to drink alcohol means to have a feast!"

The chieftain sounded so calm about it that it took Priestess a moment to understand what he was saying. She blinked: a feast. A feast. The word went around and around in her head.

When you have guests, of course you have a feast. That was all well and good. And yet...

"W-wasn't there just a battle...?"

She almost jumped out of her spot on the high seat, but the *húsfreya* stopped her with a wave of her hand. "Fear not, fear not. A *drekka* is good fortune after a battle."

"Anyway, that's what they say around these parts." There was a mischievous glint in the chieftain's eye: If this was enough to shock them, they wouldn't last long here! "I guarantee the others are doing the same. The messenger who went to demand the return of the kidnapped women is probably falling down drunk by now."

"'Nother words, they've been bought," Dwarf Shaman observed.

"Whaaa...?" Priestess moaned, but Dwarf Shaman just grinned and refused to take the hint.

The chieftain gave a dramatic sigh and shook his head. "And if the ladies have been kidnapped and the messenger bought off, there's nothing for it but to have the biggest wedding *drekka* we can throw."

It's...j-j-just...a different culture, Priestess thought, feeling herself grow faint. Beside her, the cheap-looking helmet bobbed up and down. In spite of herself, she looked at him beseechingly. People treated him as if he were some kind of freak, but in fact he was quite sensible—even if his battle strategies could be a little out there.

He said: "That's profoundly interesting."

Priestess exclaimed the name of the Earth Mother in her heart.

§

"What? We're going sightseeing? We're not taking a rest?"

The introductions were over and the banquet was still in prepara-
tion, and they were at the house they had been given. High Elf Archer,
who had claimed the second closest bench to the hearth as her bed,
was twitching her ears.

The place was smaller than the chieftain's *skáli* but still clearly well-
appointed. That much was obvious from the quality of the pelts laid
out on the benches.

"I think I'll go see the place," Goblin Slayer (who had indeed looked
very interested on the way over) said with a nod of his helmet. He
sounded quite calm. He'd already deposited their belongings in a
room with a dirt floor at the back of the house that looked like it was
probably for storing provisions.

Priestess thought back, wondering when their last proper rest had
been. *Not since we were in that cave before we went into the underground city...*

"Boo," High Elf Archer said, stretching out indolently on the
bench; Priestess didn't really blame her. The elf had already thrown
down her belongings, tossed aside her cloak, and was barefoot, having
stripped off her boots and socks. She was well and truly ready to relax,
and maybe that was that.

"I-if you don't mind, I could come with you...!" Priestess offered
eagerly; she had only just set down her things. In any case, this was a
quest, it was a job, and it was an adventure. She wanted to get a good
look at the town. And it would have been untrue to say she didn't feel
some curiosity.

The water town, the elf village, the snowy mountain, the sea, the
ruined dwarven fortress, the desert country, and this faraway land.

If I hadn't become an adventurer, I would never have seen any of them my whole life.

And so, she felt, it wouldn't be right to let this moment get away. The
sense that it would be a waste flickered like a little flame in her heart.
Not to say she wouldn't have liked to toss everything aside and just
lounge on the bench like her elder friend...

"Urrrgh…" The elf's battle with lethargy was obviously growing more intense. She grumbled, groaned, flipped over on the bench, then looked at them while she lay on her stomach.

More specifically, she gazed at Goblin Slayer with upturned eyes; he was silently checking over his equipment and getting his gear ready. She knew perfectly well that within a few seconds, his preparations would be over.

Priestess, too, was inspecting the modicum of equipment she had with her, as had become her habit.

The words that came next were a short question: "Are you coming or not?"

"…Okay, I'm coming." High Elf Archer, finally victorious over her own sloth, pulled herself up to a sitting position with all the eagerness of a cat waking up in the morning. She reached for her belongings as though nothing could have been more annoying, considered whether to take out a change of socks, then finally pulled on the ones she had been wearing earlier. As she slid her long, pale legs into her boots, she could be heard mumbling, "Never know if you'll get another chance."

"An elf? Probably will," Dwarf Shaman remarked. He was tending the fire in the hearth and showed no sign of abandoning his chosen duty.

"You don't know the half of it." High Elf Archer sniffed. "I could blink and you'd all be gone!"

"Ah yes, all things are impermanent." Lizard Priest, in the seat closest to the fire that High Elf Archer had left open for him, nodded his long head. He must have finally been able to relax a little now that they were settled indoors, but the way he curled up reminded Priestess of nothing so much as…

…*a dragon.*

A drowsy dragon, like the one she'd actually seen in the desert—no doubt it would look something like this.

"Are we sure about this?" Priestess asked as High Elf Archer rubbed her face and pulled on her overwear. Their two party members sitting by the fire gave no indication of moving, and she was somewhat hesitant to leave them there.

"Gotta have someone look after the luggage, eh?" Dwarf Shaman said, grinning widely enough to show his teeth. "Besides," he added, producing a small knife from the pile of belongings, "we've got to make some preparations of our own for this *'drekka.'* And Scaly..."

"Yes, I would rather prefer to warm my blood by the fire."

"There yeh have it."

He was right. Priestess smiled with a touch of disappointment but also a touch of relief. This was an unfamiliar land. It wasn't that they didn't trust the people here, but as experienced travelers, they knew the need for someone to keep an eye on their possessions. And it was heartening to know that there would be someone there with their companion who was feeling unwell.

"You sure you're all right?" Maybe High Elf Archer was having the same thoughts, for she gave Lizard Priest a look that was only some-what teasing.

"Ha. If the likes of this were enough to cause us to go extinct, my bloodline would have died out long ago."

"Yeah, but we were deep enough underground for molten rock. You weren't exactly fighting the cold."

"Hrmmm..." Lizard Priest had nothing to say to that; High Elf Archer laughed aloud.

"All right, see you later, then—at this banquet, I guess?"

"If yeh actually get back by then, I'll take it the town's welcome was none too warm."

"Mm," said Goblin Slayer, who had been preparing silently until that moment. "Shall we go, then?"

"Suit yourselves! Don't mind us—go enjoy the sights."

Mm. The metal helmet nodded in response to Dwarf Shaman's careless wave. They opened the door and went out, Priestess some-what frantically and High Elf Archer happily, tugging a cap down onto her head as she went.

Oh! The sun is already—

So that was why it was so dark inside, Priestess realized. And for the first time, she discovered that the night sky was blue. Perhaps it was the sea in front of her. Maybe it was because the stars had changed places in the sky. She looked up at the heavens, where the twin moons danced along with the stars, her breath fogging. It was pleasant, placing her hands near her mouth to be warmed by her breath.

"...Gosh, it's so cold," Priestess said.

"You're not kidding," High Elf Archer replied, tugging her hat down over her ears and shivering. She'd had the hat since last winter, and apparently, it had somehow avoided being buried in her room in the intervening year. Priestess remarked that it looked good on her, to which High Elf Archer replied, "Thanks!" and winked, then burst out laughing.

Banter aside, it really is cold...

At extreme temperatures, she had heard, it could become impossible to distinguish the sensation of cold from actual pain; it could even be suffocating. Priestess was amazed that Goblin Slayer could calmly take in the scenery. She was starting to think that leaving her mail on had been a mistake, whatever arguments one might make in its favor. She treasured the outfit, but in the northern lands, it felt very heavy and very, very cold.

I'll have to make sure I do some maintenance later or the freezing might take a toll.

Even metal could become brittle in a frozen land—hence why the smithy god was venerated here, or so she'd heard some long time ago. Priestess had learned a little about metal because it was considered to be a blessing of the Earth Mother as well—after all, it came from the ground.

Truly, the secrets of iron ran deep. It would be presumptuous of her to think she knew anything, having heard only a smattering. Maybe she could ask Goblin Slayer how to take care of her equipment. Or perhaps...

That princess and her lord were both wearing mail...

That was when a voice like a lute inquired: "Goodness, but is anything the matter?"

It was the *húsfreya* herself.

§

The gorgeous gold-and-pale woman stood smiling in the snow, under the dark night sky. If she had looked like the Valkyrie before, now she could have been taken for the Earth Mother incarnate. She was no longer wearing an outfit that looked suited for battle; instead, she had changed into a high-quality fur dress and apron. It showed a good deal of her cleavage, which, no longer restrained by the mail, curved gracefully, as pale as the rest of her.

The elaborately embroidered shawl, however, blunted any sense of the erotic, and she didn't look cold, either. Her dress and the rest of her outfit was likewise embroidered—it must have taken a very long time. She still had the bundle of keys at her hip, and—wouldn't you know it!—the dull black metal was carefully worked with delicate designs, as befitted a place that venerated the smithy god. With her lovely golden hair held back by a scarf, she didn't look quite like a noble from the capital, but still...

...*She's very pretty*, Priestess thought, letting out a foggy sigh in spite of herself. The woman was nothing like she would have imagined from talk of northern *"barbarians."*

The *húsfreya* saw Priestess's expression and gave her a gentle smile, then held up some pieces of cloth. "I've brought blankets. Our lands must seem cold to you."

"Oh! Thank you...!"

"We can't have you sneezing," the *húsfreya* remarked. Priestess gratefully took the proffered blankets. They were woven wool, each of them a riot of color that had obviously taken a great deal of time and care to create.

And what matters is, they look really warm!

Priestess hugged the fluffy things, suddenly looking forward to going to bed that night. She thanked the *húsfreya* again and went right back through the door to offer blankets to the other two inside.

"Certainly!" Lizard Priest exclaimed, laughing and slapping the ground with his tail; Priestess closed the door again behind herself.

"I was observing the country at night," Goblin Slayer said, and Priestess suddenly stopped in her tracks. "The country of darkness and night." He was standing in the middle of the path, looking up at the sky as snow fell, piling on his helmet, though it didn't seem to bother him. He looked like a child gazing at the stars, like a child who would never tire of counting the countless gleaming spots in the sky. "Dark forests, leaden clouds, black rivers, a lonely wind, and endless mountains." Finally, he moved his head, turning to look at the *húsfreya*. "I was told that in this land, there were only the wind, and clouds, and dreams; hunts and battles; silence and shadows... But it seems there is more."

"It seems you are a poet, good sir. Like one of our *skalds*."

"The words are not mine," he replied to the chuckling *húsfreya*, taciturn as ever. He shook his head. Priestess, however, had never heard the unusual lines he'd just spoken.

"It's a very old song," High Elf Archer said, though it was hard to read her tone.

"Is that right?" Priestess asked; it was all she could manage. *Why?* Was it the foreign land, the snow, or the night? What was it that had sometimes left her feeling disconnected since they had begun this journey?

"I was hoping to go down to the port before the feast. If it's not too much trouble."

"Goodness, now? Yes, and I shall accompany you."

"Sorry about this," High Elf Archer said from under her hat, but she was grinning. "Nothing like making a princess be our tour guide."

"I'm not bothered at all. You've taken the trouble to be here." Then they set off down the snowy path, with the *húsfreya* at their head.

Puffs of black smoke could still be seen here and there around the village, and many people remained occupied repairing ruined houses or stone walls. But each time anyone saw the *húsfreya*, they would stop what they were doing and bow. She would smile and bow politely back, and the locals would return to their work, albeit usually with a suspicious glance at the people following her.

"They really respect you," Priestess said.

"I was the only child of my father left after his passing. Though I was hardly in the cradle." The *húsfreya* looked at the villagers with something like embarrassment. "Our *konungr*, our king," she began but quickly corrected herself. "Our *goði* is really just a *bondi*, a freeman. He isn't so special or important."

"Still, can't blame anyone for wondering what's up when the daughter of someone important is showing strangers around. They think maybe she shouldn't be. I understand," High Elf Archer said, sounding surprisingly friendly. Then the high elf kicked the snow on the road, almost deliberately, and said, "Hey, what do people think of adventurers around here? That's one thing I want to figure out."

"Well…" The *húsfreya* smiled uncomfortably. "In this place, they are regarded as pirates and thieves."

"In other words, as rogues…?" Priestess asked, tapping one of her cold-benumbed fingers against her lips. Then she nodded, her breath fogging as she made a sound of acknowledgment. She thought she saw what the issue was. Probably. Even if it was somewhat difficult for her to understand it in her bones.

The Adventurers Guild itself had originally arisen essentially as a way of assuring people that the state would keep an eye on the ne'er-do-wells running around. In other words, with no Guild, "adventurer" wasn't a job—adventurers were just a ragtag bunch of uncouth villains.

Thus, even in the land of Priestess's birth, an air of mistrust clung thickly to adventurers. She could almost take it for granted that she could rely on the Guild for everything, and she was happy that way. That was how adventurers should be. But while the Guild had a reasonably long history in her own land, here, such a thing as an Adventurers Guild didn't even exist. Adventurers were nothing more than ruffians, curs, and villains.

"Sooth," the *húsfreya* said earnestly, although—perhaps in deference to her present company—with some hesitation. "Long ago, there was once a great fool who stole a golden vessel from a burial place."

"Did a dragon appear?" Goblin Slayer asked immediately. His helmet turned so he was looking straight at the woman.

Argh, again. Priestess sighed to find that even these slight movements of his still caught her attention. He was different from his usual self somehow. She couldn't say exactly how, though, and that bothered her.

"Indeed, and a terrible one. They say the whole land became a sea of fire."

The *húsfreya* continued to speak of the old story as if this history was of no consequence—indeed, it wasn't. Priestess took a deep breath of cold air, hoping to sweep away the nebulous dark thing within her.

"Dragons are very scary," she said.

"You speak as though you've seen one with your own eyes."

"I have." Priestess giggled at the way the *húsfreya*'s eyes went wide; it was adorable. Then the woman puffed out her chest like a proud child about to share a secret and said, "But it was so frightening that I ran away as fast as I could!"

§

When Priestess thought about it, she realized this might be the first proper port she'd ever seen in her life, although to her it looked much like a ship's landing built on the banks of a lake. A wharf jutted out from the shore into the water, with several boats moored to it. The resemblance between these ships and the gondolas she'd seen in the water town reinforced the impression that it was all familiar.

But the size!

"Wow… *Wow*…"

The first proper ship Priestess ever saw in her life was like a gondola big enough to hold a hundred people. (Granted, that was just her impression; maybe a few dozen was the limit…) Several oars extended from each gunwale, and a great mast dominated the center of the ship. It was all enough to make a young woman stop and stare.

But that wasn't all: There were barbarian warriors aboard, shouting and rowing the ship out into the blizzard-tossed sea. It was like something out of a child's dream. "Incredible," Priestess mumbled again.

"Mm," Goblin Slayer said from under his helmet, where he stood beside her staring intently at the boat. "Indeed."

"Does it truly impress you that much?" the *húsfreya* asked, standing on the wharf and watching them with something like amusement.

The night was already cold, and being by the water only made it colder, and yet...

Simply to have been able to see this..., Priestess thought. That alone made it worth having come here.

The ships were black shapes floating upon the ink-dark surface of the water. The prows were carved in the likeness of dragon heads, making them look like nests of sea monsters. Priestess breathed on her numb fingers and said, "Yes, it really does!" and smiled. "There is one thing that's a little upsetting, though..."

"Yeah," agreed High Elf Archer, who was holding her cap down on her head, mindful of her ears. "If only there hadn't just been a battle."

Yes, that was it. Most of the ships were intact, but several of them were riddled with arrows or showed signs of having been scorched by fire. If there was a silver lining, it was that nothing appeared to have sunk during the fighting, but it was obvious that the battle had only just ended. It was one thing to see a warrior with a scar from an old injury—but these wounds were fresh.

"Um, earlier, you said your family had shown up," Priestess began. Even though she still felt almost dizzy with culture shock, she picked up a piece of wood lying about. The damage she could see in it was recent but a bit too old to have been inflicted today. She felt a gaze on her from behind the metal helmet and nodded.

Goblin Slayer said, "Goblins?"

"Do you mean orcs?" the *húsfreya* asked in surprise, but then she laughed and waved her hands: *No, no.* "Orcs are but stupid little crybabies."

"That's what I thought."

"The family comes every year, but this year rather earlier and more often than usual."

"Ah, so that's it." High Elf Archer nodded; if she hadn't been holding her hat down on her head, her ears would probably have twitched. "I have to admit, I was kind of wondering about that injury of his. To his right arm."

"Gracious. You noticed?" The *húsfreya* scratched her cheek, but Priestess made a sound of surprise. "He was hurt?" she asked, turning to High Elf Archer even as the salty wind caught her hair in its chill grasp.

"Eh, he smelled like blood. And he kept his right arm covered with his cloak. And you didn't see him in the battle, did you?" The high elf added indifferently that she'd kept quiet about it because it wasn't good to point out a king's injury.

Was High Elf Archer just that observant, or did her sharp high elf senses help her discern the situation? Priestess wasn't sure; she knew only that she had failed to notice an injured person, and that was unacceptable.

The townspeople (*"bondi"*—was that what the *húsfreya* had called them?) had looked so calm that Priestess had simply left them.

But really…

Really she should already be among the people, caring for wounds and helping to rebuild.

The *húsfreya* noticed her worried expression. "Don't worry about my *husbondi*; he's quite fine." She smiled. "It's an injury to the bone of his right arm. He'll soon be better with some rest."

"The bone…"

But that was terrible. Even with proper treatment, there was no telling if it would knit correctly. And worse for a warrior, even if it did heal properly, one couldn't be sure it would move like it used to. Very few were lucky enough to have a cleric with miracles present at the moment they were injured. Injuries like this were one of the main reasons that many adventurers, soldiers, and mercenaries finally retired. And all of this was even more crucial in these cold climes for a man who led a martial people as their chief.

"Do you not have a cleric who's been granted miracles?" Priestess asked, eyeing the bandage wrapped around the *húsfreya*'s head. It was clear that the eye beneath had been damaged; scar tissue was visibly peeking out from under the wrapping.

"This was an offering to the sadistic god," the *húsfreya* said with a smile, sounding as if it was completely unremarkable. Then she shook her head sadly. "A *gyðja* we have, but my *husbondi* in his pride will not listen to her."

"And miracles are valuable," High Elf Archer said knowingly. "In battle, you probably prioritize the soldiers over the king."

"I know such an injury isn't fatal, but...," Priestess began, but then she wasn't sure how to finish. The *húsfreya* stared silently out to sea with an inscrutable expression. She was probably more worried about her husband than anyone, but she refused to say anything forward. Priestess was still inexperienced, still didn't know the subtleties of this place. Maybe her friends in the capital—Female Merchant and King's Sister—would have known what to do, but...

"...I'm sorry," she said after a long moment.

"It's all right. Worried as I am, it's simply that my dear *husbondi* is the stubborn type."

"I see." Goblin Slayer broke brusquely into the melancholy conversation. He had already taken a walk around the wharf at his bold stride; he now asked with interest, "And is this the 'crane' you mentioned?" He was staring intently at the wooden watchtower constructed along the shore.

It was a great, looming shadow, even darker than the night sky and sea between which it towered. Priestess had, after all, been wrong to imagine it as a gigantic arm. She realized now that it was more like a dragon's long neck.

"It's like an elephant's nose, huh?" High Elf Archer said quietly.

"An elephant?" Priestess didn't really understand, but the elf waved away her confusion.

The tower was rigged with a series of ropes that were evidently what enabled it to lift cargo up and down. Priestess's admiring exclamation took on physical form as white fog, and High Elf Archer remarked, "Humans think of even stranger things than dwarves!"

"Normally, if something was too heavy to lift, you'd have to give up, or at least call for help," Priestess commented.

"And giving up is no way to survive in this land of snow," the *hús-freya* said. A cutting gust of snowy wind came through, and she smiled as if it were a pleasant autumn breeze.

Cultural practices were shaped by the land and the people who lived there. Surely there was no single aspect of culture that every single person in the Four-Cornered World had in common. The lives these people led every day in this place must have been beyond Priestess's imagination.

And that's why...

Her amazement wasn't because their culture was so *strange* but because it was so ordinary.

"And is this the control mechanism for the crane?"

"Sooth."

Priestess's busy mind was, of course, of no consequence to Goblin Slayer, who was interested in the device itself. The ropes hanging from the crane were attached to some kind of large mechanism on the wharf. It looked a bit like a stone step and a bit like the large wooden training poles set up on the practice grounds. Several thick wooden rods radiated out from the center, and from the circular shape worn in the ground around the device, those rods were probably pushed to turn the device.

"So you have slaves turn the thing?" High Elf Archer asked.

"Yes, *prælls*."

"And that rolls up the ropes, which lifts the cargo..."

There must also have been some way to change which way the crane was facing. When repairing a ship, with hands all around, the crane must turn in every possible direction. Now, at night, they were the only ones at the port, but Priestess found herself thinking once more how astonishing everything here was.

She and others from the southern reaches regarded the people here as rustic and uncivilized. But nothing she had seen in this town made it seem like the home of barbarians.

©Noboru Kannatuki

"Hmm…" Heedless of the cold and the dark (for the night was dark despite the stars), Goblin Slayer walked over to the device. "May I try pushing it?"

"You may, but…it won't be easy by yourself."

"I suppose not." Goblin Slayer nodded, then put a hand to one of the large poles and pushed as hard as he could. The machine didn't budge, of course. The man in the grimy equipment planted his feet and shoved, but it never so much as quivered. After a while, with white fog drifting from between the slats of his visor, he could be seen to relax. "It is indeed futile."

"Well, yeah," High Elf Archer said and laughed out loud. "You'd have to be awful strong to move this thing all alone."

"Yes." The helmet bobbed up and down, scattering the snow that had fallen on it. The wind caught the flakes, carrying them off into the night. "Only a true hero could work this thing by themselves."

Priestess didn't understand why, but he sounded downright…happy about it.

§

"All right. For starters, take this."

"Is this…a horn?" Priestess asked, taking it from Dwarf Shaman and looking at it with interest. It would be time for the feast soon, so they'd returned to their lodgings and were about to head to the *skáli*. Priestess, High Elf Archer, and Goblin Slayer were each given what at first appeared to be hunting horns.

"But there's nowhere to blow into it," Goblin Slayer noted, turning it around in his hands. "So is it a cup?"

"Mm! And you'll be needing to leave your sword here…"

"That much I know," Goblin Slayer said with a nod. The ancient dwarven blade was missing from his hip. Instead, it leaned against one of the benches, catching the glow of the hearth fire in its dull, dark metal. Despite having come from some ancient ruins, it showed no sign of chipping or rust.

However, Dwarf Shaman said, "It's just a sword. Not a single enchantment on the thing. Well-made, true enough, but perfectly ordinary." While Priestess, Goblin Slayer, and High Elf Archer had been out looking around, he must have spent the time inspecting the weapon. "Disappointed, Beard-cutter?"

"No," came the response with a shake of the helmeted head. "My teacher... My master's blade was likewise undistinguished. It's enough for me."

"Figures," said Dwarf Shaman, a smile crossing his bearded face. He'd clearly expected something like this. "You should bring a dagger of some sort, though. That's practically etiquette."

"Mm." Goblin Slayer nodded again; he, and indeed Dwarf Shaman as well, both had shortswords fixed by their bodies. Speaking of matters of etiquette, the helmet and armor should probably have come off—but that was hardly an argument worth having now. Although it didn't stop High Elf Archer from giving him a dubious look.

"Just asking," she said, "but this isn't going to be one of those things where you pour a drink the wrong way and suddenly it's swords out and blood everywhere...is it?"

"With elves, maybe, but *most* people don't consider it polite to find fault with such trivial details."

"Elves don't do that, either!" High Elf Archer protested with a frown. An obsidian dagger dangled at her hip. "Think you can move?" she asked.

"Mm, indeed. I'm much warmer now, and there's a fine fire at the longhouse," said Lizard Priest, who was leaning on the archer. He had no dagger but had his claws and tail and fangs.

What should I do?

Priestess looked around in a bit of a tizzy but finally settled on simply holding her sounding staff—tightly.

"If everyone is ready, then let's go," Goblin Slayer urged.

"Oh, r-right...!" She scurried ahead, through the door—she had almost lost count how many times this was today—and outside.

I've barely seen the room we're staying in, she thought as she and the others retraced the path they'd taken not long before. It would take more than a couple of trips to learn the roads, and the whole town seemed changed under the darkness of night. She could almost have believed that if they lost the path, they would never find their way back again.

The light glowing in the *skáli's* skylight was uncommonly heartening; when they reached it, Priestess felt like she could breathe again.

"...I wonder if we'll be okay getting back," she said.

High Elf Archer looked at her with curiosity, her ears flicking with the chill. "I think so. It's only just over there."

Oh, that's right...

She was prone to forgetting that she and Goblin Slayer were the only members of this party who didn't see well in the dark. Priestess, feeling a bit embarrassed, could hardly bring herself to look at High Elf Archer, but her archer friend was frowning. Then she smiled, sort of, squinting as if she was looking at something bright, and her ears twitched again.

"Is something...the matter?" Priestess asked.

"Nah. You'll see in a second."

"—?"

Priestess had no idea what she meant, but Dwarf Shaman seemed to get it, for he stroked his beard knowingly.

Then, without the slightest sign of hesitation, Goblin Slayer pounded on the door.

"Please do come in," said someone inside. It was the voice of the *goði,* but there was another voice, too, almost drowning him out. When they pushed open the thick wooden door, they quickly discovered what it was.

Thereupon the hero discovered his mortal foe, the cursèd one, standing upon the altar.

But how could he have known that no blade, no blade at all, could touch the great ruler who had offered up the twin-headed serpent?

This inhumane villain, with a spell, he rendered moot the sword of the Four-Cornered World's victory.

The great ruler spoke:
'Twas I who lit the fire of hatred within you.
'Twas I who honed your bravery.
Will you kill the one you call your second father?

Rage rushed to the warrior's head, and he drew his faithful sword:
The keen-edged steel he'd found in the barrow, once companion to the kings of old.
But Evil only mocked him:
That sword, which has smashed armor and cloven helms, will not touch my neck
so long as my spell is not unwoven, I need not even roll the dice.
I have unlocked the secrets of steel.

But take heart!
For the warrior trusted not in his sword,
nor was his strength in the secret of steel,
but the smithy god had given him an unquenchable fire of courage.

And how was the great ruler to know?
How could he guess that the gods at the table of the heavens
were rolling their dice to define the outcome of battle
knowing that otherwise, this warrior would never pray again?

The awful ruler howled and writhed in pain
the likes of which he hadn't known before:
The warrior's blade struck true against his sworn foe.
Black steel smashed through bone, singing out in victory, and thus the warrior decapitated the villain.

Now, give ear to me,
to the legend of this great king
whose deed a thousand years from now shall still be told.

*   *   *

He came forth from the land of shadows and dark night in far-most north.
A slave he was, and a warrior, and a pirate, and a mercenary, and a general
and a king who conquered many thrones.

O King!
By your honored name, all fall before your blade.
O King, we pray for blessings upon you.

"Wow…"

It was one of the sagas. An ancient, all but forgotten song she had never heard. A tremendous tale that took a fellow with no place to lay his head all the way to one of the apogees of the Four-Cornered World. There was no instrument providing a melody, only a human voice recounting the brave deeds of a hero.

The benches lining either side of the hearth in the long building were crowded with men who bore fresh scars of battle and sang lustily along. Naturally, some kind of big game—it looked like perhaps a wild boar—was roasting on the hearth, dripping with grease. Nor was that the only main course; there was also a stew of onions, fragrant herbs, and fish like herring and cod. Then there was a table covered with apples, walnuts, and berries, as well as some kind of flat, glutinous bread. It was really, truly like being smack in the middle of a foreign banquet.

"Hoh, well come, well come. Please be seated." On the center high seat was the *goði*, the *húsfreya* attending at his right hand, who grinned widely and motioned them over. Priestess realized that the one open seat was directly across from the chieftain. Meaning…it must be for them.

"That's where we sat earlier," High Elf Archer whispered.

"_____"

Goblin Slayer offered no response to High Elf Archer's observation. He simply stood where he was and watched the men sing. "Hey, are you listening to me?" High Elf Archer said.

"...It must be the seat of honor," Goblin Slayer said at length, his helmet finally moving. "We are guests of the king." And then, without the slightest hesitation, he strode boldly through the crowd.

Even the northerners were understandably taken aback by this man who would wear full armor even to a feast. They looked at one another, whispered, and stared... Ultimately, however, they seemed to conclude that, *shrug*, he was a foreigner.

Things were calming down as Priestess rushed after him, and as for Dwarf Shaman, the crowd seemed used to the likes of him. Lizard Priest crouched slightly to make himself smaller, murmuring, "Pardon," as he went by. High Elf Archer slid lithely among the throng.

And then Priestess suddenly found herself standing beside Goblin Slayer at the high seat. "Th-thank you for...having us...?"

"But of course."

Their spot made them effectively guests of honor at the banquet.

I'm not used to this...! How, Priestess wondered, could her companions seem so self-assured? It was a mystery to her.

"Now, my good guest...," the *goði* said.

"Er, yes...!" Priestess squeaked, not having expected him to speak to her. She quickly focused back on the present moment.

The chieftain was still keeping his right arm covered with his cloak, but he looked eminently relaxed. Thinking of the *húsfreya*'s kindness earlier, Priestess thought perhaps she should say something; she opened her mouth to speak—but then closed it again when she saw the woman gently shake her head.

"Have you your cup?" the chieftain inquired.

"My cup? ...Oh!" Priestess looked down at the drinking horn she'd recently received, which she now carried along with her sounding staff. "Y-yes, I do...!"

"For you see, in this land, it's the custom for everyone to carry their own drinking cup. Good, good." The man with the wolflike face smiled as if he found the entire scene pleasant. "Very well. Someone, bring the guests wine... Er..."

"Would you, as my *husbondi* says, be so kind?" The *húsfreya* leaned toward her husband, picking up smoothly where he left off and giving the instructions. Even Priestess, just across from them, hadn't realized that the *goði* had been lost for the right words in the local language. "We have mead, *bjórr*, and *skyr*. Which would you like?"

"Er, uh, well…"

Before she could get any further, several horns of alcohol were thrust out in front of her. They were offered by one of the burly northerners; perhaps Priestess had met him that afternoon, but she wasn't sure. She held her drinking horn and fought the confusion, but meanwhile, Goblin Slayer grunted, "Hmm. Once long ago, I heard you had cider here."

"Ah, *epli* wine. Yes, give me your cup."

"Mm."

Goblin Slayer held out his drinking horn, and it was filled from a wine jug with a copious amount of alcoholic cider. Priestess reflected on how the horn came to a point at the bottom. It meant one wouldn't be able to set down one's drink until the entire thing had been drained.

"What'll you be having, then, young lady?"

"Er, um…"

Priestess, having realized this fact about the cup, was thinking as fast as she could. She'd never been too concerned about whether she was a strong drinker, but in a moment like this, she didn't want to do anything to cause offense. Their quest here wasn't just to observe but to help build friendship.

"Uh, well… What's *skyr*?"

"It's the milk of the goat."

"I'll have that, then, please," Priestess said quickly.

"Hoh," the northerner replied, his angular face softening. His craggy aspect, along with his long, braided beard, made him look a bit like a dwarf. Priestess found a thick white liquid being poured into her cup, and she couldn't help smiling, too.

"Hrm…," was the sound that escaped Lizard Priest as he looked on from beside them. He moved his hand on his long neck, waiting for the jar of wine to come around to him.

"Here, mead for you."

"Hmm, hmm, hmm…!" Lizard Priest's eyes rolled in his head as the mead was poured into his drinking horn quite without regard to what he wished for. *"Ahem*, no, I—"

"Hoh, didn't realize you couldn't stomach our wine." The words cut through the lively chatter of the banquet. Pouring the drink for Lizard Priest was a warrior with a bandage around part of his face. There were dark traces of blood as well, and he showed not the slightest sign of fear despite being confronted with Lizard Priest's terrible visage. Those around them seemed to give the man a wide berth.

He appeared neither hesitant nor worried but looked as if he wouldn't bat an eye if a sword was to be drawn right there at the feast. Lizard Priest, perhaps instinctively, responded by gladly opening his jaws to bare his fangs…

"Here, gimme that." Faster than anyone could move, faster than the *goði* or the *húsfreya* or Priestess, the delicate hand of a high elf snatched the drinking horn away. The elf princess, not remotely intimidated by human theatrics, took a good sniff of the stuff, then smiled. "Ah, lovely. You've used excellent honey in this. I love this kind of thing."

"Er… Hrm…" The wind went out of the bandaged northerner's sails, whether from hesitation or embarrassment, and he sputtered senselessly. "I'm most embarrassed to offer such a pitiful drink to a princess of the *álfr*…"

"Don't worry about it. I'll take this from him. Give him the— What was it? *Skyr*? Some of that."

"As you say, milady." The northerner bowed his head, then held out the jar of goat's milk to Lizard Priest, filling his horn.

"Ah, many thanks…," the lizardman said.

"Cheeky man. You should have told us sooner what you needed." The barbarian slapped Lizard Priest's hand, but it was unmistakably a gesture of affection. All the danger had drained from the air long ago, from the moment High Elf Archer had reached out her hand. Priestess, who had frozen when the trouble loomed, was able to relax. She glanced in the direction of the *húsfreya*, who looked like she had been feeling much the same way; their eyes met, and they shared a giggle.

"Color me jealous. A young lady of the *álfr*!"

"Indeed, indeed. A bride young for as long as she lives!"

"…What?" Priestess, listening to the easy banter of the men, blinked in confusion. Of course, she didn't quite understand what they were saying. Not exactly, and yet…

She looked over and saw the man handing off his drink to a young woman, much like Lizard Priest just had. So that charge of danger in the air a moment ago had also been just a normal thing—as she could tell from the way it disappeared as quickly as it had come. It was considered polite to drink wine, but if one was unable, a woman could help one, it seemed. Which implied that relations between men and women permitted such things here.

"Oh. Uh…" Priestess, feeling a flush rise to her cheeks even though she wasn't drinking alcohol, found herself tugging on her elder friend's sleeve. "Are… Are you sure this is all right?!"

"Hmm?" The high elf, smiling placidly at the aroma of the honey, swayed gently. "Is what all right?" she asked, indifferent.

Some words communicated whether one understood them or not. Red-faced, Priestess let her eyes wander. Lizard Priest paid her no mind, apparently savoring the thought of when he would get to enjoy the contents of his drinking horn. And Goblin Slayer, she couldn't count on him. She looked beseechingly at Dwarf Shaman, but he waved back at her as if to say, *Don't be a boor.*

He finds this funny—I'm sure of it, Priestess thought. She gave him a glare but then sighed in the knowledge that it was unlikely to have much effect on him. Finally, she looked up at the ceiling high above them, mumbled the name of the Earth Mother, and then turned back to High Elf Archer with a smile. "Never mind—it's nothing."

"No?" Her elder friend gave her a curious look, but then her eyes sparkled and she said, "Ooh, it's starting!"

Right. The thing to do now…

The thing to do now was to set aside unnecessary concerns and focus on enjoying the feast to which they had so kindly been invited.

Once the *goði* was certain that the drinks had made their way to

©Noboru Kannatuki

all the guests, he rose (with one good sway) and stood across from Priestess. This was the moment when any king or noble Priestess knew would have given a long speech. But this was a new land. And the *goði* said only, "To fellows and friends!" At his right hand stood the *hús-freya*; with his left, he lifted his drinking horn. There was a roar of approval from his subjects, who began adding their own toasts.

"To long days and pleasant nights!"

"To the trials and tribulations and great deeds granted us by the Night Mother!"

"To peace!"

Priestess joined in with a cry of, "T-to peace!"

Then there was a great clatter of the draining of drinking horns, and the *drekka* got underway.

§

There was nothing of particular note to record about the feast—and yet, countless things about the feast should be recorded.

It was quite lively; one could say that much.

The first problem Priestess had was *how* to eat the food. There were only plates on the table; she didn't see any utensils. Just as she was wondering whether they were supposed to eat with their hands, every-one around her pulled out their daggers and began spearing food with them— Ah.

Never leave home without it: She had the small knife from the Adventurer's Toolkit, which served nicely at this moment.

When she tried them, she discovered that not just the flatbread but the roast boar and the fish, too, were all more robust than she had imagined and very delicious. Even if the smell of the soup, loaded as it was with onions and herbs, did take her somewhat aback. (The north-erners made their living as traders, so they were said to have herbs both medicinal and fragrant from all over the world.)

Priestess was by now familiar with how dwarves drank wine, but the northerners, for their part, were duly impressed. There were exclamations and cheers as Dwarf Shaman was served horns full of alcohol, only to drink them down as if they were water, one after the next.

Lizard Priest, caught up in the excitement, opened his great jaws and sang a song of battle passed down from his forefathers. It spoke of a black-scaled hero who defeated a giant, killed a dragon, and took to wife a woman poet with a cursed sword. Priestess remembered this story being told with a dance in the desert country, and she'd heard a similar tale in High Elf Archer's village as well.

But the story, as they say, changes with the teller. The birdfolk dancer had portrayed it as a poignant romance, told from the perspective of the poet. In Lizard Priest's jaws, it was a war song of the victory of a ferocious lizardman who walked the world with his great metal staff in hand. He charged toward every monster he saw, intent on doing deeds worthy of the songs of his lady love. It had a certain purity, like a dragon's breath, and perhaps that made it a romance in its own way.

Whatever the case, it must certainly have been a strange and unusual story to the northerners. Just as their story of their own hero had been unfamiliar to Priestess.

Perhaps it was only natural when one of the men called out to Goblin Slayer, "Say, haven't you got any stories of your own heroics?"

"I've done no heroics," he replied, gulping down cider, and then, before Priestess could interject, he nodded. "I've hunted goblins, though."

"Orcs, you mean? Numbers they have, but no guts."

"Filthy, rotten cheaters, they are."

"I agree." The helmeted head nodded up and down.

"And fighting them with this many people is no picnic, either."

"Absolutely." Another nod.

"So how many have you killed?"

"…" Goblin Slayer fell silent and stared into the distance. He seemed to be thinking very seriously. "I have, on occasion, taken on perhaps a hundred of them at once."

The northerners dissolved into gales of laughter. They meant no harm by it; it was a joyous sound.

Huh, I've never heard that story, Priestess thought. Maybe she would have a chance to ask sometime. She wondered if he would tell her. Perhaps she should ask now. As she thought, she brought the drinking horn to her lips, sipping delicately at the contents. The *skyr* had a sour, unusual taste, but she thought it probably qualified as pleasant. She almost thought she could understand why Lizard Priest might beat his tail on the ground and cry, "Sweet nectar!"

Her thoughts were interrupted by the *goði*, in high spirits, who said, "Do you know what they say of my wife in the capital?"

Priestess, realizing she had missed her chance, looked around and discovered the northerners all looked vaguely amused. Their expressions seemed to say, *Here we go again.*

"They call her the One-Eyed Bear! Can you believe it?"

"Er, oh…"

The chieftain brought his fist down on the table, drinking horn and all; Priestess could only nod along. She'd heard people in the cold reaches liked strong wine—but the *goði*'s face was red, and his eyes were watery. "They can only say that because they've never been here!"

Maybe it was the way of this land that nobody spoke against him for acting as if he were one of them.

"She may have been trapped up here in the north, but my bride is the sweetest in the Four-Cornered World…!"

Ah. It's just that they like him personally…

Even Priestess felt a flush rise in her cheeks at the chieftain's unabashed declaration of love.

"Ha-ha-ha! Our *goði*! Even he can't steal honey from this wife, though!"

This drew a surprised look from High Elf Archer, whose face was red for a completely different reason from Priestess's. How many horns of mead was she on anyway? She certainly seemed to be enjoying it, given how she was constantly sipping at her drink.

"Just so! During the Dwelling, the *goði* fought a demon like a giant bee."

"Dwelling?" Priestess asked.

"'Tis when a man lives at his bride's house before the *bruðsvelja*, the wedding."

"So he wrestles with the thing and plucks the creature's leg off!"

The chieftain smiled ruefully as his companions told the tale with relish, but he shrugged easily. "My opponent had no sword. If I brought my weapon, it would have made things too easy."

"Huh! That's really something!" High Elf Archer said, laughing uproariously. (How much of the story did she actually understand?)

Then again, maybe it really is an incredible story...? Priestess, perplexed by a variety of words she didn't recognize, nonetheless drained her drinking horn. She set it on the table and rose from her seat, saying, "Please pardon me a moment." She was a little worried about the *húsfreya*, who had left her place before all the storytelling had started...

§

"Phew...!" Priestess let out a breath as she departed the *skáli*, putting the hubbub of the banquet behind her, released from the press of people. The cold wind that gusted outside was a tremendous relief, overheated as she felt simply from having so many people in one place.

I see...

She thought maybe she understood what it was like to drink wine. She went walking along over the crunching snow, feeling that things were somehow cheerful and bright despite the night darkness. Was it the stars or perhaps the twin moons? In any case, it turned out not to be too hard to find the *húsfreya*: All the footprints, presumably of people coming to the banquet, led up to the longhouse, but just one set went away.

Don't have to be a ranger to follow this trail.

Even she could do it. Priestess could tell whether the distinct prints belonged to a goblin or not.

She was behind the longhouse, on the edge of the village, but not so far away that the light and the chattering voices didn't carry to her. The *húsfreya*, surrounded by the twinkling, dancing snowflakes, turned when she heard Priestess's footsteps, her one good eye squinting as she smiled. "Gracious, heading to bed already?"

"No." Priestess smiled back, shaking her head. "Just getting some air." Priestess stood beside her and exhaled again, white fog drifting from her mouth. "Thank you so much for today. I can't believe there's boar and everything, even though you just had a battle…"

"A *drekka* is always like this! And how can we fail to show hospitality to our visitors?"

She added that even if one's mortal enemy came to one's home, if they came as a traveler, then it was only generous to welcome them in. She really did sound as if she considered it perfectly natural.

"That's amazing," Priestess said, unable to come up with anything more articulate or incisive. And so long as you took your foe into your home, they would know they were also your guest, even if they were your enemy. Two sworn foes, not forgiving each other but testing the limits of each other's magnanimity… It was astonishing.

While Priestess was still busy looking impressed, the *húsfreya* shook her head as if she could see it all. "I suppose that my *husbondi* has begun his usual diatribe?"

"Ah—ah-ha-ha…"

"The fool," the *húsfreya* murmured; Priestess pretended not to hear her. Nor to notice that her face was red.

What should she say? She knew what she wanted to say, but she couldn't quite put it into words.

But… Well.

In fact, what she wanted to say could be summed up quite simply.

"…He's a wonderful husband, isn't he?"

"Mm…" The *húsfreya* nodded but didn't say anything more, not immediately. Her hand brushed the bundle of keys at her hip. The girlish gesture made Priestess wonder if in fact the *húsfreya* was not much older than she was. "With this face, not a one would have blamed him had he broken off the engagement in disgust."

"I think it's lovely."

"Then you don't speak the truth."

"I mean it!" Priestess giggled, her laughter likewise fogging in the air. "In the water town… Well, in a big city near where I live, there's a bishop like you." *Her eyes.* Priestess motioned at her face, then said firmly to the *húsfreya*, "But she's a wonderful person… And I think you must be wonderful, too."

"………Is that the case?"

"Yes. Yes, it is."

"Is it indeed…?" The *húsfreya* let out a long breath. The white fog mingled with that of Priestess's exhalation, and they danced off into the sky together. "…The Four-Cornered World," the *húsfreya* said after another moment. "Is it not a very large place?"

"Yes… It's vast."

It really is.

Priestess had thought that this was the edge of the world. That if she went beyond the mountains looming in the distance, a place she had never been, that that would be as far away as it was possible to go.

But of course, it was no such thing. The people who lived here interacted with people who lived even farther north. The encounters between these people were brutal in a way that Priestess couldn't imagine. Beyond the eastern desert, too, there must yet have been a great deal of the world. And there was even more she had never seen past the forest to the south. For that matter, though she lived on the western frontier, she didn't know what might lie even farther to the west.

Worlds, people, everything: How many tales there were of vanished peoples and forgotten realms. Just as Priestess hadn't known that story of the hero.

It was impossible to say, *It must be like this*, to assign a definitive value to something. It simply wasn't possible for anyone. And this revealed that whatever was in question must be something infinitely valuable.

Huh… I see, Priestess thought, finally comprehending the true nature of the dark mist that had seemed to cloud her heart. She realized it had been there since before they'd left on this journey, since the time of the dungeon exploration contest. She simply hadn't grasped it.

For *him*, for Goblin Slayer, to show an expression like that—to show any emotion at all. To Priestess, he was an object of respect, perfect, decisive; he had trod the path ahead of her and was complete. He hardly ever showed anger. He was impeccably calm and collected, or so she had imagined him.

But that was wrong.

He had wanted to come to this land for reasons Priestess didn't know. He'd had a boyish dream of the place, a wish in his heart. He'd had hopes for the journey and was enjoying himself.

Ah! What a thing this was. There was more to the slayer of goblins than slaying goblins!

"Hee… Hee-hee-hee!"

"Is everything all right?"

"Yes… Everything's fine." Priestess wiped at the tears that had formed at the corners of her eyes as she laughed, the night breeze catching her golden hair. "I was just thinking, there are so many things I don't know. I can't forget to keep learning."

"Very true… Ah, say!" the *húsfreya* called abruptly.

"What is it?" Priestess asked, turning toward her.

The other woman's skin, paler than the snow, was flushed rose-red, and she was grinning with unmistakable mischief. "The *rrr…rrrain…*" She took a deep breath. "The rain, I explained, stays—" She cleared her throat. "The rain, I explained, stays mainly in the plain!"

"Wow…!" Priestess clapped her hands.

It was a little stumbling and spotty, somewhat juvenile and not terribly proficient—ah, but still.

"You said it…! And so perfectly!"

"I did it…!" The *húsfreya* was so cute the way she proudly clenched her fist that Priestess had taken her hand before she knew what she was doing. It was small and scarred, rough and angular…

It's a wonderful hand, she thought, clasping it; the *húsfreya* looked away shyly. "*Ahem*. I am not yet anywhere near it," she said. "You'll not mention it to my *husbondi*, will you?"

"You've been practicing?!"

"My *husbondi*, he has his heart set on taking me to the capital," she said, adding that she could hardly have him become a laughingstock.

It was clear she felt the exact same way as the chieftain—and the exact opposite way. Priestess was sure the young northern ruler thought of the *húsfreya* as his fair lady.

"I really do think you're wonderful. I mean, both you and your husband."

"Mn…"

Then the *húsfreya* invited Priestess to the bath. It was "washing day," she said, and it was the custom to bathe, even if it was immediately after a battle.

The *bathstúva* was a steam bath, a familiar arrangement: Water was poured over a stone statue of the Deity of the Basin that was heated on the hearth. What was unusual was the bubbling water that they used to clean themselves, which elicited a little shriek of surprise from Priestess.

The *húsfreya* giggled at her, but she herself regarded Priestess's mail with open curiosity. Then again, she'd brought her obviously important bundle of keys into the bath with her, so she was hardly in a position to judge. Priestess had observed that all the women at the banquet had had keys at their hips, and she was starting to understand what they meant.

On the *húsfreya*'s bare skin, illuminated by the faint but uncanny light, there was an almost translucent pattern. It ran from the eye usually covered by a bandage, extending toward her heart as well as down one arm. It was a white tree.

Yes, that was it: It looked like a great tree spreading its branches. It hardly seemed to be the work of human hands. Without quite meaning to, Priestess found herself studying it, and the *húsfreya* showed her the scar as if revealing something deeply important.

"A blessing from the gods, this is," she said. A holy scar of the sadistic god, bestowed in her youth. The heavenly fire had scorched her body, scarring her and taking her eye. It must have involved a pain Priestess could barely imagine. Yet, at the same time…

It's what enabled her to meet the kindest of people.

Be it Fate or be it Chance, the gods in heaven rolled their dice and wove their stories. It was up to people's free will how to walk their

©Noboru Kannatuki

paths. If the man the *húsfreya* had met hadn't been willing to be together with her, she wouldn't be here in this place at this moment. Just as Priestess wouldn't be, if the man she had met hadn't decided to save a rookie in a goblin nest.

Truly, truly, the Four-Cornered World burst with things even the gods couldn't imagine.

"I know that it is because of the pain in our lives that the joys are precious," the *húsfreya* said.

"Is that…the teaching of the sadistic goddess?"

"Sooth."

No doubt it was Priestess's status as an outsider that allowed her to think this land wonderful. They had held a feast for her. Everyone she met was kind to her, or at least accepting. The culture here demanded the welcome of travelers, so that food was prepared for them, lodging was given to them, and they were surrounded by warmth.

And yet—and so—actually living here would be something else again. Here in this beshadowed country where it was cold and frozen, and the sea was rough, and there was battle, and the days were dark. How hard must one struggle to earn one's daily bread amid the falling snow and hard ground and cruel waves? The people were as rough as the landscape, blood was a daily sight, and battle was something to be joined at a moment's notice.

But still…

Still, she thought it was a good place. She thought these were wonderful people. She absolutely, sincerely believed it.

"Behold."

"Oh…!"

The *húsfreya* pointed outside the window of the bath at the night sky beyond. Rainbow lights glittered in the sky like a canopy.

CHAPTER 4

GAME OF THRONES

"I wish to present a gift to the honored *goði*!"

Every eye in the room fixed on Priestess, who was clasping her hands and speaking forcefully. It was the morning after the feast, and the party had been invited to the *skáli* for breakfast.

The *húsfreya* blinked, unsure what Priestess had in mind; as for the chieftain himself, he stopped eating and looked at her, trying to divine what she might be doing. Even her party members gave her perplexed looks.

"Sorry... I hear what you're saying, but maybe you could say it just a little softer..."

High Elf Archer may have been a high elf, but she was still subject to the toxic effects of alcohol—perhaps this was precisely because she'd said that the pain of the hangover was part of the fun of drinking. No doubt the Wine God favored her for refusing to recant what she herself had said.

"I wish to present a gift to the honored *goði*."

"I see," High Elf Archer mumbled and nodded. She frowned, groaned, and took a sip of some plain boiled water. She also seemed to be surprisingly fond of the thin, hard-cooked flatbread with which she was currently stuffing her cheeks. "First I've heard about it, I think..."

"Yes. Because this is the first I've said of it."

High Elf Archer shot a suspicious glance in the direction of Goblin Slayer's metal helmet. He inclined his head as if to say, *What?* The archer looked up at the ceiling, where the morning sun was seeping through the thin leather of the skylight.

"I understand that a warm welcome is expected by the culture here," Priestess said, smoothly and naturally. "But surely it can't be right to let such a fine reception go unrequited."

It was impossible, she felt, that all of this could have been purely out of the goodness of their hosts' hearts. She was learning that, admirable as pure altruism may have been, it was much easier to accept that everything had a reason.

And if I explain it this way, I'm sure they'll be more likely to accept this from me...!

She didn't yet seem to conceive that this very understanding was a sign of her own growth.

"Fine by me," Goblin Slayer said with a nod, and Priestess let out a breath of relief. "We do at least owe them for the food and lodgings."

"The Trade God smiles upon official negotiations. His blessing must warm a land as cold and hard as this one," mentioned Dwarf Shaman. He took a sip of what would've been the hair of the dog for anyone else; for him, it was just another cup of mead. He looked quite pleased with himself. "You've had contacts with my people as well, as I think the honored *goði* well knows."

"Ha-ha-ha. Needless to say, I didn't give you lodging expecting anything in return," the chieftain replied, laughing.

Visitors were to be welcomed no matter who they were—that was hardly unusual. It demonstrated the generosity of the master of the house, or the chieftain, or whomever. Many were the old stories of poor travelers who turned out to be the messengers of the gods, with those who rejected them meeting disaster and those who welcomed them being blessed with good fortune... Perhaps the very commonness of such tales pointed to their nature as didactic parables. *Those who couldn't be bothered to spare anything for those who begged for just a single night's lodging would eventually come to a bad end*, they seemed to say. The rejection of the messenger sometimes came first and sometimes later. Consequences had a funny way of preceding their cause at times.

It was said that some villages even taught: *If someone is surrounded by enemies, protect them, whomever they may be.* To suggest that this was merely in hopes of a monetary reward would flirt with spitting on another culture.

"I know, sir. And that's why I wish to offer this not as payment but as a gift." Priestess—whether she was aware of all this background or not—smiled.

"And what gift might this be that you offer?" inquired Lizard Priest.

A "good priest" must not only be devout but also articulate enough to explain the teachings to people. Lizard Priest, a virtuous cleric indeed, rolled his eyes in his head.

"Well," Priestess said with a nod. "With the honored *goði*'s permission, I wish to petition the Earth Mother for a miracle of healing, for his sake."

"Hoh!"

"My!"

The *goði* and the *húsfreya* exclaimed almost in unison.

The chieftain seemed impressed that Priestess had noticed; it was clear from his tone that he didn't think for a second that the *húsfreya* had spoken to anyone of his wound. The *húsfreya*, meanwhile, sounded rather more unsure; her tone was difficult to place. Her one good eye—the one not hidden by a bandage—flitted restlessly back and forth between her husband and Priestess. She didn't speak up, though, but chose instead an uneasy silence, biting her lip.

"It's true that my right arm is injured and that miracles are precious in battle. It's more than I could wish for." The chieftain's eyes flicked toward his wife, and his expression relaxed into an easy smile. "And you wish to offer it not *to me* but *for my sake*, I see."

"Yes, sir. For the teachings of the Earth Mother say: 'Protect, Heal,

Save.'" Priestess nodded, making herself suppress the smile she'd had on her face until a moment ago.

Confronted with this, the chieftain let out a breath and shook his head resignedly. "Far be it from me to deny the request of one of my guests." Then he stretched out his right arm, which had remained hidden under his cape until now, on the armrest of his high seat. Bandages ran from his upper arm all the way down to his wrist, a bit of blood oozing out. It looked painful, but it was by no means a sign that his wound had gone untreated. To the contrary, the arm was carefully wrapped in fresh linen, tied tight and true.

It was important to make the wrappings tight enough to stanch the blood, but if they were too tight, it was possible for the rest of the limb to rot and fall off. Priestess had heard that in places where the sadistic god held sway, there were strange ways of treating wounds, such as opening them further. *But this first aid was obviously heartfelt*, she thought. And who might have provided this treatment? The idea alone warmed Priestess's heart.

She was shown right in her guess by what the chieftain said next.

"Wife... No, let me say, my dear one. Behold and observe this wound on my arm."

"My..." The húsfreya blinked her remaining eye.

The chieftain sighed dramatically. "You're so quick to pout, my dear one, when I ask anyone but you for help."

"Y-yes, I suppose sometimes...!" Her lovely cheeks, as pale as snow, took on the hue of roses, and her voice became that of a blushing maiden.

It was a little much for the others to stomach, all this sweetness between the *gyðja* and his *húsfreya* right at breakfast. It was quite touching and all, but the adventurers all averted their eyes—all, that is, except Priestess and Goblin Slayer. Not, of course, that they didn't understand what was going on.

The húsfreya quickly straightened up in her seat, while the chieftain cleared his throat. "If you wouldn't mind taking our guests to the captive," he said.

"Mn," squeaked the *húsfreya*, looking at the ground in embarrassment. It was probably a sound of agreement, for the chieftain nodded, satisfied. Then he looked Priestess in the eye and said, "I must receive this gift of your healing miracle, then, and you shall speak to the prisoner as well. Would that be all right?"

"Yes, of course!" Priestess's modest chest naturally puffed out as far as it would go, and she brimmed with confidence. And that was the end of it. The subject that had so suddenly interrupted breakfast was resolved harmoniously, and the eating resumed.

High Elf Archer, drinking hot water out of a cup (unlike the night before, an ordinary one), smiled. "You're getting used to this, aren't you?"

"You think so?" Priestess asked quietly. She meant it quite literally; the question came neither from embarrassment nor humility. "I can only hope…"

"Not like we have any right to talk. Am I wrong?" High Elf Archer asked the others, and she sounded genuinely amused. Maybe the warmth of the water was finally reaching her insides. Or perhaps it was the pleasure of an older friend watching her younger counterpart grow and mature.

"You're right," Goblin Slayer said, laconic as ever. Then he added, "It's not bad," as if he was offering his thoughts on the cooking.

"You don't think I overstepped myself?" Priestess asked.

"No," Goblin Slayer replied. "As I said earlier, I don't mind." He munched some of the thin grilled bread through the slats of his visor, then sipped some soup that appeared to have been made with fish stock. "You considered it and decided for yourself, and therefore, I doubt there should be any problem."

"…Right!" Priestess nodded, feeling as if these words from the man sitting beside her made everything just fine.

Whenever you attempt something, judging success or failure entirely on your own can be a challenging prospect. Without the acknowledgment of someone else—someone you trust—it's hard to convince yourself that you've done the right thing.

No sooner had she breathed a sigh of relief than Priestess felt that particular hunger one feels after just getting up in the morning. Like any young lady her age, she wanted to avoid her stomach growling, so she put a hand above her navel and gently pressed against her stomach. Suddenly everything—the flatbread, the fruit piled in its bowl, and the fish soup—all looked delicious. She was sure the tastes would all be surprising, including the seasonings, which must be quite different from anything they used on the frontier. Then she thought back on the dishes they'd been served at the feast the night before—and now it really seemed her stomach was about to growl.

"Well, before any miracles or what have you...," Dwarf Shaman began somberly. He'd been silent until this moment, but now he spoke like a sage who had seen an underlying truth of the Four-Cornered World. "We'd better have something to eat!"

Lizard Priest promptly gulped down an entire pitcher of goat's milk, crying, "Sweet nectar!" and slapping his tail against the ground.

§

"O Earth Mother, abounding in mercy, lay your revered hand upon this child's wounds."

"Hoh! The pain subsides...!"

A soft light glowed where Priestess had placed her palm, and the Earth Mother's healing fingers brushed the prisoner's wounds.

The prisoner in question was the man with the bandaged face who'd had the staring contest with Lizard Priest at the banquet. He, too, had been granted a room and invited to the feast as if he was not a prisoner but a guest. The way he lounged at the house to which the *húsfreya* guided them was enough to bring a smile to one's face. Priestess didn't think too hard about it, accounting it as simply another cultural difference.

Still, the man said, "This is quite astonishing. You've done well to lead me away once more from the Fields of Joy." Priestess was very happy to see the man smile, giving no hint that he was anywhere close to death.

"The Valkyrie says you still have many brilliant deeds to do," she told him.

"Ha! I shall have to keep going, then!"

It was true that the people of this land charged toward the abyss of death of their own accord.

But to decide how you want to die has something to do with deciding how you want to live… I'm pretty sure.

To spend one's life deliberately in a chosen purpose was not something to which a disciple of the Earth Mother could object. Protect, Heal, Save: So long as these pillars remained unshaken, there was no change in what she had to do.

Finally, relieved, the *húsfreya* stepped forward. "And what is it that brings you here so suddenly?"

"Are you sure about this?" Priestess asked, to which the *húsfreya* replied, "'Tis the role of a *gyðja* of the sadistic god."

A shrine maiden of the sadistic god, she'd said, was at once a healer of wounds and a torturer of prisoners. Priestess saw that the teaching of the sadistic goddess was to exult in the pain of injury at the same time as love of life. At least, she grasped this intellectually…

But is it really okay for us to be present at this interrogation…? she wondered with a sidelong glance at the *húsfreya*, who was prepared with an instrument that looked like either a particularly cruel scalpel or a torture device. In that she felt little or nothing, perhaps her emotions had been dampened as well.

"Ah, milady *húsfreya*. I've no intention of playing the defiant prisoner. Let me speak." And thus the prisoner with the wounded face began to talk.

He and his people hadn't meant to come to take brides so suddenly, he said. Pillaging another village in the name of finding brides was not necessarily frowned upon. However, that didn't mean one could neglect a proper *festalmal*, or engagement ceremony. The two would swear vows to each other and share ale, and the groom would remove the veil his bride had worn for a year to repel evil spirits. Failure to respect this *bruðsvelja*, the wedding ceremony, was unthinkable.

"True, there has been much battle, but…"

"But nothing can take precedence over the holding of a feast, is that not so?" Lizard Priest, who obviously felt he very much understood what the man was saying, nodded eagerly.

High Elf Archer looked at him dubiously. "Excuse me…?"

"Did milady ranger not prefer a lavish wedding ceremony?"

"Well, yeah, but…"

"And would you not prefer a man strong enough to prepare such a ceremony—or at least to come and carry you away?"

"Ah, that's it—that's it exactly!" the prisoner exclaimed.

"Indeed, indeed," Lizard Priest said, nodding amiably.

High Elf Archer looked to Dwarf Shaman for help, then Priestess, but what could they say?

"Ha-ha…," Priestess offered.

"It's important to keep an open mind, Long Ears," Dwarf Shaman said bluntly. Maybe, in light of the exchange at the banquet, they felt they couldn't say anything careless.

Most importantly of all, banter between High Elf Archer and Lizard Priest was, of course, not in the least the point of this convocation. The *húsfreya* spoke up loud and clear, sending a chill through the air. "Yes. However… You attacked our *ætt*, our clan, yet there hasn't been a *þing*"—a legal assembly. In this case, she seemed to be speaking not as the shrine maiden of the sadistic god but as the wife of the *goði*.

It was true that in receiving the *goði* as their leader, they had chosen to come under the kingdom's umbrella. But that didn't mean that all the northerners had chosen to obey the kingdom. Then, too, neither did it mean that they were necessarily hostile. The northerners were sworn to guard against the barbarians from even farther—which is to say, the encroaching forces of Chaos. Amid the ceaseless battle and the never-ending flow of blood, somehow they managed to maintain peace.

At least, so far...

But if there was to be unrest in the north for any reason, that would mean trouble. It would invite catastrophe. The storm would become a whirlwind of Chaos that could swallow up not just the kingdom but the entire Four-Cornered World.

Goblin Slayer, who had been sitting in one corner of the bench and listening quietly, now asked a single, cutting question: "Goblins?"

The prisoner went quiet. After a moment, narrowing his eyes suspiciously, he nodded slowly. "Sooth."

All Goblin Slayer said was, "I knew it."

"Wha—?" Priestess asked, blinking in surprise. "You mean, you thought it was goblins all this time?" Was everything he had done until now, including the things that had surprised and confused her, aimed at that end?

"I heard some talk of it at the banquet," he explained brusquely.

Priestess, meanwhile, had been so engaged by the atmosphere at the feast that it hadn't even occurred to her to listen to what people were actually saying.

Guess it's important to stick around at times like that...

She would have to be more attentive to things she perceived as difficult to handle. Though of course, slipping away to chat with the *húsfreya* was a special memory for her, as well.

"Besides, I expected as much," Goblin Slayer continued, interrupting Priestess's thoughts. "Because of the ones we encountered under the mountain. They weren't built like the ones from the south. But their numbers were too great and their equipment too varied to have moved from somewhere else." (Although, he added, their equipment, skill, and numbers were not *that* great.) "Thus, I decided it was best to assume that they were survivors of a battle to the north."

"Quite the shrewd observer, you are," Dwarf Shaman commented.

"Naturally," Goblin Slayer responded. "For I knew the warriors of this land would never be defeated by goblins."

"Truly, I must agree," said the prisoner. "The Vikings, the People of the Bay, would not be bested by the likes of orcs."

Even if, at times, one might be ambushed, wounded, and then finished off. That wasn't the same as being defeated, though. Their spirits would never be broken. The harsh north wind had forged these Vikings into a courageous people. Both these men here seemed to harbor an innocent faith in this conviction.

Ahhh, I see...

If it hadn't been for her epiphany the night before, Priestess would certainly have been confused at this moment, as well. It was just like her own infatuation with *him*. Her faith that he would never make a mistake.

For him...

For him, this barbarian hero from the north, the one Priestess had never known, was the same thing. He was sure that the warriors who hailed from the same land as that great fighter would never give in until the instant of death. It seemed almost an article of faith for this person called Goblin Slayer.

"The pigheaded little beasts were riding on ships, they were." The prisoner with the wounded face, seeing that he was speaking to someone who understood him deeply, became increasingly voluble, gesturing as he spoke. The goblins had come sailing on ships to attack. And so proud of themselves, too, he sneered.

But it was nothing special. He sounded as impressed as someone from the frontier when some lost goblins happened to stumble upon a village and attack it.

Once? That was one thing. But two times, three times? Again and again, unwilling to be intimidated or to learn no matter how many times they were destroyed?

"That has to mean there's a nest or something, right?" High Elf Archer, listening with her arms crossed, asked with a wave of her pale hand. "You just have to find it and smash it."

"I'm afraid 'tis not that easy."

Naturally, this northerner, the survivor of a hundred battles, ready to charge into any fight, would have realized that much. And if there was a reason that, having realized it, he couldn't do anything about it, it could be only one thing.

"The ships haven't come back, have they?"

"Even so." The prisoner nodded. "Not a single *helskip* war vessel we've sent out for trade has returned home."

Needless to say, not one person thought this was the doing of goblins. Why should they? No northerner was afraid of any goblin. They were, however, afraid of draugs. And they feared the fell spirits of the sea.

Then of course there was the chill of the frozen earth, its cruelty, which visited itself upon all equally, struggle as they might. All things in the Four-Cornered World were equal. All received blessings, and all suffered. If one could not deal with these things, then destruction was the only fate that awaited them.

Hence why the northerners first rushed to their relatives in hopes of scaring up some material goods, a stopgap solution only. At least with the connection to the kingdom to the south, they wouldn't starve in any event.

But not to actually ask for help... I don't know about that...

"Well, this is, in practice, another country now," Lizard Priest responded to Priestess's brow-furrowed question from his place curled up on the bench closest to the hearth fire. "Bride-taking may be simple trade, but asking for provisions or reinforcements—that's politics."

Matters would get bigger, everyone's problems would come to the fore, and things could end up more chaotic than how they started.

"I see," Priestess said. "I think." She cocked her head, not sounding wholly convinced. She put a finger to her lips and thought ("Hmm..."), but still it didn't quite seem to come to her.

"Gotta be a matter of face," Dwarf Shaman drawled; he was making a show of gulping down some mead where he sat on the bench. Alcohol proved quite fortifying against the cold, and he was having a drink with breakfast—or just perhaps continuing his drink from last night. And there was nothing and no one in the Four-Cornered World whose mind worked faster than that of a dwarf enjoying alcoholic spirits. "Imagine any kind of warrior begging for help: *Some goblins beat me! I've got no money! Help me!* He'd be a laughingstock."

"Oh…"

That much, Priestess could certainly understand. She, of course, knew little of a warrior's pride. And yet—and yet, even the most pitiful excuse for an adventurer could never imagine behaving in such a way. If someone could be sent running by some goblins, left to beg others for a bit of help, why had they even become an adventurer at all? Adventurers were a rowdy, uncivilized lot. They made their way in the world by their own strength.

That first adventure, that first party, those first friends. They were painful memories for Priestess; each time she thought of them, she felt a throbbing ache, like a thorn stuck deep in her heart. And yet, it was precisely because of those memories, precisely because all of them had fought to the bitter end, that…

"You're right… That would never happen."

To beg for help because of your own humiliating incompetence? No one wanted that.

"This is…most troubling…" The *húsfreya* looked grim.

Fighting the forces of Chaos that pressed down from the north, fighting their own "northern barbarians," could almost be called the northerners' duty. And now this was the northern edge of the kingdom. They couldn't run away. They had to make their stand—show their valor.

The goblins, they would manage somehow. But—a sea devil. *Something* that refused to let any ship return home safely. Whatever it was, it lurked somewhere beyond the sea of ice.

"……" Priestess took a deep breath, filling her lungs with air, then let it out again.

She and her friends were adventurers. Adventure was what they had come here for. It was why they were here. If everyone from *that* time had been here now, she knew what she would have said. And the people who *were* here now—she was sure they would understand.

"It's all right…isn't it?" she asked hesitantly.

"Sure, why wouldn't it be?" High Elf Archer replied. Her laughter was as beautiful as a ringing bell, and she winked with genuine elegance. "You can count me in. I think it sounds like fun. Even if I'm not thrilled to know there are goblins involved."

"As for myself, to add the sea to the terrible chill… My goodness…" Lizard Priest, still curled up, stretched out his neck as if the trouble was obvious and rolled his eyes in his head. Priestess had known him a long time now, though; she would have known if he had really thought it was too much bother. Instead, he said, "However, all the more reason why I must show my prowess in battle."

"Because nagas don't run away, eh?" Dwarf Shaman chuckled, wiping some drops of wine from his beard.

"Indeed!" The long head nodded.

"If the girls and even Scaly here are going, then my dwarf self can hardly beg off, can I?"

"Sure can't!" High Elf Archer laughed. "A wine barrel should float even on the sea!"

"And an anvil'll sink…"

"Bah, you're heavier than I am!"

And then the two of them were off and arguing, just like always. The *húsfreya* and the prisoner looked downright flummoxed, but Priestess laughed, a girlish giggle of relief and happiness and gratitude that bubbled up naturally from within her.

Then she asked the last of them, "It's all right, isn't it?"

She was speaking to the one in the grimy leather armor and cheap-looking metal helmet, and he replied nonchalantly, "I don't mind." His usual clear, decisive tone. "It's your adventure—you conceived of it, and you decided on it."

That gave her a greater push than anything; on the strength of those words, Priestess got to her feet. She turned to the *húsfreya* and said, proudly and clearly, "Leave it to the adventurers!"

§

"Listen, I appreciate the offer, but…"

They were back at the *skáli*. Unlike that morning, however, the *goði* was now surrounded by a crowd of other northerners. One could easily imagine that they were convening a council of war based on the information the *húsfreya* had gotten from the prisoner. And why were the adventurers, outsiders, present?

"They're going to help?"

"Adventurers—are they not thieves, rogues? They may go into battle, but they would be among the first to die."

"Across the great mountains they may have come, but rogues they remain."

The northerners' faces told the tale as they stood with their arms crossed.

In short, this is a problem of trust, Priestess thought. She kept an ambiguous smile on her face—a trick she'd learned from Guild Girl—even as she gave a little sigh inside. There was a time when she might have been panicked by this reaction, but now she was at least able to hide the shock, more or less.

Adventurers were an uncouth bunch. She'd heard that only their kingdom had an Adventurers Guild. (Or did other countries have them, too?) Which meant that the status tag hanging from her neck, the one she valued almost as much as her life, meant little in terms of "trust" to a great many people in the world.

And this was one of the places where it carried no weight. They'd been lucky this hadn't been much of a problem in the eastern desert country when they had visited…

As Priestess was thinking it all over, Goblin Slayer broke in. "Where is the problem? Is it that you don't trust us? Or that you have no confidence in our fighting prowess? Which is it?"

"You certainly get right to the point," the chieftain said with a wry smile.

"If it's a problem that can be readily solved, then we should solve it as soon as possible," was all Goblin Slayer said. "So?"

"I don't believe an *álfr* would indeed be a thief." This response came not from the chieftain but from one of the other northerners. Several others nodded, chiming in, "Just so," or, "Indeed." It seemed as if they all had a voice here. It might be the *goði* who sat on the high seat, but it appeared everyone was equal in the council.

What struck Priestess more than that, though, was the great trust they seemed to have in High Elf Archer. As a Porcelain, Priestess had often been looked down on as an adventurer, but she had at least been respected as a cleric of the Earth Mother. Here, though, hardly anyone paid her any mind—but High Elf Archer they revered simply for being a high elf.

And here Priestess was pretty sure that her much older friend was only acting all aloof because of her hangover!

I guess trust involves a lot of different things... The time, the situation, and the people—virtually anything could change everything. It was, honestly, a very reassuring revelation for Priestess.

"You all may have come across the mist-laden mountains," one of the northerners said.

"But us, we ain't seen you do it," said another.

"So if you were to see us, then?" Goblin Slayer said.

"Mm," replied yet another northerner with a nod. "Show us what you're made of."

"Hoh, a test of courage." *Wumph.* Lizard Priest leaned forward like a dragon waking from sleep. The northerners didn't fear him, so it must have been either from sympathy or consideration that he kept his huge body curled into one relatively small space near the hearth. But now, his blood was warmed by the fire, and the anticipation of battle pulsed in his blood... "If possible, I would like to perform mine at the hour when the sun is highest in the sky, ideally while sitting beside the fire."

...or not.

Everything about him curled up again—from his long neck to his tail—and it seemed Lizard Priest had every intention of nesting down right there.

Thinking about it, if they were going to head even farther north, they would naturally spend most of the adventure tromping through the snow. And rare was the moment on a cold adventure when one had the luxury of curling up by a warm fire. Refusing to miss even a moment of such warmth—was that not, in fact, rather naga-esque?

"We'll let you know when we really need you, all right?" Priestess called to him, and having received a shake of his tail in response, she turned back to the room. She put a finger to her lips in thought. "How should we handle this, then? We can't have a fight, so maybe a contest of strength... But in that case..."

"Say, isn't it true that around here you lot prefer to...yeh know...?" Dwarf Shaman, having finished his mead, was now enjoying a *bjórr*. He sat cross-legged on the bench, looking entirely at ease (although for reasons quite different from those of Lizard Priest). Priestess, who deep down inside still felt a tad nervous, was honestly jealous.

Nonetheless, she asked, "What's *'yeh know'*?"

"Dunno what they call it around these parts. The name changes everywhere you go. But it's, yeh know, this." He mimicked grasping something with his thick fingers and tapping it against the table.

"Yes, indeed, we have it." The chieftain grinned, baring his fangs, leaning his chin on his right hand as if to flaunt how the *húsfreya* had healed him. "All four corners of this world are the gods' game board. Shouldn't adventurers, then, test their skill upon the game board themselves? Dear wife?"

"Very good, I should think. Riddles might do as well, but before a battle, a *hnefatafl* is good luck." The *húsfreya*'s snow-white countenance set firmly, and she nodded. The gaze of her unbandaged eye ran across the adventurers like lightning. "As *gyðja*, we will accept a match from any challenger, whosoever they be."

Before Priestess could speak, Goblin Slayer said sharply, "Very well." He met the woman's gaze squarely from behind his visor, as if to say there was no problem. "We need proof of our strength on the board, then."

"Sooth."

"In that case..." Goblin Slayer's arm moved. His hand, wrapped in a rough, well-used glove, landed on Priestess's delicate shoulder. She gulped a little when she felt him squeeze firmly. "This young woman will do."

"Huh?" Priestess sounded absolutely ridiculous.

She looked to the right: Goblin Slayer's helmet was gazing directly at the *húsfreya*. She looked to the left: High Elf Archer was playing innocent, Lizard Priest was nodding, and Dwarf Shaman was taking a drink. She looked forward: The *húsfreya*'s eye was ablaze as she stared at Priestess, as if she could see directly into her heart.

Priestess blinked. *"Huh?!"*

§

"In short, 'tis a game of war."

On the table that had been placed by the high seat, spanning the hearth, the Four-Cornered World was spread out. In other words, it was a square, with spaces carved in it, decorated with engraved characters: a stunning wooden board. Two armies stood upon it in battle array, differentiated by their colors: white and red. At first, Priestess thought they were made of the teeth of a sea monster or some such thing—but no, this was tin, a so-called "white metal."

The armor of the king and his soldiers was sculpted in fine detail, their clothing represented with delicate brushwork. Each piece was a riot of color, with swords and helmets, and even the sparkling of the gems that adorned them, carefully painted in. The banner bearing the letter *omega*, fluttering in an undetectable wind, made the pieces look as if they might come to life and start marching around this very moment. They looked like nothing so much as actual soldiers who had been shrunk down to the size of a finger.

It wouldn't have surprised Priestess a bit to learn that this board and these pieces had some sort of magic spell or blessing on them. One thing, however, *did* surprise her.

"The, uh, red pieces are surrounding the white ones—is that right?"

The two armies didn't stand confronting each other across the field;

rather, the white army was hedged in by the red one on every side. Priestess, studying the board with a serious expression, put one thin finger to her lips and glanced down.

The northerners—big, burly warriors—crowded around, seemingly less with real interest than with the attraction of a spectacle. Fear, horror, an inability to think straight—any of these would have been perfectly natural reactions for a young woman in this situation.

"I've never seen this game before. *Hnefatafl*, you called it...?"

Priestess, however, looked up without a trace of fear, meeting the gaze of the player sitting across from her.

"Yes, precisely," replied the *húsfreya*, smiling as if, for some reason, Priestess's attitude made her happier than anything. "If the white player is able to move their *konungr*, their king, from the 'throne' at the center of the board to any of the corners, he escapes, and the white player wins."

"So that means that if the surrounding red army is able to capture the king, they win, right?"

There really is something almost ritualistic about it. She wasn't sure whether it was the movement of the *húsfreya*'s fingers over the board, the tone of her voice, or the craftsman's art displayed in the board and pieces.

From the four "corners," out beyond the board. Priestess didn't know what that could signify.

"...And how do the pieces move?"

"Straight forward or back, or from side to side, as far as they wish until they strike another piece." With her fingers, beautiful despite, or perhaps because of, the battle wounds they bore, the *húsfreya* slid one of the red pieces smoothly along and back again.

Okay, got it. Priestess nodded a couple of times. No diagonal movement. Which meant...

Priestess stared intently at the battlefield of eleven by eleven rows, 121 squares. She'd played a tabletop game once, sometime before—a game that had involved trekking across the Four-Cornered World to

©Noboru Kannatuki

slay a dragon. This world with its square spaces was just one battlefield in one corner of that one.

At the same time, the abstracted nature of it made this version of the Four-Cornered World, boiled down to a few dozen squares, seem vast.

Yes. It seems tremendous…at the same time as it seems very small.

That was how the battlefield looked to Priestess. There were too many pieces, both allied and enemy, to run around willy-nilly. And because the king was in the center, he would need two moves at the absolute least to reach any of the corners. And that was only if the path was already free of impeding enemy soldiers…

"It looks like I'll have to take out some pieces. Can pieces be captured if they land on the same square?"

"No. Rather, by sandwiching them between two other pieces." The *húsfreya* flicked her fingers, controlling the white and red armies almost as if by magic. A piece caught between two pieces, or else between another piece and the throne, or else between another piece and a corner, would be taken. The only exception was the king: So long as he was in the vicinity of the throne, he could be captured only by being surrounded on all four sides.

A game of sheep and wolves, then, Priestess thought, remembering something they used to play for fun back at the temple of the Earth Mother. There had been so many young children there—herself included—and nobody could live by faith alone. The older nun with the beautiful brown skin had taught Priestess how to play, and when she had gotten some experience, she'd instructed the even-younger girls.

As a child, Priestess had been especially happy when she was able to beat her erstwhile teacher, but as she grew and took on new roles, she saw that the sister had been holding back with her.

She was so good at that game.

Priestess couldn't help a smile of nostalgia, even if she knew this wasn't really the time. She felt less like she was playing a war game and more like she was engaging in that familiar childhood pastime.

"So what if I pass between two of your pieces in one of my moves?"

"That's all right; your piece is safe."

"I see…" Maybe it was the way Priestess nodded at each rule, confirming all the details: The chieftain, watching them from his high seat, spoke as if offering her a lifeline.

"If you need to make some notes, that would be all right."

"?" Priestess gave him a look of curiosity. "No, thank you, I'm fine."

"Sure?"

Yes, she was. She nodded. On all her adventures thus far, she had never written any notes. "I just want to make sure I understand the rules. Might I ask for a practice game before we have our proper match?"

"What do you think, dear wife?"

"I think it's quite all right," the *húsfreya* said with a placid smile and a nod. "Neither at play nor in earnest is a young maiden my enemy."

"I hope that doesn't mean you'll take it easy on me," Priestess said. She faced the game board squarely, ready to go. She would be in command of the white army. "Because even your play, you should treat earnestly…!"

And then the battle began.

§

"Hey, are you sure about this, Orcbolg?"

"Sure about what?"

This conversation, of course, was taking place among the adventurers, who looked on with bated breath. Arrayed around Priestess as she studied the board, they had their eyes fixed on the battle unfolding on the tabletop. The embattled white army was doing its best to fight its way past its red opponents, but…

"I've got to be honest; I don't think she can win," High Elf Archer said, dropping her voice even lower and whispering to the metal helmet. Perhaps it wasn't very politic to rain on her much-younger friend's parade as she stared intently at the board. But at the same time, to fail to analyze one's fighting strength while on an adventure could hardly be called a good thing, either.

But Goblin Slayer, for his part, only tilted his head in puzzlement. "Is that so?"

This guy…

He was always so serious, but at that moment she couldn't stand it. She huffed quietly.

"I was so sure, Beard-cutter," Dwarf Shaman said, his wine in one hand and intense interest on his face. "I was so sure you were going to take her on yourself." This strange adventurer was, after all, the party's leader. It would naturally be he who answered any challenge for a demonstration of skill.

"No, that would be me, then," High Elf Archer said, puffing out her modest chest proudly and flicking her long ears. "For elves have hardly ever lost a battle."

"That's because when yeh live long enough, you're bound to win eventually."

"Say that again!" High Elf Archer managed to yell in a whisper, a neat trick, but she didn't harangue Dwarf Shaman any further. After all, her precious friend was in the midst of an intense confrontation. That was more important than sniping at a sarcastic dwarf.

Goblin Slayer, also appearing deadly serious, said quietly, "I'm not very good at board games." High Elf Archer and Dwarf Shaman looked at him as if they couldn't believe what they were hearing. "We did some tabletop practice before the dungeon exploration contest, and it didn't go well."

He added in a whisper that the dice just never seemed to go in his favor.

Now the elf and dwarf looked at each other, and Lizard Priest laughed aloud. "Hence why you always have sought my opinion?"

"Instead of relying on my own ideas, it's quicker to ask a specialist." Goblin Slayer nodded firmly. He understood every situation perfectly, his judgment was always right, and he always led them directly to victory…

...was exactly the kind of idiotic thinking Goblin Slayer never wanted to fall into. He felt that if he possessed that kind of genius, he would not be hunting goblins.

The snake's eye was always waiting. It could mean failure or much ignorance. The amount that other people knew was always greater than the amount that he knew. And that being the case, there was only one question that bothered him.

"Has it been a nuisance?"

"Perish the thought." Lizard Priest lifted his head from beside the hearth (perhaps he was finally warm enough) and looked at the board. He was just in time to see another white soldier be pincered by the red army and captured. Yet Priestess, thoughtful but not worried, made her next move, and her next, moving her pieces along. If those soldiers had been living people, they might or might not have trusted their commander, but they would have moved without hesitation.

"It is the leader's role to be decisive and swift. It's not as though you simply accept what I say wholesale." Lizard Priest's eyes rolled in his head, and he looked at Goblin Slayer. "Milord Goblin Slayer, you are a fine leader."

"...I see." Goblin Slayer grunted softly; then from within his helmet, he could be heard to repeat under his voice, "I see..." He said, "That's good, then," and fell silent.

For a time, the *stofa* was dominated by the sound of the two young women shuffling pieces around. The onlookers continued to hold quiet conversations, exchanging their opinions of the game in whispered tones. High Elf Archer's ears must have been able to pick up every word without so much as trying. She, if anyone, ought to have known which way the room was leaning, but she looked troubled.

"Maybe we shouldn't have let the girl do it, then? Maybe we should have had this guy handle it." With the words *"this guy,"* she nudged Lizard Priest gently in the neck with her elbow and sniffed.

"Did you not know?" For the first time, Goblin Slayer looked away from the board, turning toward High Elf Archer. His gaze behind his visor was that of someone seeing something they could hardly believe. "She is a far more capable adventurer than I am."

§

"Hmm... Hmmmm..."

Priestess looked at the board, now well into the mid-game, and made a perplexed face, just as the gods in heaven sometimes did.

This doesn't look good for me...

She'd sought to break through the center of the enemy formation, but that now appeared to have been a mistake. Although the red pieces were divided into four groups, there were twenty-four of them, as opposed to just twelve white pieces. If she tried to meet force with force, her king would be struck down and never get away.

And thus she found herself—disappointingly but inevitably—in the current situation.

The red army, after all, was not a bunch of goblins. They were grizzled old hands who were just as capable as the white soldiers. The number of battles they had survived since this board and its pieces were born into the world far outstripped the number Priestess had been through.

The king was safe so long as he was in the vicinity of the throne—but only the king. Other soldiers could be trapped and crushed against the throne. The corners were the same. Which meant...

"This is a siege game, isn't it?"

She'd been distracted by the word *"throne,"* but the way to envision this was as a castle, a stronghold. And the area around the throne was the ramparts. That explained why the other soldiers could be cornered and destroyed against it.

As the one entrusted with these soldiers' lives, Priestess didn't intend to give up until the bitter end, but even so, she was starting to see her limits.

"You're quite right. Speed is your friend," the *húsfreya* said, presumably pleased to see Priestess fighting so hard. Where Priestess frowned, the *húsfreya* smiled as she moved her soldiers around the board. "And that makes checkmate."

"Oh…!"

She'd been careless—well, no, not really. It was simply the consequence of being cornered bit by bit. To escape, to reach one of the corners, the king had to press himself against one of the far edges. Deny himself one direction of movement. That was where the enemy could lay a trap. And Priestess had walked right into it.

"Haaah…" She sighed deeply and stretched herself out on the table. Careful not to touch the board, of course. "It's tough, this game…"

"You find it boring?"

"No!" Priestess said, looking up with conviction. "No, not at all!"

Indeed, it was hard. The rules were simple, but the game was deep. Or…perhaps all games throughout the world were like this. Simply played but rich and profound. There were no guaranteed ways to win. Would it even be interesting, if you could win a game so easily?

"What would you like to do? Would you prefer to take red for the next round?"

"Let's see…" Priestess put a finger to her lips, barely noticing the grinning *húsfreya*. A small sound escaped her as she thought, and then she shook her head with fresh certainty. "Thank you. But no. May I try playing as white again?"

"You're quite certain?"

"Yes, ma'am!" Priestess smiled so brightly, one would never have believed she had just lost a game. "I have a little experience with siege battles myself, you know!"

§

Having said that…

There was no way Priestess could win. The shrine maiden of sadism, who administered *hnefatafl* as if it were a holy rite, and the devout follower of the Earth Mother simply specialized in different fields.

What's more, a beginner who had just learned the ropes would simply never outplay an experienced commander. That would have been blasphemy against every game.

The king of Priestess's white army was once again taken without managing to escape. However, she exclaimed in admiration at each new play, by turns agonized and overjoyed by the swinging struggle of attack and defense taking place on the board.

"I see...

"Wait, you can make a move like that?!

"Amazing...!

"One more game, please!"

Her face was bright with each exclamation.

Of course, in a real contest, there are no do-overs. That's to be expected.

"I was treating that as the real game, but how can I refuse?"

If her opponent, the *húsfreya*, was willing to accept it (even if with a wry smile), then there was no problem at all.

Over and over, the two young women moved their pieces about the board, the tapping and clicking echoing throughout the room. Priestess's play was not very impressive, but ever so gradually, she showed improvement—or at least began to get used to it. In the end, though, she couldn't possibly hope to prevail over her foe, the *húsfreya*.

The northerners began to whisper among themselves until finally...

"You can't press there. Keep a soldier over there." A voice, sharp yet solemn, spoke. It was the prisoner, scars still fresh on his face.

"Huh? ...Oh!" Priestess blinked, then returned her piece to where it had been and gazed at the board. She counted the squares with her fingers, considered the position of her forces versus those of her opponent, and then exclaimed, "Oh! Yes, of course...! Thank you very much!"

"'Twere nothing."

Priestess moved her piece to a new location (*tap, tap*) and made a huff of triumph. It must have been a pretty decent move, because for the first time, the *húsfreya* said, "Well, now...," and began looking troubled.

Naturally, though, the other onlookers weren't about to keep their peace at this. "Hey, now, no advice!"

"That's right. The audience should be seen and not heard! It's not fair!"

"What's not fair? I just helped a young lady in trouble," the prisoner said, crossing his arms as if this was the most obvious thing in the world. He fixed a mocking smile on his face. "And you call yourselves Vikings—you're a sorry lot!"

"Ooh, now you've done it!"

It was, perhaps, a testament to their self-control that these hot-blooded people had stayed quiet for so long. They pressed close around the players and all began shouting at once.

"Go right!"

"No, up!"

"Yes, there."

"No, not there!"

"Pick up that piece!"

"No, it's too soon!"

"Move your king!"

"No, wait!"

"This is ridiculous! Is that move even legal?!"

"I'll show you what's legal!"

"Hey, somebody bring a *hnefatafl* board!"

"Ahhh, it begins!"

Boards were veritably slammed down on benches, and a slew of contests began. And then the people watching *those* games started shouting, and drinking, and singing. Well, if it wasn't noisy now! The silent observation of the battle from a moment ago seemed as if it had never existed.

"Well, now..." The *húsfreya* smiled again awkwardly. There certainly wasn't going to be any more council going on in the *stofa*.

"Hrr... Hrrrr... Hrrrgh...!" High Elf Archer's ears were trembling. "Hey, I wanna try this *hnef...hnefatafl*, too! Teach me!"

"Hoh...! We cannot turn down the request of an *álfr*...!" The northerners prepared a board reverently, and one of them sat down across from her. Dwarf Shaman couldn't help but smirk at the affectations High Elf Archer's young opponent tried to show before the woman with whom he was infatuated.

The dwarf sipped a thin *bjórr* (it had taken some doing to decide which beverage to enjoy after his mead) and nudged his friend next to him. "Say, Scaly. Sun'll be high soon." Indeed, it was already high in the sky, sunlight pouring into the *stofa* through the skylight.

"Hrrrm... Which, I suppose, means I must do what I must do." Lizard Priest heaved himself up and requested a game from the nearest available northerner. "And, of course, some goat's milk," he added. (He would never forget that.)

He and his opponent were soon surrounded by a rotating cast of northern observers. The meeting, which had begun as a grave and serious council of war, appeared to have gone offtrack. How many of the northerners even remembered that this was supposedly going to be a "test" of the strange visitors from the south?

Goblin Slayer and the chieftain, watching the entire situation unfold, shared a brief exchange:

"I've won."

"So it would seem!"

The point hadn't really been to win at a game of *hnefatafl*. It had been to convince the northerners, the Vikings, to recognize the party's strength. It was second nature to Goblin Slayer to ensure that the victory conditions were always clear. And from that perspective...

"One—one more game! Just one more, please!"

"You're quite obsessed! There will be no end to it." Despite her tone, the *húsfreya* was smiling and lining her pieces back up. What else could make her act that way? Likewise, why else would the northerners start giving advice of their own accord, or open up to the party, even start having conversations with them?

"Because the girl is an adventurer," Goblin Slayer said. To him, the logic was clear as day.

"I don't exactly *feel* like I've lost..." The chieftain followed the metal helmet's gaze to where the two young women were alternately agonizing and rejoicing over their battle, and he let out a chuckle.

Yes, it would be blasphemy against games for a brand-new player to handily beat a far more experienced opponent. But for a brand-new player to *enjoy* the game as much as an experienced opponent—that was like a revelation from the gods.

That was what games should be. All those who prayed knew that this was what the gods who watched over the board of the Four-Cornered World wanted. For the scene before Goblin Slayer now was the very picture of how the gods enjoyed themselves.

"...But lose I have," the chieftain said.

"No." Goblin Slayer shook his head. "We won."

Yes, the victory conditions must always be clear.

She was an adventurer. Their rest was over. The enemies were goblins. It was the same as always. Nothing had changed.

Therefore, something else followed naturally:

"We're going to kill all the goblins."

"Are you...sure that's all right?" Female Merchant asked, but even she wasn't sure what she was asking or of whom. There were several people in the young king's throne room who might have been appropriate interlocutors.

The king himself, for example, or the silver-haired lady-in-waiting who stood like a shadow, or the cleric of the Earth Mother who was cheerfully reviewing some paperwork. Having cajoled her way into being sent as an observer from the temple to the frontier, she hardly seemed bothered by her brother's tough but fair advice. She had possessed a merry disposition born of ignorance and naïveté, but through cruel experience, it had begun to transform into an unmistakable strength. It was enough to make Female Merchant smile—and, admittedly, feel a little jealous.

"Seems there's a great many things that require our attention," muttered King as he wrote a report. "Where does it start, I wonder?"

"Perhaps from the moment we installed one of our country's knights as chieftain in the north?"

"Ha-ha-ha! Now, there's a mistake." King grinned and tossed aside the quill pen he had been using, grabbing a new one instead.

How many does that make this month? Female Merchant mused, counting in her head. She let out a tiny sigh. Quill pens might be an extravagant luxury, but they were also consumables. They had to be shaved and sharpened several times a day. Nonetheless, King couldn't simply use the cheapest available products. Both the ruler who used them and the merchant who had procured them for him would have been the object of much chatter and scorn.

But then if I find rich products for him, the twittering only continues...

Politics made everything more difficult. Female Merchant had become all too familiar with that fact of late.

"His father was northern nobility. He grew up here in our land, but he was born among, and his blood belongs to, the people of the north," King said. He was sharpening a new quill pen with his dagger, pleased at the chance to take a break from his paperwork. "They say he killed someone in a blood feud and had to flee."

"Blood *fyood?*" asked King's Sister, who was lounging on a bench. She pronounced the word awkwardly, unsure what it meant. "What's that?"

"The northern way. When a member of one clan dies, the matter is resolved through revenge battles and killings with the other clan." The silver-haired lady-in-waiting was staring out the window, hardly acting as if she was in the presence of the royal family.

"How barbaric," Female Merchant said before she could stop herself; her brow knitted, but she worked hard not to let anything more show on her face. She knew, at least from the reports, that there was more to the northerners than just battle.

But King simply laughed. "It *is* barbaric." He was taking undue care inspecting the tip of his quill, eager to delay his return to work as long as possible. "That's why the northerners settle most things with indemnities and avoid battle."

What if an agreement on the indemnity couldn't be reached? Female Merchant shook her head gently. Did she have to ask? Just think of the environment that had forged those fearsome northern dwellers.

"And—how do I put this?—it has something to do with expunging the family's guilt, but..."

Female Merchant was intrigued; the young king was hardly ever lost for words. "Your Majesty?" She cocked her head politely but received a dry laugh in return.

"He's my uncle."

"Your uncle, sire?" An unusual word here. "At that age? And…a northerner?"

"That vagabond? My father took his older sister as a concubine and welcomed the wanderer and his father as generals."

"Ah…"

It was a common enough story. Typical—although everyone would have their own opinion of it. A royal or noble absolutely needed a son; one could even say it was their duty, in a way, to take precautions if need be. A mistress, a concubine, a lover, or any number of other things. So long as they were of appropriate status, it might even be called a good thing.

A bizarre murder, for example, might turn out to have been an attempt to get rid of a hidden prince, the result of seed sown carelessly in a prostitute. Such hellish tales could be found if one went far enough back in the past.

Even the fact that I'm in this room…

Was that why the red-haired cardinal had exited in such a hurry, leaving only herself and the attendant? (King's Sister notwithstanding.) *Is that really what he was thinking?* She understood: It wasn't overbearingness on his part, nor was it simply to cause trouble. Although to agree to the implied invitation would be to invite catastrophe on herself later.

"I'm not sure about any of that…," King's Sister mumbled, kicking her legs as if to say none of it had anything to do with her—another runaway. The kicking would have been unladylike in a dress; in the vestments of a cleric, it was that much worse. Female Merchant looked uncertainly at the lady-in-waiting, who simply shook her head in an *oh fie* gesture.

Maybe it's okay. This wasn't the temple. It was the castle, King's office, her older brother's personal chamber, and there were only friends around. Female Merchant knew well that it was hard to find such places and such moments.

"My dad died when I was little anyway," King's Sister added.

"That was before the battle in the Dungeon of the Dead. Father… No. Let's drop the subject." King waved a hand as if trying to wave away the conversation, meeting his sister's surprised look with a grim one of his own. "In any case, about the time of the battle with the Demon Lord, it finally seemed that they might be able to repay the indemnity."

And when he had gone up north, he had been able to help a certain clan that was in dire straits… He met a princess, fell in love, got married, and became king. He and his queen seemed to be quite close.

It was like a saga, Female Merchant thought. Like one of the ancient ballads playing itself out upon the earth.

One might wish to be like them but certainly could not be. She herself was the same way. To realize one would never be like the heroes of those songs was painful—but that was what made them shine so bright and seem so beautiful.

Perhaps the reason they couldn't speak publicly about it here was precisely because these were the deeds of someone in a foreign land, a follower of a foreign religion.

"That was the battle when the Hero appeared, isn't it?"

And, above all, because of the radiant exploits of that young girl. It was only natural to favor the deeds of one's own heroes against those of other countries.

"I didn't know that familiars of Chaos had appeared in the north as well."

"Thanks to the Hero, we were able to clean them up right away. But there were always going to be vestiges, leftovers."

It was the glory of the northerners, one heard, to fight with their own "northern barbarians." The barbarians. An army of Chaos that had come from far away. But the battle was growing fierce, too fierce for them to carry on alone. And so…

"So they came to us."

"And we happened to have a knight who had married one of their princesses. Nice and simple."

"So," King said, "where is the problem?" Meanwhile, he finally gave up any pretense and simply tossed the quill pen down on the desk.

Female Merchant smiled slightly as she extended her pale fingers, taking the quill and dipping it in the nearby inkpot. "Only that it seems likely to inspire unrest."

"Some nice, ambiguous chatter will fix that." The young king sniffed with boredom, then rested his chin in his hands like a waiting lion.

Those who hated him would be expelled; those who loved him would be honored. Those who wished for unrest would be put out, while those who sought harmony would be his friends. If things were explained that way, then people could find whatever other justifications they wanted for each individual instance. The fact was that no matter what he said or did, there were always going to be people who saw it as unsatisfying or unfair. He didn't have the time to entertain every single one of them.

And yet, I can't actually fall into that mindset, either. Such is the duty of being king.

"The talk is of why you would have sent a survey now, of all times," offered the silver-haired lady-in-waiting, who sat by the window with her arms crossed. "And frontier adventurers, of all people." She didn't look very interested—but then, she never did; figuring out how she really felt was not easy. At the moment, her small, doll-like face was looking squarely at King; her eyes, like beads of glass, were narrowed in a squint.

Why did one have the sense that her gaze was equally directed at King's Sister?

"Anything personal in the choice?"

King denied it categorically. And again: not possible. But the repetition sounded less than convincing. "It's certainly a matter worthy of the attention of Silvers… But we also had the recommendation of the bishop of the water town."

"And the Temple of the Earth Mother made the same recommendation!" King's Sister said brightly. The young ruler glanced at her, then let out a sigh.

Female Merchant placed her pointer finger gently to her lips, then nodded. "I must admit, I have felt some concern, a sense that Chaos was brewing in the north…"

Such feelings were always born of a bevy of small details, notes, and information. For example, there had been quite a few sunken merchant vessels lately. That in itself wasn't strange—sea travel was dangerous, sea-based commerce was dangerous, and it would have been even more unusual if *nothing* ever sank. But even so, it seemed to be happening a little more than usual recently. They were beginning to see shortages in goods from the north.

The northerners were not simply warlike barbarians. They were also accomplished seamen and merchants. Suppose that the goods they conveyed, the trade they did via the northern sea, was ever so slightly disrupted. It would be like a drop of ink in a great river— nothing would immediately and obviously change.

And yet, nobles and merchants with something dark in their back-grounds were suddenly holding their breaths. She could see shadows on people's faces.

Was the world in danger? Was it time for the Hero to make her appearance? Hardly. But still, there was something sneaky that couldn't be overlooked. Something that slipped out of the corners of people's mouths or lurked in the margins of written papers with their rows of letters.

Detecting such things was, the lady-in-waiting had taught her, pre-cisely the basis of cloak-and-dagger operations.

I sense Chaos. That was what Female Merchant thought whenever something caused the brand on the back of her neck to prickle.

"I agree." King leaned forward, head still in his hands, looking completely in earnest, and smiled like a lion. "Which is precisely why we adventurers have to jump into action, isn't it?"

"Majesty…"

With King looking like he might leap up and throw on his armor at any moment, Female Merchant could only sigh.

What really bothered her was the realization that it didn't bother her.

CHAPTER 5

Vikings

The northerners moved with astonishing alacrity. If their enemies had been draugs or a sea monster, that would have been terrifying—but goblins inspired something less than fear. If the *goði* said this was their battle, though, then so it was.

> Loot may be lost, a family may fall,
> and my own life will wither in time,
> but great deeds
> wrought by mine own hand,
> precious are they,
> for they never fail nor fade.

Fires were lit, and the warriors shouted and cheered in time with the incantation of the shrine maiden—that is, the *húsfreya*. If they killed the foe in battle, if they overmastered life in pain, then the Fields of Joy awaited them. For the Vikings, battle itself was a holy rite. For all were given one life equally and would be questioned as to the fruits of their days in this world, and battle was one of the great affairs therein.

Priestess had half given up on understanding it, simply accepting that this was the way things were. But there in the middle of all that commotion...

"Huh? Goblin Slayer, sir, you aren't going to use that sword?"

They were in the lodgings they had been granted, getting their equipment ready, and Goblin Slayer was gazing at the sword. He sat on the bench with the dwarven blade laid across his knees, studying it. It was wide, and thick, and sharp. Nothing remotely like the strange-length swords he usually used. This sword was nameless and not enchanted, but even the untrained eye could see that it was a very fine piece of work.

"No," Goblin Slayer said, letting his fingers brush the clear surface of the blade. "I don't intend to." He set the bare weapon carefully on the bench beside him. The black metal gleamed like starlight in the reflection of the hearth fire. Goblin Slayer gazed at it a moment longer, then grasped the hilt again, holding it up toward the skylight to see it.

"Yeah, that thing's too long for you, Orcbolg." High Elf Archer, her giggle like the ringing of a bell, was already set to go. Looking like a myth in motion, she tugged her hat tight and spun in place as she waited for everyone else. "I wonder if they even make swords at the weird length you like around here. Have you tried asking for one?"

"The *goði* lent me something from the armory," Goblin Slayer responded, still looking at the dwarven sword. He didn't sound particularly interested.

Indeed, a barbarian shortsword was settled safely in the scabbard at his hip. Priestess had heard that in this land, it was typical to fight with the sword in both hands, although she didn't know exactly how it worked.

I guess it's not that different from fighting with a sword and a shield, one in each hand.

Her friend Female Merchant had once mentioned fighting with a rapier and dagger, too. And she had another thought...

"You're able to use pretty much any weapon, aren't you, Goblin

Slayer?" Very much unlike herself, who had struggled even practicing the flail for the holy ritual.

"It's a personal style I developed," came the answer from under the helmet. "I have no special mastery of anything. And the way I use weapons is somewhat idiosyncratic."

"Well, I cannot imagine this is a place where losing a longsword or two would do you much harm." A muffled voice came from beneath a lump of down feathers. The scaly tail sticking out behind it was the only hint that this was Lizard Priest's cloak.

Priestess grinned a little and gave the soft feathers a quick pat. They were so soft that if she could have, she would have liked to give them a big hug—but this was hardly the moment.

"I believe I will have to hold out for the underwater breathing ring until we are aboard ships." They would be on a sea of ice. The thought revealed that Lizard Priest's caution was eminently justified.

They had been out on the sea once, just briefly. (Were those gillmen doing all right?) But even so.

"I wonder if my mail's going to be okay…" Priestess was quite concerned about her own equipment. If she should tumble into the water, the weight of the mail would drag her down. And although an underwater breathing ring might save her from drowning immediately, it wasn't all-powerful. "I know some northerners will be coming with us, so it shouldn't be that much of a problem, but…"

"Yeah, 'cause they're all front-rowers!" High Elf Archer tugged her hat down, stuffing her ears inside. She seemed to like the hat, but it looked a little tight—maybe that was part of the fun. "I've always wondered. You and Orcbolg both—isn't that stuff ever unpleasant?"

"You mean the mail?"

"Uh-huh." High Elf Archer nodded, and indeed, other than her cold-weather gear, Priestess was dressed in her usual light armor.

As a matter of fact, in this party, only the two humans really wore proper armor. There was High Elf Archer, of course, and Dwarf Shaman was a spell caster, while Lizard Priest had his precepts. For that matter, not everyone would smile on even Priestess's modest use of fighting wear.

"It felt really heavy at first," she said, rolling up the hem of her cleric's vestments and patting the mail beneath. The oiled metal felt even cooler than usual to the touch. "But I found that if I cinched it around my waist with a belt, that helped. And I'm used to it now."

"And you don't get cold in that?"

"Eh, I manage…" Priestess smiled noncommittally.

"I can hardly believe it," High Elf Archer said with the slightest of smiles. "I mean, you humans. The whole idea that you would even try to live in a place like this…"

"What do you mean?"

"I mean this place practically screams, *Don't live here!* So don't! Most people would just give up." Instead of building houses, making thick clothes, putting up with the cold, and otherwise adapting. "I can hardly believe it," the high elf murmured again, almost as if praising their ingenuity.

"Humans are sometimes called 'the common folk'—perhaps it's because one finds them everywhere!" Lizard Priest said, evidently as impressed as High Elf Archer, even though he was supposedly a much stronger kind of creature than any human. Even in his thoroughly feathered state, he couldn't have lived in this land. It wouldn't have been an exaggeration to describe this as a sort of defeat for him. "That name is no exaggeration. Even if they do have the arrogance to declare themselves the apex of creation," he went on.

"Ha-ha…" Even after these years together, Priestess didn't always grasp Lizard Priest's humor. He didn't seem to be genuinely insulting humans, though, so no worries.

"I'll need a scabbard," Goblin Slayer muttered to himself, quite apart from the chatter of his colleagues. After seemingly endless inspection, he had laid the dwarven sword back down on the bench. He seemed sorry to leave it, though, and for a moment, it looked like he might simply pick it up again. Priestess was at a loss as to why the weapon seemed to mean so much to him.

"When we get back, yeh should find some smith to take care of it for you," remarked Dwarf Shaman, finally speaking after having worked silently to organize his bag until that moment. A veritable shop's worth of items had appeared and disappeared as he rearranged his bag of catalysts.

"Gee, take your time, why don't you?" High Elf Archer said, pursing her lips, but the fact that she hadn't actually bothered him was a show of consideration in its own way. Then again, perhaps it was only natural: a spell caster's spells could determine the destiny of a party.

"......" Goblin Slayer, however, fell silent at Dwarf Shaman's suggestion.

"What's th' matter?"

Was he...*surprised*? Priestess couldn't see the expression on the face behind the visor, but that was the sense she got.

"...Yes," he said after a moment, nodding. "That's good." Then he nodded again. "...I'll do that."

§

The fleet of ships cut through the water, leaving a white wake behind them in the ash-gray sea. The northerners' boats hardly ever sank in this water; they literally seemed to glide over the surface. They wound their way among the lapping waves like a snake among the hills.

"Wah—pbbt!"

This mode of travel, however, encouraged the waves to come crashing up over the side of the boat, and one of them temporarily stunned Priestess. The spray from the water that came flying off the brave-looking dragon head at the prow soaked her as thoroughly as a rainstorm.

"You will be careful not to fall, yes?"

"Y-yes...!" Priestess nodded as best she could, clasping the side of the ship as the *húsfreya* supported her from behind. The *húsfreya* was dressed much as she had been when they first met, in raiment of battle that almost seemed to impart an air of holiness to her. The fact that even here and now, she still had the bundle of black keys hanging from her hip, as if they were of utmost importance to her, warmed Priestess's heart.

Every glimpse she got of the ocean, though, seemed to be of a black slate, and she understood why they claimed that hell lurked just below the surface. Strangely, though, Priestess didn't feel fear. Countless oars pushed through the water smoothly, in perfect rhythm, propelling the boat forcefully along.

The source of that strength lay in the arms of the brave warriors seated along either side of the vessel. Each one looked like an army unto himself, and they rowed in perfect time. The gunwales were rounded to protect the rowers, the sign of a ship of war.

Supposedly, the oars could be retracted into the boat, although Priestess couldn't imagine it. This, she was told, was what they did when relying exclusively on their sails—and when she looked up, she saw a sail of woolen material above her. It inspired confidence to see the sheet full of wind, and it granted the ship more speed yet.

These Viking ships were moved by the clever use of both oar and sail. Observing all of this around her, she found, banished the fear and replaced it with…

Wait… Why do I feel downright…excited?

Clutching her cap to her head, Priestess stood unsteadily on the deck among the rowers. Every ship rocks, but this one rocked less than she had expected—testament, perhaps, to the Vikings' skill. Then she looked to either side and saw several more ships accompanying them across the sea, the fleet forming a wedge shape. They traveled almost in a straight line, and her ship was at the head—in other words, in the vanguard. That meant they dealt with the worst of the waves, and Priestess exclaimed, "Eep!" again as another blast of water soaked her.

"Yes, because the *goði* always is first into battle," the *húsfreya* said, giggling as she gave Priestess her hand and helped her along the deck. Priestess noticed a profusion of rocks at their feet—stones for ballast, perhaps—as they headed to the middle of the ship. A tent was set up by the mast, serving as the *helskip*'s cabin.

"So we know where we're going."

"Of course. To exactly the destination you dragged out of that prisoner."

There among piles of equipment, the *goði* was holding a council of war with the party. Priestess entered the tent and bowed, the grimy helmet answering her with a silent nod. She continued bowing as she approached the barrels surrounding the table.

"I think we can assume there's something in the waters from which our ships didn't return," the *goði* said.

"And if there isn't, then we should proceed directly to searching for the goblin nest."

"Mm." The chieftain nodded. He wasn't wearing a helmet, but he was already in battle array. His equipment, of which mail was a prominent part, made him look every inch the native northerner. The only difference, perhaps, was that he had no beard... (*"I did wish he would wear one, and I asked him to once,"* the *húsfreya* had confessed shyly to Priestess.)

"Goblins don't possess the art of navigation on the sea, do they?"

"They don't," Goblin Slayer declared. When it came to anything involving goblins, he showed scant hesitation.

But it's true..., Priestess thought, straining not to miss a single word over the sound of the waves. They had, in fact, encountered goblins on boats in the sewers below the water town, but they had merely been riding the vessels, not piloting them. She suspected it was impossible for goblins to row together to work with—or fight—the wind and the tides the way the warriors of the north did.

"The secret of mounted riding the goblins have stolen, but as for long-distance travel by sea, I believe even if they possessed the knowledge, their character wouldn't let them do anything with it. They couldn't stand a journey like that."

"If they simply floated here on the wind and the tides, then I can take a guess at their location..." *Hmm.* The chieftain stroked his chin, then asked a question that seemed to simply occur to him, almost carelessly: "What do the goblins mean to do about getting home?"

"They haven't thought about it," Goblin Slayer said brusquely. "They only ever imagine things going well for them."

That was how goblins always were. And they thought themselves very smart. It was what made them so ugly to deal with—arrogant and cruel. They might be the weakest monsters in the Four-Cornered World, but they were still monsters. And if one could not prevail against goblins...

"Then, too, even we aren't sure how to deal with the sea monster," the chieftain said with a bitter smile, looking out toward the northern sea, which frothed and tossed—in other words, just like it always did.

The board they were on was beyond human ken; it must be home to a great many things that defied the imagination. They hardly knew what was beneath their feet, and discovering what was beyond the ocean was a true challenge. Even if one sailed with the "wiki" of the Vikings, it would hardly result in a comprehensive encyclopedia.

"You may find thinking about it bears little fruit," Lizard Priest said, taking a big bite of cheese to fill his stomach before battle. With his long tongue, he licked up some crumbs that got down onto his chin, but nonetheless he sounded quite important. "If you have the data, you can kill it. *How* to do so is a question that can be answered later."

"Pure dumb chance, is that what you're saying?"

"I'm saying that it's essential to maintain the flexibility to respond to a situation as it develops." In-very-deed.

The chieftain looked at Goblin Slayer, somewhat befuddled. Goblin Slayer nodded. "This is how adventures go, or so I have heard," he said.

"In-very-deed!"

The chieftain might find these words confusing, but they were cheerful in their own way. Goblin Slayer looked to the horizon. Even one living as a northerner found that there were limits to human sight on board a boat. However...

"Shouldn't you be able to see it soon?" A high elf atop the sails, now descending like a fluttering leaf (*shwip!*), was another matter. She stretched out like a cat, then tested the string of her greatbow with a twang. "An ugly boat. Maybe about…twenty, I guess? All goblins."

"Sounds to me like we'd better get spells ready." Dwarf Shaman, who had been huddled up to conserve his stamina, stood. For spell casters and clerics to conserve their strength was something of an ironclad rule, be it on an adventure or in battle. "I assume you have wind masters on the other ships as well. A little bout of Tail Wind won't throw off your formation, will it?"

"Oh, I-I'll help…!"

Priestess, eager to show that she was there, too, gripped her sounding staff tightly. Whatever those around her might think, she felt she hadn't yet properly proven herself. She had lost all her games, even if the *húsfreya*, the *goði*, and the other Vikings had praised her performance. It was, in fact, understandable if she felt she had to put on an especially good show here.

"…No." The *húsfreya* smiled at Priestess, who was giving her a questioning look. (She didn't even notice the chieftain, who was watching her with a smile as if thinking that if he had a daughter, she might look like this.) "First come the stones."

§

The goblin found it all thoroughly distasteful. Hateful, even. As he always did.

He always ended up losing out, while those other cheating bastards got all the goods. And now, just when he had thought a little luck had come his way, it was the others who were having all the fun with it.

For example—yes, the humans around here. They went everywhere in these big vehicles (boats or ships or something, they called them), strutting around like they owned the place. Even though without their boats, they would have been nothing, would have had nothing to brag about.

One day…

One day, the goblin would drag that arrogant young woman to the ground and hurt her as much as he liked. True, he'd only seen her at a distance, but he was sure that clear-eyed look on her face was arrogance. Just imagine her face if he jammed something in that eye of hers! Either the remaining eye or the damaged one—perhaps he would start with the damaged one. That seemed to promise a more protracted and enjoyable infliction of pain.

Even as he entertained these fantasies (for which even the word *ridiculous* was too generous), the goblin grumbled about the unfairness of his situation. He hadn't made any special effort to change things—but nonetheless, he was quite certain it was everyone else's fault that nothing had changed.

Except that, not long ago, something had. One day, something had come washing up on the shore near their nest. Yes: boats. Boat after boat, sideways on the sand like toys a child had tired of. They had holes in them, broken timbers—all very annoying, but they would do. The goblins didn't even question the fact that there were no sailors aboard. They were well aware how stupid humans could be; it didn't surprise the goblins that some humans had simply thrown away their boats.

Anyway, now that was all over. Boats! Boats! Boats!

The days when those sons of bitches got to lord it over everyone else were over. With boats at their disposal, now it was the goblins who would show they were the strongest.

And indeed, it went well chasing away the fools who had no boats. They fled to the south (not that the goblins knew that word)—fools that they were. There were only mountains there. They would starve and die soon enough.

When it came to the orders of the chief of the horde, though (the stupid, overbearing, unfit chief!), well, there was hardly anything more aggravating. He wanted them to push the boats out of the harbor, out to sea—in this cold! The goblin yowled and complained, but he did it—but it was others who got to actually ride on the boat.

Those who went beyond the sea didn't return.

Bunch of trash! They must be living it up somewhere, for sure...

Thanks to those louts, the goblins' fleet of boats had gotten smaller and smaller, until this was the last of them. And it had certainly left *him* waiting a long time for his chance to ride on one…

"E-eyagh! Ahhh, i-it hurts…!"

The goblin decided to let the weeping and shouting of the writhing girl before him, pinned on his spear, soothe his anger. It had been such a good idea to cart her along on the boat, although he'd now been enjoying her for so long that her voice was growing weak.

She was a padfoot—a member of the dormouse people, not that the goblin knew or cared.

When the weather started to let up a little, walking around stabbing your spear randomly into snowdrifts was a great way to pass the time—because every once in a while, you might be rewarded with a cry of "Yeeek?!" Then it would be time to get the polearms and the hooks and drag those snowbank-snoozing idiots out into the cold for a little fun.

And once she stops moving, I can eat her.

"GOORGB!!"

"Ahhh… Hrngh…?!"

"GBBOG! GGGBBOROGB!"

"N-no… Nooo, stop! St— Hrgh!"

He looked around; there were several other playthings on the deck, buried under his companions. A few of them had ropes around their necks and were hanging from the big stick (none of the goblins quite knew what it was for) in the center of the boat.

As for this goblin, he was intensely envious of his companions. He didn't need this half-dead toy—he wanted something that still had a little spirit left. After all, the others had only taken them by playing a nasty little trick.

Sometimes, a goblin died when he was attacked by a bear, but that happened only to the stupid ones. *This* goblin was not like that—he had never made such a mistake!

"*Hhh… Hhhh… N-no more…*"

Still, couldn't she pipe down just a little bit? The boat kept shaking, covering him with vile, salty water. He hated it. He knew whoever was controlling the boat was to blame, even if he didn't know who that was or how they were doing it. If *he* were the chief of the horde, he would do a much better job of making the boat go. All brawn, no brains, that was the idiot's problem.

If I pitched her into the water, maybe it would be a little quieter around here…

"Argh… Ahhh! Hngh—no! N-no…"

The goblin grabbed the girl by the hair and tugged violently, getting a clump of it out of her head and a scream out of her throat. He dragged her toward the side of the boat. She fought and flailed, and in his anger, he kicked her.

Quite pleased with the quiet sniffling of his plaything, he leaned out over the side, preparing to heave her overboard headfirst.

At that moment, though, he saw something in the distance. Was that…a boat? A human boat? A whole horde of boats!

"GBBB…!"

A smile spread across the goblin's face. The humans thought they would win simply because they had boats, but they were wrong, wrong, wrong. Maybe they had the one-eyed girl with them. But if they didn't, that was fine, too. If he played his cards right, he could become the chief of the boat.

To do that, though—he hated it!—they would have to get their boat closer. He turned and was about to shout to his useless fellows.

"GOROGB…?"

That was when a wave of stones came crashing in.

§

"Tyrrrrrrrrrrrrrrrrr!!!!!!!!"

Crying praise to the Valkyrie, the northern warriors fired rocks at their enemies. Stones flew from the battle line of ships, followed by a hail of arrows and then of spears. Priestess watched them, guessing that they were trying to raise the draft in order to speed up the vessel. In battle, heavy stones were just that—deadweight. It was only logical.

What really astonished her, though, was the Viking warriors' skill.

She had seen with her own eyes what a fine slinger Goblin Slayer was, but still they amazed her. When she saw a warrior with a spear in each hand, she'd wondered what he was going to do with them—and then he had flung them in sequence, first the right, then the left!

Even as she stood with her staff at the ready on the raging seas, it was enough to make her catch her breath.

Nonetheless, Priestess's full attention was on the enemy force ahead.

"GRB! GROORGB!!"

"GROOROGB!!"

"GORG! GGGBB!"

They're terrifying...

Priestess shook with fear—not cold—in spite of herself. For those things the goblins rode aboard, one hesitated to call them ships.

Yes, they resembled the seafaring vessels of the northerners. But they were full of holes; the masts were broken and the sails tattered. And where the sculpted prow should have jutted proudly out were tied the bodies of those who have words. All the equipment that should have been maintained and cared for was filthy, with hardly any evidence of its former beauty.

The oars slapped the water haphazardly, like the legs of a flailing bug. They didn't ride the wind, nor the waves, but were simply carried along. That was no ship. Not anymore. It was the skeleton of a ship. A seagoer's rotting corpse.

Yet, even at a distance, it could be seen that the goblins were sure that they controlled the north wind and commanded the seas. In the way they brandished equipment, had their way with women, and cackled horribly, there was no bravery, no pride. There was only a fathomless cruelty, only a pale, superficial imitation of what they imagined themselves.

Although it had been only a short while, although there was so much she still didn't understand, Priestess had been exposed to the northerners' culture. And that was why she understood so clearly: *This is blasphemy.*

That ship—that thing—was a floating goblin nest. Nothing more.

"GOROGGB! GRGGB!!"

"…!" High Elf Archer, wielding her greatbow, called out faster than Priestess's eyes could widen: "Counterattack incoming!"

Precisely because they were merely imitating, the goblins had no sense of range—they simply assumed they could do whatever the humans could do. They flung spears, arrows, and rocks, and when those weren't available, they simply tore up the boards of the deck and threw those. The vast majority of these projectiles, of course, merely plopped into the sea between the two ships, disappearing into the expanse with only a ripple to mark their passing. Even the shots that made it across largely broke up against the hull. The goblin attack was only a crude copy of the human one, much like the arrowhead attack Priestess's party had suffered back on the snowy mountain.

If that had been all that Priestess was observing, she might have maintained her detachment. But amid all the filthy green flesh, she could see glimpses of pale skin, too: women. And she could see one of them being grabbed, to be thrown mercilessly over the side of the ship into the black waters…

"Ah—!"

Oh no…

It happened at the moment she was having that thought.

The pips of the dice are completely evenhanded to all, adventurers and monsters alike.

One of the goblins flung a stone ax, and with what must have been a miraculous roll, it arced through the air, groaning as it went. It described a great peak, and then, despite its height and speed and steepness, it dropped straight down.

Priestess looked up and saw it. It filled her vision, the blade coming directly toward her.

She had no chance to scream or do any other such useless thing. She simply threw herself to the ground, curling up into a ball as best she could…

"Hmph."

Whack. A hand wearing a grimy leather glove reached out and caught the ax in midair. Almost before the grunt was out of his mouth, the warrior in the cheap-looking metal helmet had launched the ax back in the direction of the enemy force. It was like the weapon was moving in reverse—except this time, it was spinning in little circles, and its arc was even steeper.

"GOBBB?!?!" There was a death cry, accompanied by a general hubbub.

"That's the first one."

"Thank you so much...!" Priestess got to her feet, pressing her cap to her head. Her cheeks felt a bit hot. She was embarrassed by her mistake, but she was tickled by the looks of astonishment on the faces of the Viking warriors, almost as happy as if they had been amazed by her own deeds. She put a hand gently to her modest chest, protected by her mail, and said, "We have to help her...!"

"A captive," Goblin Slayer observed. From across the waves, the voice of one who had words could be heard, barely. Goblin Slayer was decisive as ever: "We'll need to jump across."

"Classic maneuver. We'll come up alongside for boarding as fast as we can..."

Almost before the chieftain could finish, though, Goblin Slayer was shaking his head. "We need that thing again," he said. "Water Walk!"

"Comin' right up!" Dwarf Shaman said, and then he cried out to the stormy sea: *"Nymphs and sylphs, together spin, earth and sea are nearly kin, so dance away—just don't fall in!"*

At the same moment, Goblin Slayer kicked off the side of the ship, launching himself into the sea with a spray of water. The sea was very nearly frozen; that cold would stiffen your muscles and make it all but impossible to breathe, let alone swim. But the sprites supported Goblin Slayer's weight for the instant before he kicked off again, bouncing from wave to wave, leaping through the froth. He looked like he was running through a cloud of butterflies, and he showed just as much hesitation.

And on his hand was Spark, the ring of breathing.

"Ahhh..." To the young woman, tormented by goblins and then

thrown into the sea, it must have looked like a flash of hope. Summoning the last of her depleted strength, the dormouse girl grabbed hold of the filthy leather armor and clung on. Goblin Slayer, in turn, hugged the girl to his chest. So that he could turn away from the goblins, of course.

"GOROOGGBB!"

"GBBB! GOROOGBB!!"

And if it is the way of goblins to be willing to shoot someone in the back after he's been foolish enough to throw himself into the sea...

"I wish you'd tell me when you're about to go charging into action!"

...then it is the way of a party to support a friend without hesitation and without question.

Even as she shouted, High Elf Archer danced through the air, her wooden arrows piercing sky and sea. One goblin unlucky enough to have aimed into the air found himself pierced from skull to jaw, his bow twanging and the arrow falling uselessly away. By the time he was tumbling into the ocean without even a scream, High Elf Archer was kicking off the mast of the ship.

On the next beat, she leaped up, her great yew bow raining arrows and death onto the goblins below.

"If yeh play around too much, you'll drop bow and arrows and all right into the water!" Dwarf Shaman snapped.

High Elf Archer laughed, although this hardly seemed the time. "As if I'd do anything that stupid!" she called, landing right back where she had begun. She exhaled slowly, brushing aside some hair that had fallen over her forehead, as if to say a high elf could do anything. "Even a weak little bow like this would feel bad if it got laughed at by goblins."

"I guess *most* bows are like little girls' toys by elf standards," Dwarf Shaman said, shaking his head with an annoyed huff. He hated to compliment the long-eared lass; it always went straight to her head.

But instead, he turned away from his familiar verbal sparring partner and spoke to Lizard Priest, who was still wearing his down cloak.

"I'm not expecting much here, Scaly, but I thought I'd better ask…"
He smirked, because he knew what answer was coming. "You want
Water Walk yerself?"

"I will get in that ocean after the town has turned to dust, good
sir," Lizard Priest said. He heaved himself to his feet, raising the huge
Viking shield he was carrying. Then with a "Many pardons," he
pushed past some warriors to the side of the ship, where he draped his
tail over the side, toward the water.

The warriors could only watch in confusion…until Goblin Slayer
grabbed hold of the tail, and Lizard Priest pulled him up like a fish out
of the sea.

"Sorry. That's a help."

"Think nothing of it…!"

The dormouse girl in Goblin Slayer's arms had reached the limits
of her strength and lay limp on the deck when he set her down.

"How is she?"

"Let me have a look…!" Priestess said, already hurrying over to the
pitiful child before Goblin Slayer had finished his question. Protected
by Lizard Priest's shield, Priestess checked the girl over quickly, getting a sense of her situation.

Priestess served the Earth Mother, abounding in mercy—if not as
devoutly as the shrine maiden of the sadistic gods served her deity.
Protect, Heal, Save. Priestess had been granted more than miracles to
help her achieve those ends—that was what made her a cleric. The
girl's actual physical wounds were light. The starvation, hypothermia,
fatigue, emaciation, and lack of sleep were far more serious, poten-
tially fatal.

"But she's all right now…!" Priestess said. *I'm sure she'll live.*

Priestess cleansed the girl's body promptly, then wrapped her in a
blanket and cloak. She needed some first aid for her wounds, as well,
but right now, the top priority was to keep her warm.

"Think some wine'd help?"

"Start with just a little, please. We have to make sure she doesn't choke on it," Priestess said, deliberate but not hesitant, grateful for Dwarf Shaman's offer of assistance. "It will help bring her around. But wine alone will leave her without enough water in her body…"

"Mm. Don't worry—I've got that in mind."

Dwarf Shaman took the girl, who seemed as frail as a withered branch, in his arms and laid her down amidships. It was the safest possible location, where she would be protected from the waves, the wind, and the rain of arrows. Dwarf Shaman poured a bit of fire wine into her mouth; Goblin Slayer kept one eye on them and grunted.

"What do you think?"

"One supposes there are more captives. And breath rings or no, Water Walk remains essential."

The ships were getting closer, and more projectiles than before could be heard bouncing off Lizard Priest's upraised shield. He, however, paid no heed to the *thwack, whack, bump* but only bared his fangs in his great jaws. "I think it may be high time we boarded the enemy ship."

"I agree," Goblin Slayer said with a nod. "Bring the ships together. We're going to fight our way across."

"…" The chieftain, neither amazed nor unduly impressed by this, simply smiled. He, too, agreed; this was stupendous.

The way these people worked with one another, it was much like how accomplished Viking warriors worked—although with its own subtle differences. At this moment, they were witnessing the "adventure" of which adventurers always spoke. Something was spreading among the northern warriors observing this, who knew they were seeing something unusual and precious.

It was all worth it, the chieftain thought.

"I suppose this means we need an adventurers' organizational up here as well. Think so, dear wife?"

"Oh, please, do not be silly," the *húsfreya* replied, her prim, sharp profile turning a bit sullen. "We have not been bested yet." What sweet expression would the woman make when her loving husband realized she was pouting? Even there in the middle of battle, Priestess couldn't help a giggle as she imagined it.

Naturally, the *húsfreya* had taken notice of her new friends' actions with her one good eye—how could she not? The faraway princess muttered, "Don't tease me," then took a deep breath. The adventurers had shown their mettle. Now it was her turn.

Taking a deep breath of the freezing air and turning in to the waves, the shrine maiden of the sadistic god called out: *"When the wind blows, let us cut timber; when the sun shines, let us go to sea. O maidens, cleave to the darkness and shun the eye of day!"*

Now—now it was the Vikings' time.

§

"Fylking! Battle formation!"

"GOROGGB?!"

"GOG! GOBBG!!"

The vessels collided with a crash, hooks biting into the enemy ship to ensure it couldn't escape. The goblins panicked—belatedly—and tried to shove the hooks away. Those who failed found themselves kicked and shoved out of the way, but it was too little, too late.

"Chaaaaarge!!"

"Hrrrahhh!!"

With one word from the *goði*, who stood at their head, the northerners came piling onto the enemy ship.

The goblins watched as their companions who had been unfortunate enough to be first in line turned into showers of blood. They swung their own weapons: rusted swords, half-broken spears, and crude clubs. But it was a useless show of defiance in the face of the great-shields the northerners carried. The boat rocked on the waves, but the Vikings kept their footing, a wall of shields, the very image of the *skjaldborg*.

"Puuuush!"

"Hoooo!"

"GOROGGB?!"

The wall absorbed the goblin attack and shoved forward, bashing with their shields. The stunned goblins stumbled backward, wobbled, and then fell into the sea. Some backed away in terror, others tripped and fell, while still others howled in sheer incomprehension of the circumstances. The one thing that was true of all of them was that the sea gave no refuge, no place to run.

The goblins began pushing and shoving one another, caught between fighting and fleeing, rocking the boat violently.

"No mercy!" The chieftain grinned, baring his fangs, and kicked a goblin head that lay at his feet. "Press the advantage!"

"Hrrraaahhhh!"

Spears cracked, axes howled, swords cried out, and six-sided clubs roared. The goblins' resistance was futile and easily crushed, death rattles escaping them as readily as their filthy blood. Those who attempted to use the captives as shields were forcibly separated from their hostages, their skulls soon split by black steel blades. The northerners confiscated the chest representing the goblins' meager loot, and the monsters who clung to it they kicked into the icy waters. They could not be prevailed upon, could not be begged for mercy. To kill, to take the women and loot, and to sing songs of victory was their joy.

"*Gygax*! Praise the gods!"

"*Gygax! Gygax! Gygax!!*"

"O Arneson, Master of the Black Moor, behold my deeds!"

"*Jackson*—praise all the gods! Glory be to Livingstone, King of Traps!"

Hack and slash! The stuff of Vikings! The Vikings!

Yes, out in the open field, or in a cave, or in a dungeon, goblins might take one unawares and strike a fatal blow. But here on the northern sea, with a song of ice and fire rumbling across the waves with their great battleships...

"We would never be bested by any orcs!"

The Vikings, the People of the Bay, were utterly at home on the water.

"Guess there's not much for us to do now that the battle's started," High Elf Archer remarked.

"I think you're right," Priestess said.

But despite the friendly exchange, they were hardly letting their guard down. The fight to board the goblin vessel might have been successful, but freed captives were pouring back onto the Viking ship, and there were wounded to tend to as well. It was the adventurers' role to protect and treat them, though they hadn't nearly enough hands to do it.

In the center of the ship, the *húsfreya* looked after those with especially grievous wounds, working her deeds tirelessly. Alcohol or vinegar would be used to clean out injuries—these tended to be especially common on the right side of the body, the side that wasn't protected by the shield—which would then be stitched up and wrapped in hempen cloth.

The *húsfreya* probed wounds with tools Priestess couldn't have distinguished from torture instruments, removing arrowheads and shards of sword. The way she even occasionally closed off blood vessels, brilliantly stanching the flow of blood, left Priestess wide-eyed. In the temple *she'd* been raised in, they had only been allowed to use miracles at times like this, and yet...

The northern warriors might have been Vikings, but they were still human. The probing of the wounds sometimes provoked screams and cries. But the *húsfreya* would snap, "What are you, a child? Even an infant wouldn't yowl on account of the likes of this!" She only very rarely administered painkillers—poppy or henbane.

"These people are all right now...!" Priestess said.

"And I thank you! Very well, now these..."

"Right...!"

She's incredible.

And here Priestess was, actually fighting alongside her. It inspired a sense of pride in Priestess as she pattered this way and that around the boat, carrying bandages.

And then there was Lizard Priest, his massive form casting a shadow over the women he was protecting. "Gracious, I fear I've not been of much use..."

"Then just keep on keeping everyone safe…!" High Elf Archer said as she flashed by his elbow, kicking off the gunwale and firing another arrow. Her bowstring twanged like a zither, each note portending the piercing of a goblin skull. She might be on a rocking ship, aiming at targets on another rocking ship, but it didn't matter: Elves shoot not with the eye or with their own skill but with the heart. The northern warriors were fine archers in their own right, but even they could hardly hope to match a high elf.

If a contest of spells was to begin at this moment, admittedly, that would change the face of the battle again. But…

"Looks like they've got no spell casters, from what I can tell," Dwarf Shaman observed, seeing that at present, he didn't appear to be needed.

In battle, it's ultimately the commander's leadership that determines the course of events, and *their* leader was on the front lines. The way he slashed with his sword, shouting and yelling, leading the Vikings ahead—yes, he was the chieftain indeed. A foreigner he might have been, but it seemed he had earned his position, that he was seen as far more than simply prince consort.

A glance at the *húsfreya* revealed her smiling with a hint of pride— vicariously sharing in her husband's deeds, no doubt.

Well, every land has its own heroes, Dwarf Shaman thought. To insist on stealing the spotlight always and everywhere would be sheer arrogance. Even the great Hero, who plunged into battles for the fate of the world, wouldn't horn in on someone else's goblin hunt.

This place had its own tales, as Dwarf Shaman's homeland had theirs. These never-ending stories were not one single heroic narrative but a continuing cycle, a saga.

"How does it look?" The unexpected question was posed to Dwarf Shaman by, of course, Goblin Slayer. After rescuing the hostages and further reducing the goblin numbers with his slinging ("Ten, eleven"), he was stepping back for a view of the battlefield.

In a pitched battle like this, adventurers became limited in what they could do. They might want to help fight the good fight, but if outsiders joined that unflappable formation, they were more likely to be a liability than an asset. And of course, Goblin Slayer was not going to simply be a liability.

"Hoh. Asking me, are we?" A smirk came across Dwarf Shaman's bearded face. "Well, if nothing else, I think we know who their leader is."

He was referring to a goblin on the wreckage who was large enough to loom over his companions and was obviously giving the orders. Like Goblin Slayer, he was holding back from joining the battle proper, but unlike Goblin Slayer, he was squawking and shouting.

"GOOROOGGBB!!"

The goblin ostentatiously wore a rotting bear pelt; he was large even by the standards of the northern goblins, who tended to be bigger than southern ones. Still, the word *hob* didn't quite fit him, and one hesitated to call him a champion.

It was the *húsfreya* who declared: "Some nerve he has, pretending to be a berserker...!"

The man she loved, her people, could never be outdone by the likes of goblins.

"I agree," Goblin Slayer said with a nod. "Whatever he pretends to, he's still just a goblin."

§

There was an invader there, a very silent presence, unnoticed by anyone.

From the deepest depths, he hunted his prey and ate, guided only by light and sound.

For him, it was like a drumbeat he heard while dozing; the days were pleasant.

Then again, perhaps to call them *days* wasn't quite right, for never once had he been concerned with the march of the sun or moon.

He had never even wondered where he was at any given moment.

For him, the entirety of the four corners consisted of his own hunger and the question of where his next meal was located.

He existed to eat, and so long as he existed, he *would* eat.

It mattered not when this place was, nor where this moment: When he sensed commotion above him, he knew that this was the time.

Hence, he reached out his hand.

It was the only thing that seemed real to him in his ephemeral, death-transcending sleep.

Thus, by the time they realized that he was approaching, that he had been drawn to them...

It was all too late.

§

Whoosh: The sea exploded. A geyser of froth shot upward, lifting the boats beneath it as easily as if they were twigs. The vessels broke up in midair and came cascading down in pieces that sent humans and goblins alike running for cover.

The party's ship was still safely on the water, but a massive wave shook it violently, and those aboard tumbled to the ground with a sensation like they were flying through the air. One of them exclaimed, "Wha—?!" although it wasn't clear who. They supported themselves as best they could by grabbing onto the gunwales, falling to all fours, or, if they were Lizard Priest, bracing with their claws and tail.

Even the northerners were taken aback (so we need hardly mention the goblins' amazement). They looked up, wide-eyed; then they saw it.

Or, wait... *Did* they see it? Beyond the geyser of spray, there was nothing. For what was there was only the atrocity that attacked indiscriminately from the black depths of the sea. If they could assign what they were seeing any significance, it might look to them like a mouth. A great maw lined with fangs that existed only to consume.

The only thing they could comprehend was that the jaws had emerged from the depths, writhing, moaning, squirming. Those who hadn't managed to land in the water, sadly, found themselves chewed to pieces and swallowed by those jaws. Seawater came down like a storm, mixed with pink mist and gore and sundered limbs. It was enough to make a person doubt their sanity—at times, even to rob them of words.

When the great wave had them in its grasp, it was the only sound they could hear, for it drowned out all others.

"Ahhh… Wh-what was that thing…?!" Priestess, clinging as hard as she could to her staff, got unsteadily to her feet. "Was it a Sea Serpent?! But it was nothing like the one we saw before…!" This creature seemed to have nothing in common with the sea monster they had encountered some time ago. That creature had been frightening, to be sure, but nowhere near as terrible as this.

"My very goodness! I wonder if it might not be related to mine own ancestors…!"

"It's coming from below!" High Elf Archer cried, clinging to Lizard Priest, her ears flicking furiously. She even forgot to draw her bow. "And it's coming back!"

She was right: *Whoosh!* There was another great eruption of the sea. Swallowed up by the pillar of water this time was the ship right beside the one the adventurers were on. The warriors, who had been in the midst of fighting the goblins, disappeared into the waters, looking as if they couldn't believe what was happening.

"Ah… Ahhh?!" the *húsfreya* cried. Was it for the loss of her comrades or because the ship shook so badly that it threatened to capsize? Or—was it from the fear that the ship her *goði* had boarded might be the next one to be attacked?

"A beast! A beast comes!"

"Damnable draug…!" The northerners couldn't restrain their yells and cries.

What held terror for those without fear? The devil of the sea. The unknown master of the abyss.

Although naturally, this was hardly enough to put them at a disadvantage against some goblins…

"GOROGGB! GOOBBG!!"

The goblins, who understood nothing of the situation, took this to mean that the enemy had been weakened through the goblins' own strength. Or perhaps they felt that the humans were fools to be afraid of such a thing and that *they* were different. Freshly invigorated, the goblins made to strike the northerners before they could shore up their lines.

"So the roll was...*snake eyes*." Dwarf Shaman scowled. He took a gulp of his wine, of which he had spilled not a drop despite the tossing of the boat. "The wheel of karma turns. It might turn us right over at this rate...!"

The situation was bad. The music of battle crescendoed, the shouting of warriors mingling with their death cries, and then there was the ocean, boiling up again.

This was not a battle anymore. An attack by an unknown monster did not call for soldiers. Who could be expected to leap straight into this whirlpool of chaos?

Who else? Adventurers.

"All right...," Goblin Slayer said softly. "What's next?"

He could tell one thing: That was no goblin.

CHAPTER 6

DEEP RISING

It had been spoken of since the Age of the Gods: the consuming appetite, The Greed, the rising deep.

"GOOROGB?!"

"Hrgh—ah—ahhhh?!"

Those who were taken by the waves could scream and struggle, but it was no use; they vanished to their dooms. Human and goblin alike, all were equal before the voracious appetite of this monster.

Truly, it was a scene from hell. Where first there had been one geyser of water, soon there was another and another. Could it be an army of terrible monsters appearing from under the waves? The battlefield became a maelstrom of chaos, confusion, and killing.

"Husbondi!"

Thus it was understandable that there should be abundant joy in the *húsfreya*'s voice as she called out: Clad in black armor now covered with reddish blotches, the *goði* returned, dragging one of his companions.

"Hoh, dear wife, I've returned!" he shouted, sounding no more concerned than a child who had been out to play and every bit as cheerful. It was almost as if he wasn't bothered by the sea devil wreaking havoc—but things weren't going to be that easy.

Still vibrating with the thrill of battle, the chieftain took the canteen his *húsfreya* offered him and drank lustily, then said, "So what *is* that thing?"

It was Goblin Slayer who replied. "I don't know." He stood by the side of the ship, observing the battle with the yelling warriors and screaming goblins and howling waves, then added: "But it's not a goblin."

"And it looks like blades work perfectly well on it!" the chieftain said, passing the canteen to his men and telling them to drink. *Boosh.* He dropped something on the deck: one of the monsters, cut clean in two. So the stuff dribbling from his sword must be the creature's blood.

The creature jumped and bounced on the deck, demonstrating a frightening level of vitality as it continued to twitch and writhe. Someone exclaimed, "Eek!"—was it Priestess or the *húsfreya*?—while High Elf Archer groaned, "Ugh."

"Think we can drag it up out of there?"

The chieftain's question was simple, and Goblin Slayer's response was equally so: "What do we do after that?"

"We kill it."

He sounded so nonchalant, but the tentacle at his feet was proof that it could be done. Resting against his sword as if on a cane, the chieftain smiled, baring his fangs, then shrugged. "At least, we ought to be able to have a good, long fight with it. So long as the goblins don't interfere."

"All right." With that decision made, Goblin Slayer acted quickly. Because he had been told that decisive judgment and decisive action were crucial. "The usual plan. Can you do it?"

"Thing's awfully big." Dwarf Shaman, although clearly intrigued, frowned as if to ask whether they were really doing *that*. It was an unpleasant way to use a spell. "Might be nice to be a little closer... Say, Long Ears. Where would you reckon is directly above it?"

"Blargh... Don't tell me you want to get inside it?" She hated the thought, but the frown that contorted her face detracted nothing from her beauty—perhaps one of the benefits of being an elf.

She leaned out as far as she could, Lizard Priest wrapping his arms around her waist to support her. In the distance, another pillar of water appeared. Another *boom*, taking with it another ship—goblin or northerner, it wasn't clear.

High Elf Archer knew they had to hurry. Her long ears twitched back and forth; she squinted her gemlike eyes and looked deep into the water, then drew a breath. "That guy in the bear pelt. I think it's around there, maybe… The thing's so big, it's hard to be sure."

"That's where we'll go, then," Goblin Slayer declared. They had to kill the goblins anyway. He made sure the northern sword was secure at his hip, and he nodded. He'd asked them to shave it down to a strange length, so it felt familiar—but it was still sharper and more polished than he was used to. He turned his helmet to look at Priestess. "What will you do?"

There was no hesitation in her voice. She spoke firmly and clearly. "I'm coming with you…!"

"I see."

It was decided, then. They would wager everything on defeating the sea devil. Quickly.

"How many spells and miracles do we have left?"

"I've only used the one. Been able to conserve 'em otherwise," Dwarf Shaman said.

"M-me too! I haven't used a single miracle today." Priestess glanced at the *húsfreya*, letting out a breath of relief. "…Because they can do so much healing even without miracles here."

Ah, she thought, *I still have so much to learn.* There were so many in the Four-Cornered World who deserved her respect and admiration, who had gone before her. Witch, Sword Maiden, and now the *húsfreya*-princess of this northern land—could she become a woman like them?

I know I have to decide what kind of adventurer I want to be.

Priestess remembered what Female Knight had once said to her. It felt like good fortune to be able to make the choice.

"You gonna use your Purify miracle?" High Elf Archer inquired.

"That's dangerous, so no," Priestess replied flatly—maybe there was still some youth in her that needed to come out.

"The same for myself," Lizard Priest said, keeping one eye on Priestess. "I am managing to cope with the cold, but still..." He helped High Elf Archer down; she jumped like a cat.

"Thanks."

"Oh, hardly." Lizard Priest rolled his eyes in his head. "I thought perhaps I should leave a Dragontooth Warrior to guard the ship. It would make a fine messenger as well."

"Try not to scare anyone," Goblin Slayer said. Was there anyone there who realized he was making a joke? Priestess giggled to herself. "But go ahead."

"Yes, of course. Very well, then..." There was a rattle as Lizard Priest produced a fang from his pouch, tossed it to the ground, and then brought his hands together in the unusual lizardman gesture of reverence. *"O horns and claws of our father, iguanodon, thy four limbs, become two legs to walk upon the earth!"*

Even as they watched, the enchanted fang began to swell and grow, until it took on the shape of a soldier. There was a murmur among the northerners at the appearance of the Dragontooth Warrior; meanwhile, the adventurers nodded to one another.

"We're going in. Our first priority is to cast spells"—Goblin Slayer looked at the sea—"on *him.*"

"S'pose I'd best save Water Walk, then. Be careful—won't do any of us much good if we go falling in."

"We should probably put on our breath rings ahead of time." *Mm.* Priestess put a finger to her lips in thought. She noticed that it had gotten much colder, a strange thing to observe at this moment. "I'm glad we were able to rescue the dormouse girl, too; that makes me feel better. Assuming she doesn't get eaten..."

"That's up to luck and the heavens now," High Elf Archer said. She chuckled with some resignation, tugged gently on her bow, and shrugged. "Don't screw it up, okay? If *you* fall, all of us together won't be able to pull you back up."

"Mm! Yes, it is time to make my stand. How could I face my ancestors if I was defeated by a little freezing water?" Lizard Priest made an energetic noise, then hefted Dwarf Shaman's stout form onto his shoulders. Everything was ready to go.

With this council of war complete, the adventurers knew what they had to do next, and they moved eagerly to challenge the monster. Their courage was like that of the northerners and yet different—it was the courage of adventurers.

"The honored smithy god, I've heard, stores up courage in those who pray…" The *húsfreya* smiled, her one eye glinting.

"We need them, don't we?" the *goði* said, clasping his sword. "These adventurers."

"Mm…" The *gyðja* of the sadistic god nodded at her beloved's words, then took a deep breath of the sea air, filling her ample chest.

Loot may be lost, a family may fall,
and you, too, will one day die,
but I know
that one thing ne'er fails nor fades:
great deeds grasped
by the dead.

From her mouth flowed the high words of the gods. Words of prayer that praised the adventurers' and the warriors' deeds of valor.

The dice could be heard rolling in heaven, where they acknowledged the *gyðja*'s wish. Certainly the adventurers running across the great plain of the sea heard it.

The die was cast. As such, one needs hardly say what was to happen next.

But if one did, nonetheless, wish to put it into words, it would be very simple.

"Go forth, adventurers…!"

The adventure began.

§

"O Earth Mother, abounding in mercy, grant your sacred light to we who are lost in darkness."

"GOOROGBB?!"

"GOBBB?! GOBRGBB?!?!"

The fight began with a flash in the midst of the storm, like a star descended to earth. Priestess, charging forward with her party members, held her sounding staff high, its light searing the goblins' eyes.

"Outta my way!" High Elf Archer, unleashing a literal hail of arrows, kicked writhing, screaming goblins aside to open a path.

"Jump!" On Goblin Slayer's signal, the adventurers, running along the boat, kicked off the deck. They cleared the spraying, frothing gap between the two ships, secured to each other with hooks, in the space of a breath and pressed forward. "Twelve…!"

"GBBOGB?!"

As he landed, Goblin Slayer mercilessly kicked a goblin in the head. There was a dry snap of the spinal cord cracking; he immediately slammed the goblin to his right with the Viking sword. "Thirteen!"

"GOOB?! GBGR?!"

There was a whistling sound and a spurt of blood as the goblin collapsed, his throat slashed. Goblin Slayer didn't even spare a glance at the body as he went past. The enemies were many, and his destination was far away.

The goblins left behind him began to recover from the shock of the holy light, jabbering to themselves. A high elf. A sweet little servant of the Earth Mother. The goblins hated all adventurers but especially these ones. They were just giving chase, their hands full of a random assortment of weapons, when—

"Hrrrngh!"

"GOROGBB?!?!"

—a single blow from a great, powerful tail literally swept them away. Right, left. Their attacker might not be able to bring his claws or fangs to bear, but for this descendant of the fearsome nagas, his tail was deadly enough. He didn't have to be a Euoplocephalus; his tail was all muscle, like a living whip.

The battered goblins tumbled away from the ship, catching their companions up with them as they went. If any of them was alive as they sank into the ashen waters, it didn't matter; they wouldn't be coming back up.

"Good gods, your cloak is soaked!"

"I didn't account for a sea voyage!"

The exclaiming Dwarf Shaman was on Lizard Priest's back, where he had a firm hold on the down cloak and was observing the battle-field. How hard was he going to have to concentrate; how many sprites was he going to have to call, to cast a spell on something so huge? Monster though it may have been, the thing was a creature of the sea. It would be more intimate with the sprites of water, air, and ocean than he was.

"Well, sometimes you just have to trust the dice...!"

"Here it comes again! From below!" High Elf Archer shouted, her ears twitching fast. Then a great impact sent their ship rising into the air.

"Yeeeek...!" Priestess couldn't hold back a scream. She tried to keep her footing even as the sea appeared to rise like a wall, looking as if it would overwhelm them.

No—she realized heaven and earth had switched places.

By the time she registered that the boat had been overturned by the sea devil's emergence so close to it, it was too late. Priestess found herself thrown clear, tumbling through the air; she squeezed her eyes shut...

It's all right... Even if I fall in the water, I can still breathe...!

With her eyes still shut, she reached out with her sounding staff, seeking any sort of clue, doing all that she could do under the circumstances. She knew falling in the water wouldn't kill her, at least not immediately. And if you gave up, then your adventure really was over. She couldn't allow herself that.

Ah! May she have the blessing of Septentrion, the north wind!

"Are you all right?!"

"Yes!"

Goblin Slayer grabbed her outstretched staff and pulled her up. Piercingly cold water struck her body, but she was not in the heart of the sea.

The party, lucky enough to have been flung free of the rolling vessel by the sea monster, succeeded in landing on top of the overturned ship. Although whether it was lucky that they were now able to witness the destruction of the other ships by the creature's tentacles at close range was debatable.

Goblins and northerners alike who had been flung off their ships found themselves mercilessly consumed. When one realizes that with a single misstep, the adventurers might have met the same fate, one begins to think that the dice must have been smiling on them today.

"That is definitely *not* a horde of water snakes! I don't know what it is, but it's something incredible...!" High Elf Archer, shaking herself dry like a cat, sounded awfully upset and un-high-elf-ish.

Yes, they were safe—but only for the moment. The capsized ship was like a leaf battered by the waves, and it was still sinking. With the hooks that had once kept the ships bound to each other broken, they had no way to get where they were going.

It was beginning to look like the only thing that awaited them was disappearing into the icy depths...

"I...I have a grappling hook!" Priestess said, producing an item from the Adventurer's Toolkit that she never left home without. How many times had it saved her skin?

"Good!"

She handed the grappling hook to Goblin Slayer, who took it and, with an exquisite throw, hooked it onto the nearest ship. They kicked aside goblins who scrambled to reach for the rope, then jumped off the sinking vessel.

"GOORGGB!!"

"Fourteen!" A goblin waiting for them on deck got a sword to the brain like a nail in a coffin, and that was the end of his life. A person could fall in love with a blade this sharp. He almost didn't feel anything as he cut down goblins with the northern sword; blood simply flew.

Forward they went, producing a mountain of corpses in the process. Then they jumped to the next ship, working their way across the sea.

"You know, Orcbolg, I notice you haven't done a lot of throwing this time," High Elf Archer remarked, even as she let loose an endless stream of arrows. "Starting to get attached to your toys?"

"Ha-ha-ha! Pretty unusual for Beard-cutter!" Dwarf Shaman laughed, but Goblin Slayer didn't answer them.

Because first, he had to kill the goblin in front of him. "That's fifteen…!"

"I can see it!" Lizard Priest called. Goblin Slayer, kicking off the goblin's corpse, turned in his direction. A collection of bodies hung from the mast—corpses of women, who or what they once were no longer discernible. The remains whipped wildly in the wind.

They were a banner most awful. Beneath them, the goblin leader, so far from leading his troops from the front, was jabbering and cocky.

How very goblin-like. That was all Goblin Slayer had to say about it.

"I'm going to jump!" he shouted, and then he pushed off the gunwale and leaped for the next ship.

Because first, he had to kill the goblins in front of him.

§

Damnable fools!

When he saw the adventurer boarding his ship, the first thing the goblin felt was rage toward his fellows. None of them did any work. They just yelled and shouted and did whatever they wanted.

The moment they opened their mouths, it was nothing but "Graah, graaah!" "Do that for me!" "Do this for me!"

And yet, look. They hadn't even been able to stop that stupid human.

Yes, all the humans were stupid. It seemed the man causing all the commotion was their leader—but how idiotic could you be? What were they thinking, having the most important of them jump into the fray first? It was precisely because the leader was smart, and strong, and great that the horde was powerful. If the leader died, was that not the end of everything?

It was exactly because no one else understood this that he had to go so far out of his way.

The goblin chieftain snorted in disdain and took a firm grip on the shining battle-ax in his hand. It had been on the body that had been wearing this bearskin cloak, and the chieftain was confident that it was a weapon fit for a leader. The blade glowed with a mystical light that even a goblin could tell was magic. This goblin knew that as long as he possessed it, he wouldn't die.

Even while all this was going on, the boat was shaking as the surface of the sea erupted, *ba-boom, ba-boom*. Goblins and humans both were flung stupidly into the sea and eaten. But *he* wouldn't be eaten, the chieftain knew very well. For he was the chief, categorically different from those fools. With his levelheaded observation of the battlefield, he would never be thrown off his feet like they were—obviously.

Yes, situational awareness, that was it. The goblin leader took a few proud, threatening swipes with his ax. Just the sound of it slicing through the air was enough to cow the other goblins and make them do as he said. And it made captives, whether human or padfoot, cry out in fear, which pleased the chieftain.

"GORRGGBB…!"

And so he was somewhat vexed by the attitude of the adventurer leader: a man who, with his pitiful equipment, was clearly on a lower level than the goblin. He didn't even seem to flinch! Not that the chieftain could really tell, since the adventurer wore an expressionless metal helmet.

Bah, who cares?

The adventurer obviously thought he would win, but if the chieftain killed the leader, then it would all be over. The stubby little dwarf, and the apathetic lizard carrying him, were no match for the goblin. If he could just kill this man in front of him, then the high elf and the skinny little girl would be his. He would break their arms and legs, have his way with them until he tired of them, and then—if they were still alive—he might see fit to toss them to his lackeys.

Needless to say, he would do the same with that accursed one-eyed woman. Ooh, she would chirp if he tore out that other eye!

The goblin chieftain could see his future victory, right there, just beyond the adventurer in the grimy armor. Assured of his superiority, the goblin laughed. And it would all start with taking care of this man right here!

"GOOROOOGGBB!! GOOROGGBBB!!!!" the goblin chieftain howled, swinging his ax so hard, it seemed he was trying to summon up a storm. If he landed a hit on the adventurer's head, it would crack his skull clear through his helmet, while if he caught one of the man's limbs, it would be lopped off, armor and all.

No one could possibly maintain their composure in the face of this display. Look—the adventurer wasn't even trying to draw his sword!

"GOOOROOGGBB!!!!"

But of course, this didn't mean the goblin would show him any mercy. Had the adventurer not killed other goblins? This was a simple, fully justified case of revenge.

The goblin, his head full of these goblin-y thoughts, raised his ax to deliver what he was sure would be the coup de grâce…

"GOOROGGBBB?!"

The next instant, he found a twisted blade, crueler than he could imagine, biting into his arm.

§

"GOOROGGBBB?!"

The upgraded southern-style throwing knife did exactly what

Goblin Slayer had come to expect it would and sliced the goblin's right arm clear off. Still holding the battle-ax, the limb whirled through the air. Before it landed, Goblin Slayer was already kicking off the deck.

The goblin was babbling, but there was no need to listen; it would have been pointless.

Now he saw it, the strength of the tempered steel blades of the northerners. How something like sacredness dwelled within them. Truly awe-inspiring.

Berserkers: warriors in bearskins who knew no fear. A word with which to inspire terror. They chewed up shields, tore people apart, could even pull gods limb from limb. Nothing could be more awful.

And yet...

Why should I be afraid of a goblin?

He might fear a great barbarian who could not be intimidated, but at a goblin cowering for his life?

"GORROGGBB?!"

With his right hand, Goblin Slayer pulled out the northern sword. Short, of a strange length, but polished to perfection. He had no qualms at all with it. It was wasted on him.

The goblin was holding the stump of his arm and bellowing. Thrashing with pain, weeping and jabbering, cursing everything he could think of.

The distance would be closed in one, two, three. Normally Goblin Slayer would aim for the throat, but this goblin's throat was a bit big. The belly would be enough.

And then the sea will do the rest.

"GOROOGGBB?! GBB?!"

His blade met virtually no resistance as it drove into the goblin's guts, like he was stabbing a snowbank. He gave the hilt a twist to make sure he did plenty of internal damage, and the goblin let out a choked scream.

"This makes...sixteen!"

The monster was reaching his one good hand toward Goblin

Slayer—was it a spasm of pain or did he think he was begging for his life? Whatever it was, it didn't rise to the level of resistance.

Ah. Yes.

Goblin Slayer reached out with his own left hand and tore the bear pelt away.

"This is more than you deserve."

Then he gave the goblin a merciless kick. *Thump.* There was a spray of filthy blood as the sword came out, and the goblin went tumbling into the freezing ocean. There was only a dull splash as he hit the water—a fitting end for a goblin. The waves would carry him away shortly, and he would be gone.

Meanwhile the ax, which had continued to spin through the air, finally landed on the deck with a thump of its own.

In one hand, Goblin Slayer held a rotting bear skin. In the other, the ax. He let out a breath.

"I knew…" He slid the sword back into its scabbard, stuffed the pelt into his item pouch, and nodded once. "…*this* was more suited to throwing." He sounded satisfied as he tugged on the string tied to the southern-style knife.

He had no regrets at all, having it upgraded. It fulfilled a different purpose. At least, different from his other equipment.

"How are you doing there?" he asked.

"Oh, we'll manage somehow!" High Elf Archer shouted, letting off another volley of arrows. "If that *thing* doesn't eat us!"

Goblin Slayer replaced the throwing knife in the sheath on his back and ran up the deck, which was bouncing in the waves.

Ignorance was a sin, but it could also be bliss. The goblin chieftain's ship was drifting closer to the sea monster—or monsters; he didn't know if it was a whole swarm of them or just one. And yet, the goblins appeared completely unbothered—for they were goblins, after all. High Elf Archer and Priestess were battling furiously to keep them at bay as the little monsters argued about who was to be the next chieftain.

"If we could just…use a spell, then I think…the rest would be…!"

Priestess might not be the strongest, but she'd survived more than one battle like this. She had a lot to learn about wielding her staff as a combat weapon, but it was more than enough to keep the goblins from getting too close. Protected by the two women, Lizard Priest leaned over the side of the ship with Dwarf Shaman on his shoulders.

"All right, I've got 'im!" Dwarf Shaman cheered, clenching his small but doughty fists in the air. The way he raised his arms was very spell caster–ish; it almost looked like he was reeling in a fishing rod. "Keep those feet firm, Scaly!"

"I shall! I daresay I'm not eager to fall in…"

For a lizardman from the south, the northern sea must have seemed a terrible thing—but his people lived in the marshes, so they had a certain affinity with water themselves. Lizard Priest's sharp claws bit into the deck of the boat as it tossed and reeled and was soaked by the waves as if it were deliberately trying to throw off its passengers. He held out his ample tail for balance.

Dwarf Shaman gave a sharp tug on the invisible fishing rod, grinning as if he could feel it catching something under the water. And then he roared to the sprites, seeking to enlist their help in dragging his quarry to the surface: *"Nymphs and sylphs, together spin, earth and sea are nearly kin, so dance away—just don't fall in!"*

The sea exploded—not metaphorically but literally. The battered boats were shaken like candy in a bottle, slammed together by the waves. The geyser of seawater blocked out the sun so that everything suddenly went dark. And the spray turned the world white—but none of this could conceal what emerged.

"OOCCCTAAAAAAAAAAAALLUUUUUUUUUUSSS!!!!!!!"

"Wha—?"

"Heek…!"

The sight was enough to rob one of sanity. Confronted with the writhing creature that emerged from the sea, anyone would find their grip on reality under assault.

Now it was clear why they had initially taken it for a whole swarm of giant sea snakes. It was a mountainous, towering collection of tentacles bending at impossible angles, and flesh, and fangs that consumed anything and everything. It was a cephalopod-like creature that looked as if its parts had been stuck together with clay—but it was a single monster. The master of the abyss, who had dwelled in the deep perhaps since the Age of the Gods.

"Hmm," Goblin Slayer grunted, while everyone else stood stupefied. He sounded less surprised than he did eminently sure and satisfied as he said: "I knew these people couldn't be defeated by mere goblins."

§

"Ha-ha-ha-ha, now, this is a big one! A real big-name hunt!" A hero dove across the stormy sea, leaping from one rotting hulk to another. A man with black-steel mail and a steel sword in his hand. A knight who had come from the south to the north to be a *goði*. He was accompanied only by a single silent Dragontooth Warrior acting as a shield bearer.

Of course, the sea devil with its monstrous appetite would not overlook even something so small as this. Now awakened from its drowsiness by having been dragged forcibly up to the surface, its tentacles all struck at once.

If anyone was to deride the hero's sword as a mere blunt instrument, however, it would only be testament to their own ignorance.

"Hrr…n!"

A single sword, a single swift strike. The chieftain stood his ground—indeed, pressed forward, cutting loose the tangle of tentacles. He spun his greatsword over his head as the feelers all but stumbled over one another to reach him, slicing through them.

The tentacles, which had come at him like stabbing spears, were thrown up and back, and he brushed the roots away with the flat of his blade. A crimson banner seemed to fly above his head. Brandishing his blade right, then left, he continued to push forward. Training upon training, practice upon practice: This was simply an utter mastery of the fighting arts.

"OOCCCTAAAAAAAAAAAALLUUUUUUUUUUSSS!!!!!!!"

It was impossible to say, really, whether the sea creature felt pain. Or whether it had reason or was even sentient. He'd cut off a handful of the creature's seemingly infinite tentacles, but there appeared to be as many of them left as hairs on a person's head.

Still—the sea creature howled. Maybe it was just a yawn or maybe was directed at the insect who had awakened the monster from sleep, but it was unmistakably a howl.

All aimed at one simple human in front of it.

"Today," the *goði* said, baring his fangs, his voice almost melodic, "is the day you die…!"

The sound of steel and the sound of the uncanny beast collided with each other. Writhing tentacles shot forward with what seemed enough force to destroy a single warrior.

The chieftain didn't take a step back; in fact, he pushed forward instead. When one was wielding the sword, one could not stop moving. The momentum itself was what led to the next attack. The protecting sword ought always to be pointed like a stake at the heart of the enemy.

Talho! Lebetz! Alte, basso!

The sword was everywhere, and yet it couldn't possibly parry every single attack. The Dragontooth Warrior and its shield took a blow in the *goði*'s place, crumbling apart. "Brilliant!" the chieftain shouted and continued to press forward, ever forward.

Yes: The chieftain's sword had certainly reached the sea monster.

No problem, then. Just keep hitting it, and it will die.

When the ship beneath his feet began to break apart, he leaped to the next one, sweeping aside the thorns of flesh with his blade.

The chieftain stood, and struck, and cut. With each stroke, blood flew, flesh was rent, and all of it crashed over him like a wave.

The way his breath fogged in the air revealed how hot the chieftain's blood was. O gods, behold his deeds! See the battle of the hero and the devil of the northern sea. This creature was a warlord of Chaos, a major playing piece, on a scale with Hecatoncheir or a battlemech. And here a single unique unit was facing it down.

This was it, the radiant adventure evoked by the adventurers. For all the many adventurers in the Four-Cornered World were radiant, shining stars.

"...A berserker is quite a sight to see, isn't it?!" the *húsfreya* said with a smile as she watched the man she loved do battle, unperturbed by the crashing waves.

The northerners saw all this and looked at one another. What were *they* doing? Just pissing about with goblins who didn't understand at all what was going on? Look, had the adventurers not held up their side of the bargain? While the northerners had been shocked, and shaken, their formation broken, the adventurers had worked as one to pull the devil from the deep. And now the northerners simply watched their *goði* fight. They watched, unable to do anything, as he and his sword alone confronted the beast.

But consider—just consider. When people saw them later, the survivors of this battle, what would they say? When they saw the helmets, armor, and shield without a scratch? The swords without so much as a chip in the blade? What would they think? Had these Vikings, they would wonder, been content to let the adventurers fish the enemy out of the sea and then merely stand by as the *goði* fought it?

They had defeated the small fry. Done their jobs. Was that why they had looked on as the hero finished things?

To be seen in such a way, to be thought of in such terms—they couldn't bear it. A true warrior preferred death to living with dishonor.

"...*Gygax!* Praise the gods!"

"*Gygax!!*"

The warriors shouted, loud enough to be heard by the ninth pillar of the Circle of Eight, the great god who had gone beyond the stars.

So what if they died? One of their brothers would take up the fight and another after him. What did they have to fear?

"GOROGGB?!"

"GOB?! OROGGBB?!?!"

Such conviction was unknown to the goblins, who were and would only ever be possessed of but little wit. All they knew was that the cowed and hesitant warriors were suddenly charging forward, disdaining wounds and injuries. There was no way the likes of goblins could cope with such a push.

The air shook with the shouting of the warriors, the death rattles of the goblins, and the bellowing of the storm.

"Who cares about any sea monster? For my husband is without fear…" And thus, the *húsfreya* smiled. The prince whom she loved more than anything could never be defeated by what was before him. "For he is the bee-wulf, the bee hunter!"

The squirming tentacles became whips of flesh, striking the chieftain's armor almost faster than the speed of sound. The chains of his mail jumped aside, his flesh was split, and his blood flew. But so what? In exchange for that single blow, the *goði* had a chance to drive at the heart of the beast.

"Hrrrahhh…!" Even as he moved in, the flesh-spears were stabbing at him, but the chieftain parried to one side and then the other and pushed another step closer.

He let the momentum of the slashes carry him into a corkscrew motion, flying from the prow of the ship toward the monster. This was one of the master's techniques with the two-handed sword. The Fourteenth Form, which meant death.

The steel blade sliced away the monster's tentacles, sending them flying, the creature spewing terrible fluid higher than the waves.

"OOCCCTAAAAAAAAAAAALLUUUUUUUUUUSSS!!!!!!!"

"From my ship, speed! From my shield, strength! From my blade, blood!" The *húsfreya* sang out her own prayer, louder than the roaring of the sea devil. The light that spilled from her one good eye became lightning that ran along her arm. Then the light became electricity that struck the *goði* in the heart.

"And from my maiden fair, a kiss! These I seek!" The lightning enveloped

©Noboru Kannatuki

his body, coursing around him, leaping through space to the top of his helmet.

In Priestess's eyes, he looked like a stag with golden antlers. Yes: like the horns of the great god that every child imagined on the helmets of the fearsome Vikings.

The lightning ran onto the chieftain's sword, swelling its size, making it ever larger. The chieftain grinned and brought the sword back toward his shoulder, preparing to swing.

It is pain that gives life its joy.

It is the searing heat followed by the shock of cold that tempers steel.

A god of steel wreathed in lightning. A true miracle, bestowed by the blessing of the husband-and-wife gods.

This, this was the all-cleaving blade known only to those who had uncovered the deepest secrets of steel.

"Hoh, adventurers!" the chieftain shouted, taking aim at his mortal foe. "On my mark!"

§

"Goblin Slayer, sir!" It was Priestess who acted before anyone else, raising her sounding staff, with Spark on her hand.

The furious sea. The ship that threatened to break apart beneath their feet. The massive sea devil. The horde of goblins. The fight they were still in the middle of. The journey north. Adventure.

Precious moments, all. Inspiration came like a dawning light in the back of Goblin Slayer's mind.

"Tail Wind, now!"

"You got it!"

Even though he had just fished a gigantic monster out of the ocean, Dwarf Shaman didn't look tired, and he acted without a moment's hesitation. He understood well that at times like this, this man, Goblin Slayer, would always come up with something.

"O sylphs, thou windy maidens fair, grant to me your kiss most rare—bless our ship with breezes fair…!"

Even as the sylphs of the northern sea sang and danced, they reached out a hand to their friend. The wind began to batter the ship—which was really just some rotting wood barely holding the shape of a boat. The gust was powerful enough to catch even High Elf Archer off guard and send her stumbling. She glanced in Priestess's direction. Her cherished but much younger friend was standing at the prow of the ship, her staff held high, praying for all she was worth.

Boy, she's really become something to be proud of.

Priestess herself was probably the only one who didn't realize it. Humans were quick. That made the elf a little jealous and also a little bit sad.

"Oh, for… It *always* turns out like this, doesn't it?" High Elf Archer said with studied cheerfulness, pounding Lizard Priest on the back. "One more stand. Let's not go falling down now…!"

"Mm, I quite agree."

High Elf Archer raced across the deck, giggling at the way his tail tickled as it brushed past her legs. Whatever Orcbolg was up to, it would bring down that sea monster. And if the high elf's arrows could hit it at all, they would whittle away the creature's hit points.

Although granted, she did grumble "Ugh" when she saw Orcbolg pull out the bottle full of greasy liquid. "I thought I told you to stop acting like a Hylar dwarf."

"This is a different plan," Goblin Slayer said calmly. "Get ready."

"Ha-ha-ha…"

I'm so going to kick his ass when we get home.

But even that thought was somehow reassuring. High Elf Archer kicked off the gunwale, pulling back on her bow and loosing an arrow.

"OOCCCTAAAAAAAAAAAALLUUUUUUUUUUSSS!!!!!!!"

Then fire glowed in Goblin Slayer's hand. The black liquid in the bottle was beginning a conflagration, and he flung it—down through a hole in the deck.

This was Medea's fire, petroleum, or Iranistan's oil. Whatever you called it, it was…

"Fire water."

Boom. There was a great roar, accompanied by an eruption of flames. Immediately, the fire began to lick at the whole ship, charring everything black, shining all around…

"O Earth Mother, abounding in mercy, please, by your revered hand, cleanse us of our corruption."

From the midst of this, how could the gods fail to hear the plea of a young girl?

Her soul-shearingly pure prayer reached the Earth Mother—who must have smiled a little when she thought of where this prayer was going. But still she granted it, her delicate, invisible fingers brushing across the corrupted goblin ship, purifying it.

There might be flames all around, but this was unmistakably a holy wind blowing past them. Although, since the fire was sucking up all the oxygen, it would have been tricky to breathe without their breathing rings.

The fire devoured the speed of the ship, sucked in the wind behind it, growing stronger as it consumed.

"I knew this ring would be necessary if we used this much fire," said Goblin Slayer, who had checked his facts ahead of time. Then he took the battle-ax bequeathed to him by the northern warrior and put it in the belt at his hip. He gave a disinterested "Hmph" regarding the goblin arm lying at his feet and kicked it out of the way.

There was no turning back now. There was only one thing to do.

"Release the spell!" Goblin Slayer shouted. "We're jumping!"

"You're on, Scaly!"

"Understood…!"

"Heek?!"

"Your ass is gonna get *so kicked*!"

Goblin Slayer grabbed up Priestess, while Lizard Priest put Dwarf Shaman on his back, and High Elf Archer flew merrily through the air.

Then the adventurers put an end to their adventure.

§

The goblin grinned to himself, grateful to his own good luck. He was covered in wounds, he had been stabbed in the belly, and the stump of his arm had been inundated with saltwater, agonizing it. But despite it all, the goblin was alive. Even if only just.

He'd clung to the side of the rolling ship, and that had saved him. The foolish adventurers had foolishly overlooked him, like the fools they were. One day, he would make them regret it.

He had done nothing wrong, and yet, look how he had been treated. Surely he was entitled to do the same to them.

Struggling with his single remaining arm, the goblin managed to crawl across the deck.

His head just wouldn't stop spinning, though.

"GOROGB…?"

Suddenly, he noticed there was fire everywhere. It should have been too hot to bear—so why did he barely feel warm?

The air, however, was deeply unpleasant. It made him want to retch.

The goblin cursed everything he could think of, but he was in fact rather satisfied with his current situation. The ship seemed to be speeding along for some reason. That would help him. And he had survived. Thus, he could always come back. And then he would find those adventurers, and someday, he vowed, he would kill them…

"GORRGGB?!?!"

The last thing the goblin saw as he looked up was the vast, black emptiness within the yawning jaws.

§

Up on the surface, the roar of the lightning dragon resounded. The blade of electricity struck true, slamming into the sea devil, and meanwhile, the burning ship became a flaming spear piercing the monster.

"OOCCCTAAAAAAAAAAAALLUUUUUUUUUUSSS?!?!?!"

The monster bellowed and reared back. The lightning-shrouded sword and the burning ship were both terrible weapons—and yet, they were not enough. Neither could land a final, critical hit.

What shocked the creature more than anything else was the great sacred flare, the likes of which it had never experienced before. The weight of the "holy ship," carrying the blessing of the Earth Mother, overwhelmed the sea devil.

And then the effect of Water Walk wore off.

Monster and ship both hit the water with an enormous spray of foam and sank. Down they went, then farther down. The great mass of them, which had been supported by the water sprites until that moment, slammed into the sea.

They sucked a massive flow of saltwater down with them—which then rebounded. It caught up the abandoned hulks floating on the battlefield, the surviving goblin, and the northerners in a single tremendous wave.

"Hold steaaadddyyyyy!"

But the Vikings, the People of the Bay, ate massive waves for breakfast. They weren't worried about the goblins or about the sea devil—for they were with the people they lived and fought with every day. At a single order, without panic and without hesitation, they grabbed their oars and began rowing.

Even the least of the northerners was a formidable warrior and an unimpeachable sailor.

"GORGGB?!"

"GORBBGG?!?!"

And the goblins, needless to say, were not.

The goblins, without the least sense for ships or the sea, could hardly even struggle. They were simply swallowed up. Consumed. No goblin would emerge from these waters alive.

Nature in the Four-Cornered World was absolutely fair to all. It bestowed its blessings upon those who could adapt—and upon those who couldn't, destruction.

Perhaps it would be most accurate to say that the northern sea settled everything with its own hand.

§

"Good gods, but you do the wildest things," the chieftain said with an exasperated smile. The sky had changed completely and was now bright and sunny.

The adventurers had jumped from the flaming ship, passing the sea devil and the lightning sword. They were hale and healthy as they stood on the deck, watching the sea gradually regain its calm.

"Is that so?" Goblin Slayer asked, cocking his head, seawater dripping from his helmet. "I only did what I always do."

High Elf Archer gave him a good, sound kick, sending him sprawling. She pointed and laughed, but Priestess hurried up to her. "I-it was my idea, so…!"

At that, High Elf Archer looked up at the heavens and covered her face. But whatever she was wishing for at that moment, the Earth Mother—averting her eyes herself—probably didn't hear it.

Lizard Priest, observing the three of them, rolled his eyes merrily in his head, while Dwarf Shaman grabbed the wine at his hip with some resignation. "Do yeh really think that killed it? I mean, something that big? Not entirely confident m'self…"

"Hmmmm." Lizard Priest sighed heavily. "Even if it did, I very much doubt whether that thing was the last of its kind."

"Aw, who cares?" At his friend's joke at the spell caster who had done more than anybody else this time out, he glugged down some wine.

"If it ever comes back…it just means another *drekka*!" The *goði* looked at the northerners, who gave a great bellow of victory up to the heavens. The rescued prisoners wept and embraced one another, argued with the other northerners, and generally made a lot of noise.

The chieftain, listening happily to the hubbub, smiled. "Was I as heroic as you'd hoped of me, my dear—?" And then he spoke the *húsfreya*'s name.

She chuckled and said, "Oh, my dear *husbondi*. Your accent is showing again."

"Oops!" The chieftain scratched his cheek in embarrassment. He still had a lot to learn. *"Ahem...* Dear wife. I do thank you always," he said, making sure to sound like one of the northerners.

The *húsfreya* leaned toward him: Under his helmet, his lips were undefended. She brushed them gently. In perfect common speech, she said: "I do adore you, my prince."

"_____"

"Hmm?"

"Once more! Dear wife, I beg you!"

"Heavens, I couldn't!" she said mischievously, slipping back into her accustomed style of speech and dancing away from the chieftain with a smile. The black-steel keys clinked on her hip; she brushed them with her fingers, looking endlessly happy.

"Please return these for me. Later, when there's a chance." Goblin Slayer, who had finally gotten to his feet again and was watching the two of them, spoke to a nearby northerner—the warrior with the wounded face. He had more wounds now—and Goblin Slayer handed him two weapons. The northern sword that had been at his hip until this moment and the enchanted battle-ax.

"Are you quite certain?"

"They're good weapons," Goblin Slayer replied. And then he added, "They're wasted on me."

Hmm. The scar-faced warrior let out a quiet breath, but at length he said, "I understand," and took the items reverently.

Among the Vikings, it was said that if you offered something to someone, be it as humble as a hunting knife, you ought to receive something in return. This was a land where fighting never ceased. That was exactly what made it a land so rich in the knowledge of how to avoid fights and traditions that promoted peace.

But receive something? He had received so much already.

The young lovers—the husband and wife—their joyous faces were things of such profound value here in the north.

"What really matters is this: It was a fine fight," the northerner said. "Hrm?"

"I speak of your reward." The warrior with the wounds on his face made sure he had a firm, respectful grip on the sword and ax. "You adventurers are not thieves, are you? Mercenaries, perhaps?"

"No." Goblin Slayer shook his head. It was almost a reflexive movement; thus, it took him several seconds of silence to find the words. "No...," he repeated. "Adventurers are those who go on adventures."

Adventurers were those who risked danger. They traveled the world, delved into dungeons, and faced dragons for riches, honor, renown, or the sake of the people. That was how it was supposed to be—how he wanted to believe that it was. How he wanted to be.

"I am Goblin Slayer," he said. There was nothing he hated more than having goblins stand in his way. But there was also nothing more painful than having goblins stand in his way. "For a reward... I ask that in the future, when adventurers visit this land, you treat them as adventurers."

"Is that indeed enough?"

"Yes."

Priestess, listening at a distance, thought for a moment she had misheard, her eyes widening. Because otherwise, if she hadn't... Well, it might be the first time she had ever heard such a thing. And yet, she didn't feel the tremble of discomfort that had run through her in the past.

Because—well, hadn't he done it? Perhaps it had the groaning quality of a rusty hinge, but he—he had laughed out loud.

"Yes, that is enough," he said. And then, as if it was a matter of utmost importance, Goblin Slayer added, "Also, if you could provide a scabbard for me."

CHAPTER 7

HONEY MOON

The coming of spring is heralded by a languorous sunny atmosphere that makes you want to yawn.

And indeed, that was what Cow Girl found herself doing, making no attempt to hide her audible yawn as she sat on the fence, kicking her feet. The sky was blue, the sunlight was warm, and the breeze was lovely. You could hardly have asked for a better afternoon.

"Mmmm…"

It wasn't that she was shirking work. She'd mostly finished the things she had to do today. She hadn't yet done the things that would be *good* to do today, however, or started the things that would take several days.

Awww, it's all right, she thought. On a day like today, who could blame her?

She'd finished all her jobs in time to have a few minutes to herself; there was no need to keep working. Everything pressing had been done; no one could complain if she took it easy for a while.

"Hup…!"

Cow Girl leaned her weight backward off the fence, like a child in the branches of a tree. Just like that, the world was upside down, spreading out before her in reverse. The sky was made of green grass, and at her feet there was solid blue. Back when she was a child, she'd had to wear a skirt, and she would have been scolded for doing this— they would have said it was bad manners.

Oh...huh. Maybe it still is?

If her uncle found her, she thought, he might have something to say about it—but even that was a welcome thought. He was still quite harsh about the winter excursion, but otherwise, it had been quite a long time since she'd been scolded by anybody.

Then again, just because it had been a long time, and because she found the thought welcome in its own way, didn't mean she was eager to be scolded.

Well, if he sees me...we'll worry about it then.

Cow Girl's logic was about as sound as that child in the tree branch. For now, all she felt she had to do was savor the sun and the wind and the sense of spring.

"Ooh..."

Suddenly, a decoration like a tattered rag dropped into her upside-down world. Swaying in her view from the green above her head was a cheap-looking, but familiar, metal helmet.

He had a lot more cargo than usual, but then again, he'd gone much farther than usual. He'd put away his cloak—this far south, he must no longer need it. Knowing him, she was sure that it was folded neatly and placed in his backpack. Only one thing was unusual enough to catch her attention: the gorgeous sword at his hip.

"No animals this time?" she teased, grinning at her upside-down friend.

"Mm," he grunted, coming to a halt and looking intently at her. "...What are you doing?"

"Hmm? Oh, uh..." Cow Girl kicked, flipping back upright. Then the world swiveled around, and now she could see the other side of the fence from before. Her feet hit the ground (*tump!*), and she pushed off, turning around.

There was the grimy metal helmet, just like she'd expected. She was very happy to see it. "I've been waiting."

"...Is that so?"

"Uh-huh. Sure is."

Cow Girl smiled, and he simply said, "Is that so?" again, the helmet nodding.

There was only one thing she could say to that.

"You're back?"

"Yes… I'm back."

§

The road to the farm's main house was certainly not a long one, and she enjoyed listening to him talk on the way. He spoke in brief bursts, and she had to ask him in detail about things to learn anything.

I mean, I've just got to.

He had crossed the mountains. He had killed some goblins. He had seen the northern country. A monster he didn't know much about had appeared. He had killed more goblins.

That can't be all there is to the story, Cow Girl thought. At the same time, though, she didn't necessarily understand enough about adventuring to have grasped the details, even if he told her. Take the subterranean dwarven city, for example: She couldn't quite figure out what that meant. And of the northerners—their houses, their way of life, their frozen sea, their ships—she could form only the vaguest picture.

As for the monster, he said it had many legs. The only things Cow Girl knew like that were insects.

"So it was sort of like a centipede?"

"No, I don't think so…" He shook his head from side to side, thought for a moment, and then added, "They called it a…devil fish or some such. I don't know the details. I've never seen anything like it before."

"Huh…"

It was like one thing was everything; that's how it was with him. But when she asked questions, he did answer them, and she liked hearing his piecemeal explanations. She didn't always follow, but about the time he was demonstrating with a gesture how he had tried to move a stick, she started to think:

He had fun, didn't he?

And that made her happiest of all.

"So it was good?"

"Yes." He nodded. "Although I didn't succeed in moving it."

"It was really big, right? Not your fault."

As Cow Girl spoke, they reached the door of the main house. The air inside carried the slightest chill, as if a hint of winter were still hiding within. Cow Girl's uncle was at work and wasn't back yet. It made her heart skip a beat to walk quietly into the house, just her and him.

"I'll put tea on," she said, trotting toward the kitchen.

First things first: She had to make a fire. And lighting a fire made her eager to boil water.

Thus when he said: "I have a gift for you," it was only after watching her scurry around for a moment. He said it quite seriously, setting his baggage down as she took a seat while she waited for the water on the fire to come to a boil.

"Ooh, what is it?"

"First, this."

On the table, he set the magnificent sword that had been at his hip. Even Cow Girl, who knew nothing of such matters, could see how exquisite a weapon it was. The hilt was carefully wrapped in leather, and the guard was polished to a sparkle. No doubt the blade was in similar condition. There were no obvious ornaments to speak of, but it was clear at a glance that this was a very fine piece indeed.

After all, it was only natural: As fine as the sword was, it was the scabbard that was truly beautiful. Worked with dark-steel and copper accents that were polished to shimmering, even the fur pelt was oiled and shining. Its value was unmistakable, as was the immense thought and care that had gone into it.

"Wow," Cow Girl said, blinking. "I was wondering about this thing. What's its story?"

"The sword, I found. The scabbard was made for me."

His answer was brief, but it was enough to tell her what she needed to know. He had requested specifically to have this made. He was truly blessed with the people he met.

"That's great," she said.

He was quiet for a moment, then said slowly, "I thought it might serve as a decoration."

Cow Girl folded her hands on the table, then rested her cheek against them. She knew very well what expression he was wearing behind his visor. Thus she knew what he would do when she spoke, knew he would fall silent and look at her.

"I think you should use it as a decoration in your shed."

"...Is that all right?"

"I think that would be the best fit."

"Mm," he said with a little nod, and then he took the sword, looking genuinely happy. He drank in the sight of it, then nudged the blade from the scabbard for a peek, his helmet bobbing up and down.

Cow Girl recognized it as the same way he'd reacted when he'd been bought a wooden sword at a festival long, long ago. She got up from her seat, so as not to interrupt or interfere with him. She banked the coals from that morning, and when the water (brought from a bucket) was boiled, next came the tea. She used some of the leaves the receptionist at the Adventurers Guild had given her, although as far as actually making the tea, she could only imitate what she'd seen and been told. It was fine—as long as she didn't pretend she was going to brew the most delicious tea in the Four-Cornered World, there was no problem.

"There's another, as well," he said softly as she was returning to the table with two cups. He riffled through his belongings, took out a carefully wrapped wine jug, and set it on the tabletop. He must have seen the question mark appear over Cow Girl's head, for he explained: "It's mead."

"Huh..."

She could be forgiven, one hoped, for having a completely different reaction to this than she had had to the sword.

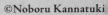
©Noboru Kannatuki

Mead—honey alcohol. Of course she knew about it; she had even drunk some. But maybe the mead they made in the north was different somehow. Intrigued, Cow Girl leaned toward one of the jugs.

"Was this a gift, too?"

"Yes." He nodded. "They asked me about my household, although I didn't quite follow."

"Your household?"

"I said that I'm unmarried but that I live with you and your uncle. Then they told me to take this home with me."

"Huh… There's quite a bit of it here. Maybe they want us to drink it together?"

The mead was fragrant despite the tight seals on the jars. She gave one of them a shake and was rewarded with a distinct, pleasing *splish*. The sound made her excited somehow.

"Maybe we should have some with dinner tonight."

"Yes." He nodded. "Although I don't know much about alcohol consumption."

"As if I do!" She giggled. "Say… Do the people of the north wear horned helmets?" Still smiling, she waved her fingers in the air, tracing two horns. "You know, like you used to do?"

"Yes." He nodded. "I saw it myself."

As the steam rose from their tea, the two talked about a great wide variety of things.

How immensely useful Uncle's cloak had been on the journey north. How the land there had been quite different from the saga the two of them had heard once upon a time, and yet just like it described. The bravery of the northern warriors. Their strength. How they were a company of heroes.

The chill of the north. The warmth of the north. The startling culture, games, and food. The songs.

The terribleness of the raging sea. The unknown monster that lurked within it. The captured women. The northern hero challenging the sea devil. And the faraway princess who loved him. How sweetly the two got along.

The massive sword the hero wielded. The great, inspiring horns that decorated his helmet.

How of the rescued women, some had returned home, while several had decided to stay and become brides of the northerners. How it seemed the cleric girl who served the Earth Mother was being talked about for promotion.

This and much, much more he told her, giving his all to speak of it in his poor style and minimal vocabulary.

She *ooh*ed and *ahh*ed at the appropriate times, occasionally asked questions or urged him on, and all the time listened joyously. It was a whole collection of stories to make the heart race.

In other words, it was an adventure.

CHAPTER 8

A Slice of Bread, a Knife, and a Lamp

It might have been years later—or just moments.

"Oof!"

A girl went plunging headfirst into a snowbank, her voice muffled by the drift. Extricating herself from the snow along the mountain ridge, she groaned piteously. She had no idea she'd caught her foot on what was called a "snow cornice." No idea that if her luck had been bad—if the roll of the dice had been bad—she would have simply tumbled straight down to the foot of the mountain. She didn't know that in that case, her flesh would have been rent by sharp rocks and ice as keen as steel.

But anyway, none of that happened. She just cursed her own clumsiness and the mischievous snow, drawing her mouth down in a frown. She shook her head, and the black hair that fell down below her armored headband billowed out, snowflakes tumbling from it. She looked like a rabbit too eager to wait for spring—and in fact, there wasn't much difference between her and such a vulnerable animal.

They were right about not going into the valley.

That was what the more experienced adventurers had told her before she left: *"Even if you get lost, don't go down into the valley. Climb onto the ridge."*

She didn't actually understand *why* this was the right thing to do. Even now, she couldn't resist the idea that the valley must eventually lead to the village. In fact, the girl didn't entirely understand what this "valley" was. She had a vague sense that it was a place water flowed to.

It was really more than a valley; it was a marshy depression, and when she had gotten lost and wandered into it accidentally, it had been awful. It was cold, and the sun didn't reach it, and you could only see down, not up, and there were piles of slippery snow everywhere, and... Well.

Next time I get lost, I'll climb on the ridges.

Yes, the girl told herself forcefully. At the same moment, her stomach gave a pathetic gurgle. She put a hand to her belly (there was nothing there to rely on in a pinch) and bit her frowning lip. She'd already wolfed down the big loaf of bread she'd gotten at the harefolk village that she'd stumbled upon.

Speaking of which...

The monster fang on display in that mansion was really something...

Would she be able to fight such beasts one day? Was she even capable of it? The thought terrified her, but it excited her a little, too.

"Oh, that's right...!"

The girl tried to snap her fingers—but they were too numb to manage it. She seemed pleased anyway.

She had realized that her canteen still contained some watered-down grape wine. She let her pack down as gently as she could (which was not very gently at all), then took out her canteen, struggling with the unusual way she'd packed things. Then she drank—*glug, glug*—without regard for how much she had left, pouring the stuff into her empty stomach.

Phew! She exhaled, slowly put away her items, and picked up her bag again, then took her time getting to her feet. Then she began to work her way down the mountain, never knowing that she was walking along the edge between life and death, with only the pips of the dice to help her.

I've never been anywhere like this before.

A cramped, tumbledown house. Her father with his cloudy eyes. A village full of people who were nothing but cold. And her, shrinking into herself.

That little girl couldn't have imagined this place—the edge of the world. Or, no...

This can't be the edge.

From where she was, she could see an oddly stereotypical city at the foot of the mountains and then the sea. Small boats—although to her they looked like great ships—traveled the waters toward the north. So this couldn't be the northern edge. There had to be somewhere more northerly. Farther away, over the horizon.

"Hee...hee!" She didn't know quite why, but that thought alone made her very happy.

Each time she ran, pushing off the snow, her pack bounced on her back, rattling around. Her cheeks were warm, and her vision was bright. From outside, she wouldn't have looked like much. Just a girl all but tumbling her way down a snowy mountain. The sword at her hip looked dangerously heavy and left a line trailing through the snow alongside her footprints.

The people of her village might have pointed and laughed and said they couldn't watch this. They had half forgotten about her already. But that meant nothing to her. She was full of pride and bravery as she went along. For she carried with her that pride, and her excitement, and her black onyx charm—and that was all.

That was all she, with the @ of the *propater*, the origin, on her back, needed to push her forward. People who felt they were smarter than her could say what they pleased—but what else did she really need?

"Oh...!" the black-haired girl exclaimed when she saw a dark spot, just visible against the snow. She blinked several times against the light reflecting off the snow, but finally, she saw that it was a person—someone from the city. It was a towering man wearing fine wool clothing, with an ax in the belt cinched around his waist. The scraggly beard that covered his face made him look something like a dwarf, but he was much too big for that.

Aw… He's not even wearing a horned helmet.

She was just a little disappointed—and, yes, just a little scared—but she managed to draw a breath.

"Um, excuse me…!"

Her voice came out as small as the buzzing of a fly, even though she'd tried to shout as loud as she could. It was all she could squeeze out.

But at length, much to her relief, this man of the northerners seemed to notice her. It was unlikely he'd heard her voice; presumably he'd seen her up here. Not that it mattered to her either way.

"Hoh! Now, here's a young lass whom I've not seen before!" the man said in a voice—and with a laugh—as big as his body. "Where've you come from, then?"

"Um, uh… That way," the girl answered, shaking a twiglike arm in the direction of the mountain she'd come down. She'd followed the mountain road resolutely, clung to the cliffside, and eventually gotten across the mountain and had wound up here.

She wondered if he would be angry. If he would yell at her. What would she do if he attacked her? What items and equipment did she have with her, again?

The girl, suddenly feeling quite anxious despite the brevity of their conversation, stood where she was and shifted uncomfortably. The man took stock of her for a moment, then said, "Ah," and nodded. "You'll be an adventurer, then?"

"…! Yes, sir!" the girl replied, smiling like the sun and nodding so hard, her black hair bounced up and down. "An adventurer! That's what I am!"

Pride filled her small chest as she turned toward the Four-Cornered World and set out.

AFTERWORD

Hullo, Kumo Kagyu here! I hope you enjoyed Volume 14 of *Goblin Slayer*. This time, goblins appeared on the northern sea, and Goblin Slayer had to slay them.

Stories of heroism have been set in such places since the days of *Conan the Barbarian*. If this book was to spark your interest in such stories, I would be very happy indeed.

I've mentioned before in these afterwords about a campaign I'm in where I play a character who's only good at shooting arrows. After years of safely and successfully playing this character, I'm reminded again and again that TRPGs are really great. A boy who just liked to bullshit people about being a hero is now running all over helping the town. But he couldn't do it alone, so he enlisted the aid of a bunch of other people, relied on his friends, and finally found he had, in fact, become a hero.

The Four-Cornered World has lots of adventurers, too—and heroes—each with their own stories. Goblin Slayer might be the main character of these books, but he's not the center of this world. Hero, the runners, and even the northern *goði* and his *húsfreya*, and the adventurers on the frontier. What they do is an equally important part of the story.

I'd be glad if you also picked up *Dai Katana*, which is another side of the entire tale. I can only apologize for keeping you waiting for the final volume.

If you want to become one of these adventurers, there's going to be a supplement published for the *Goblin Slayer* TRPG. And if you want to watch these adventurers, there's going to be a second season of the *Goblin Slayer* anime.

What a world, huh? No one is more surprised than I am. First my work becomes a manga, then an anime and TRPG, then there's a theatrical movie and a supplement and a second season... It all just seems incredible to me. It's certainly not something you get to experience every day.

Like everything else, all this was possible only because of everyone cheering me on, so thank you all so much.

Speaking of everyone cheering me on: my readers, my editor, the whole editorial division, and everyone else at the publisher. Kannatuki, who's produced another batch of wonderful illustrations, and all the different artists involved in the manga version.

My gaming buddies and my creative-type friends.

The admins of the aggregator sites and everyone rooting for me on the web.

Thank you again, and I hope you'll continue to support me.

My plan is for Volume 15 to be about goblins appearing in a grassy field and Goblin Slayer having to slay them.

I'll be working my hardest on the TRPG supplement, the anime, the side story, and the new book. Nothing would make me happier than for you to enjoy them.